I0663651

Sarjikris

This book is a work of fiction. Names, characters, places and incidents are either a product of the author's imagination or are used fictitiously, and any resemblance to actual persons, living or dead, business establishments, events or locales is entirely coincidental.

ISBN: 978-1942433019

Cover by Benita Pearse

Disclaimer:

www.benitapearse.com

"Love is composed of a single soul
inhabiting two bodies."
- Aristotle

Prologue

2010

"Why am I here?" I glanced at my watch. I didn't have time for this. I had a plane to catch. I wanted to get home. Home. It wasn't home. Not really. It was just more home than here. Only, I wished home was somewhere else entirely. I wished...a lot of things. None of my wishes would ever amount to anything so why bother even wishing in the first place.

"Are you being facetious, Khaldun? You are here because you are a Sarjikris. You are here because you are a Superior. You are here because I choose for you to be here." A rumble ran through the hundreds of occupants at the foot of Bastet's crumbled tomb in Zagazig, a city near the old ancient city of Bubastis. Many who were here were residents of Zagazig, Bubastis, Cairo and various areas on the Nile River: Egypt, Sudan, Kenya and beyond. The few others who were present were scattered far and wide – like me. They couldn't hear Bastet and me talking; they couldn't listen in. But they had seen Bastet's arrival. And they could see our heated conversation.

"Very funny, Bastet. The unrest here is not my problem. I don't need you burdening me with your problems. If you want to stop the destruction of your home, your people –"

"They are your people too, Khaldun. Don't you ever forget that."

I gave a cynical laugh. "How could I ever forget? I wouldn't be here otherwise, would I?" I raised my eyebrow at her elegant, majestic feline form.

She didn't answer.

"Get rid of your leader. You have known for a long time that Mubarak's a corrupt dictator. He's depraved, a malicious tyrant, and he's destroying Egypt. Get rid of him. You don't need me to tell you this."

"True. However, that is not why you were summoned – Mubarak is being dealt with as we speak and changes are coming." Bastet's quiet answer spoke volumes; she didn't like it any more than the rest of the world.

"These will be difficult times for everyone. I'm sorry I spoke out in anger, Bastet. I pray as little blood is shed as possible."

"You are a good man, Khaldun. You always have been. This is why you were chosen, why I value your insight. Come, it is time for me to address our people."

Again, I heard the mumblings across the group of Sarjikris as Bastet and I turned from each other. It was rare I attended these gatherings. It really was once in a blue moon.

I scanned the crowd again. I hadn't paid attention before to the number of superiors and chiefs present. I stood up straight and scanned the area again. All of them were here, from every corner of the globe. This was unprecedented. The last time this happened was when...

"No, it couldn't be." I whispered upon an exhaled breath.

"Ah, it has dawned on you, Khaldun, as to why you are here?" Bastet turned to face me again.

"Why now? It's been over two thousand years since He interfered. Why now?"

"He wants to try again. That is all I know. He wants to try and save the world from disaster…according to Him."

"What? Like last time. It worked so well didn't it? So well in fact that humans are destroying both the Earth and the people this time around. At least previously their crimes didn't involve the planet. Does He really think His interference will change that, will change how humans behave?"

"Yes, He does."

This was crazy. "Do you know what He plans to do?"

"Yes. But this time I have you. You knew this day would come. You knew I'd expect you to fulfill your destiny. You are going to stop Him. You are going to prevent conception."

"And how do you propose I do this? Do you know who she is?"

"No. All I am sure of is the host will be young and innocent…again. He sees that part of the original formula as flawless."

"The Innocent One. How clichéd. Couldn't He come up with something better…original?"

Bastet gracefully laughed at my stupid pun. Then gave a nod. Her black fur shone in the moonlight, her eyes catching the twinkling of the stars. There was no denying her beauty.

"And which of his trusted…soldiers…will He choose for this…job."

Bastet chortled again. "Good choice of words, Khaldun. I don't know for sure except I believe it will be a *Mount Hermon Watcher. The Mount Hermon Watcher.*"

"*Grigori?*"

"Yes."

"Of all the ones to choose he had to pick *that* one. But that would mean a hybrid, a..."

"Yes, a *Nephilim*. And we – you – have to stop Him." Bastet turned from me again and began her ascent up the ancient stone steps.

I watched her go, unable to move. Now I understood the urgency of my presence here. Now I understood why Bastet wouldn't take 'no' for an answer this time. Now I understood...nothing.

What did she expect me to do?

Chapter One

MAY 2013

I was excited. I hadn't slept a wink, although I wasn't sure if it was from eagerness or from the man next to me who'd decided to use me as his personal pillow through our seven plus hour flight. He wasn't very happy when I woke him so I could watch our descent over London. After stretching and grumbling he turned to face me, stopped and blinked a couple of times, looked me up and down, let his eyes rest on *the ladies* and smiled. What was it about men and boobs? They were like little boys in a toy store, ogling what they couldn't have. I was sure up to the moment he saw my size C-cups he was going to complain because I caught the occasional curse word mumbled among other things before I got the *OMG, are those real* look. Well, at least he didn't say anything about my method of arousing him (a dig in the ribs when asleep wasn't the most pleasant of awakenings). Ha, 'arousing him' – talk about a good pun.

Apart from Mr Pillow-head, the flight had been uneventful. Basic. Cheap and cheerful, crammed into economy like all the other sardines in the can. The food had been inedible – apart from the chocolate bar – but the booze welcoming. I'd read two books on my Kindle – was half way through book three – because there'd been a problem with the entertainment system.

Having a window seat gave me a prime view of some easily recognizable landmarks as we circled overhead, waiting in the morning stack above London of incoming flights into Heathrow. Buckingham Palace, The Mall, The London Eye, Big Ben. Tesco: seriously, there was a flat-roofed building with TESCO written in giant letters that you could only see from above.

"Your first time in London, I take it?" Mr Pillow-head asked me.

"No. But it's been eighteen years so I have no memory of it."

"Well, welcome back then. Holidaying alone?" He was a middle-aged man, probably not quite as old as my dad but a lot better looking.

"Summer job." The captain came over the loud speakers informing the passengers and crew that we were clear to land.

Everyone had already placed their seats in the upright position, their trays folded away, their seatbelts on, and unfortunately electronic devices switched off – no Kindle to read for the last half hour. Honestly, I didn't mind – I enjoyed the view from the window too much.

"I'm Steve." He held out his hand to shake mine.

I obliged. "Abby."

"Pleased to meet you, Abby. Maybe we could go for coffee. Or meet up for drinks while you're here. Get to know each other." Steve hadn't let go of my hand. He'd moved in a little closer. Even though we'd been on this airplane all night, and Steve had never once headed to the bathroom, he smelled delicious. There was still a hint of body spray – or cologne – upon his person. With his more than five o'clock shadow – which was always sexy in my book – he was irresistible…almost.

"I don't think so." I added a disgusted look to my words as I pulled my hand out of his and proceeded to wipe said hand on my jeans. Then look pointedly at his left hand.

"I believe your wife may have a problem with you propositioning young women. And quite honestly, I find it insulting that you'd think I'd stoop so low as to sleep with a married man." I turned back to the window as I caught the final step of our landing. I refused to let this jerk next to me spoil my fun.

I was home. After eighteen years, I was home.

There was hardly a bump when the wheels hit the tarmac of the runway and I found it hard to contain my excitement. I swore my grin spanned from ear to ear.

After the plane finished taxiing to the terminal, I unbuckled my belt and collected my Kindle and small travel bag that I'd stowed under the seat in front of me. I found my sneakers under the same seat, untied the laces and put them back on. My feet were swollen and hot and cramming them into my Nikes was not fun.

The people waiting to leave, who were crammed into the two long isles, began to move. Mr. Pillow-head – I refused to think of him as Steve – had already left. Good. I quickly joined the long line and shuffled out of the open door.

The walk from the plane to immigration was long, really long. But I didn't care…until I had this sudden urge to pee. Mr. Pillow-head hadn't been the only one to not use the plane's facilities. Although I'd been living in New York for the past eighteen years, I was still a British citizen and therefore joined the fast-moving British and European passport line.

I shuffled along to the immigration guy, wishing for those in front of me to go quicker. I got my passport out ready for inspection when there were only two people left in front of me.

"Good morning. Hope your flight was pleasant." The cheerful immigration man held his hand out waiting for me to hand him my passport.

"Yes, thank-you." I was getting uncomfortable, trying not to make it obvious what the problem was, hopping from one foot to another, as he casually ran his fingers over his keyboard, checked his monitor, stamped my passport and then handed it back to me.

I quickly put my passport away safely and frantically looked for the restroom sign. I needed to find that bathroom, now.

I ran through the bathroom door to an empty stall. Fidgeted to undo my jeans quickly, still hopping around, and sat down rapidly, breathing a wonderful sigh of relief at being able to empty my bladder.

Chapter Two

Even though I'd taken some time in the bathroom to have a quick wash and to brush my hair and teeth, by the time I reached my flight's designated carousel my backpack had not arrived. I'd opted against a suitcase and bought myself a very large, framed backpack – fluorescent green – thinking it would be easier for traveling on public transport. Now, as I watched it appear from the depths of Heathrow's conveyer-belt system, I wondered how I was ever going to walk with it on my back…and not fall over.

Taking a deep breath, I grabbed for one of the straps and heaved with all my might. I managed to get it half way off the belt, over the top of a suitcase, before I had to start walking along the edge of the carousel. The buckle of one of the straps had caught under another suitcase. I stopped walking and pulled…hard. The suitcase came with my backpack and as the case tumbled over the metal edge, I lost my footing and fell hard on my ass.

Well, this was probably one time I wouldn't complain about having some good padding there.

I could feel the heat of embarrassment rise up my neck and onto my cheeks. I chortled to myself as I stood and brushed myself down. After I unhooked the unwanted suitcase I leveraged my backpack onto my shoulders and clipped the straps and waistband into place. I didn't look to see if anyone had seen me – it would be hard to miss what had happened. Instead, with a flushed face I kept my eyes

11

ahead and moved through Customs and headed straight for the Heathrow Express.

Due to the hour, the train was packed with standing room only. I rummaged through my carry-on bag and removed my Kindle. Hooking my arm around a pole, I turned my Kindle on and continued reading my third book. I sank into a world of *Jack Reacher*, enjoying the solitude. I loved my own company. Yes, I knew there were people everywhere but I didn't have to talk to them.

By the time I reached Victoria bus station, my legs ached from the weight of my backpack. And my lack of sleep was catching up on me. I was jostled constantly by the rush of daily commuters trying to get round me; I was going too slow. Trying to push myself forward I channeled all my energy into my legs to propel me onward, marching one, two, one, two.

I reached for the door to the ticket office but as I made contact a bolt of static electricity shot through my hand and up my arm.

"Ouch." I shook my hand. My heart raced, beating hard zapping my breath. I took a few gasps. I really didn't know what to make of what had just happened. And I was frightened to touch the door again, even though people were coming and going around me without a problem. No one else seemed to experience the same from touching the door. Except, there was a man – I thought – who'd moved away from me quickly too. I wasn't a hundred percent sure whether I'd imagined him or not; a dark hoodie had flickered in and out of my peripheral line of sight but I was sure his dark, olive-skinned hand had touched mine.

As my heart began to calm back down, one thing became very clear from what happened – I was turned on. I mean, really aroused. From all the times I'd received a jolt of static – New York winters were brutal for being dry and charged – I couldn't remember a time where I'd been turned on by a zap. I was embarrassed and knew I was glowing, body and eyes. I quickly scanned the people around me but all I saw were annoyed and angry faces – I was in the way.

The coach was waiting when I approached the designated bay. I gave my backpack to the driver, showed him my ticket and he put my pack in the luggage hold. I stretched out my shoulders and rubbed the back of my neck. Then checked my carry-on bag to make sure I had everything I needed: water bottle and Kindle. Yep, didn't need anything else.

There was a double seat free just one row in from the front. I settled myself next to the window and opened my Kindle to continue reading. I was supposed to be reading a soppy summer romance – something that was not my normal choice. And even though the romance novel would be an easy read, nothing too taxing on the brain, I wanted to finish my *Jack Reacher* novel first. I'd waited months for its release. Once I finished I'd have to swap to *that* one. I had promised Jen I would give it a try. I wasn't into the idea of fairytale romances at all. You know the thing: beautiful (size two) woman meets exceptionally handsome man with the requisite happy-ever-after ending. As far as I was concerned they weren't real and so I never saw the point in reading about them. But Jen had recommended this one as a good read. She promised me I would enjoy it, and said I needed something that would keep me occupied during my journey. And to give me some ideas for having a summer fling – as if I needed instructions in how to have sex with a man…not.

Jen – and her brother Jason – were my best friends, and my roommates. They were twins, although it was hard to believe. Jen was in complete contrast to Jason. Tiny, only five feet compared to Jason's towering figure of six-two. Jason was dark-haired, brown eyes like me, tanned and muscular, and Jen was strawberry-blonde, blue-eyes and a pallid complexion. Jason was boisterous and outgoing yet didn't cope well with crowds; Jen was timid until acting on stage where she loved being the center of attention. Jason was a cynic, Jen a romantic. I fitted somewhere in the middle, a drama queen as my mother liked to call me, flamboyant and chatty, but preferred to blend in with the crowd. And I lived in the real world – one that dealt with facts and little emotion…normally. And our lives together worked extremely well.

Living in New York was the first time JJ – that was my nickname for the two of them – had moved away from home. They were each other's best friend and NYU turned out to be the perfect opportunity for them to enjoy their college career. They both planned to be doctors. Something I had planned too.

I met JJ our first semester. We were all taking an anatomy and physiology course together, and hit it off. We became lab partners. Even though normally it was only two people partnering, due to the odd numbers in the class the professor allowed our team of three. We helped each other out with notes and studying. Having someone you could rely on during your college life was important – I was fortunate to find two people. And the bonus was we discovered that we had the same ridiculous sense of humor, same taste in music, and same desire to make the most of our college lives in New York City. We began to plan our schedules so that we could take other classes together. And then we found an apartment together.

I turned my Kindle off for a moment, stifled a yawn, and wondered what the time was. I'd forgotten to change my watch and because I was tired it took me a second or two to figure out the five hour time difference. The coach would be leaving soon. It wasn't full, unlike the plane. There were still plenty of seats left. It was also still relatively early and we were traveling away from London so I wasn't too surprised. The passengers varied from the very young to the old, and quite a few my age travelling alone. I really hadn't known what to expect. The only buses I'd ever been on were New York City buses, and that was rare.

I glanced out of the window and watched the driver close the luggage hold and head towards the door. As he rounded the corner of the bus he stopped to talk to someone for a minute. It was hard to see who it was, not that it mattered – I just wanted to get going.

The driver began to walk to the door again, the man he was talking to followed him. His face was shadowed by his dark hoodie and sunglasses, but it didn't stop my noticing a smile appear as he finished talking to the driver. If his mouth and smile were anything to go by he was obviously gorgeous. And mysterious with the cloak and dagger look, but that just made him intriguing. His body appeared broad, but not too hefty. The perfect V shape. Maybe I should start reading Jen's novel now. I laughed to myself; I always said there was nothing wrong with looking. Let's face it, men believed it was their right to look at beautiful women; why shouldn't us women be afforded the same opportunity if a situation presented itself.

I wasn't normally someone who made it that obvious, though. I must have been staring, gawping almost, because before I knew it he suddenly stopped where my seat was and slowly glanced my way.

"Hello." He stood to the side of my seat, not moving to his own. He was definitely attractive, and attractive men were always worth observing. But I was struggling to catch my breath, to make my perusal of his person appear to be just an interested inquiry because there was a humming, like a vibration of current, jumping between us.

With large hands resting on the headrests, his arms eased across the expanse of the seats. My eyes traced his profile in more detail now that he was closer. The sleek figure was sumptuous where his hooded sweatshirt didn't hide his biceps very well, and his jeans accentuated his long muscular legs that were planted firmly across the aisle. But it was his face that captured my interest. It was perfect, virtually flawless yet with a five O'clock shadow even though it was only ten in the morning. He'd probably been up all night. I just wished I could see his eyes – eyes exposed a person, reached into their soul.

I managed a gargled "Hi," my heart stuck in my throat beating loud and clear. Astounded by my encumbered voice, I speculated when I'd ever shied away from a man. Never. Unless of course he became intense, and then he was dumped faster than a pile of hot bricks.

The bus began to move and the man removed the small backpack from his right shoulder, and pulled his body into the double empty seat across the aisle, still aiming his smiling in my direction.

That smile…was…wow! I grinned then dropped my head a little. After flying three thousand miles, looking like

16

the back end of a bus, I couldn't believe this guy was showing an interest in me.

What was I thinking? I needed to clear my head, stop acting like a love-sick teenager. I'd left that era thirteen months ago and I had no plans of returning, not that I remembered ever behaving like that. I wasn't the dopey type. If I found a man attractive, I'd let him know; if he reciprocated we hung out, and I'd see how things went. One night stands were perfect and the conclusion I liked. Mmm, maybe if I weren't so tired I would have considered that approach with him.

I reached for my Kindle and switched it on. I hoped reading would calm the obvious blushing of my cheeks, appease my racing heart. And I tried to ignore him. But that proved difficult. I was convinced his eyes bored into me. And yet, when I plucked up the courage to peer over again, he appeared asleep, behind his very dark sunglasses and large hood.

Okay, so I still couldn't actually see his eyes, opened or closed. It was his body language that led me to this conclusion. He slouched slightly, his long legs jammed under the front seat, knees wedged into the seatback, and his head tilted towards the window. And yet, he continued to smile, his face almost animated.

This was ridiculous. I didn't even know this person, and had no intention of ever seeing him again.

I glanced down his body again, wanting one last look. His hands, one was resting on the shallow window-ledge, the other on the seat next to him. His hands, large, dark. His hand...I remembered. It was *his* hand that was on the door. His hand that sent a bolt of electricity through my body. His hand that switched on my sexual appetite with one touch.

Chapter Three

The journey to Peterborough passed by quickly with few stops, and the coach headed straight for the main terminal. I had a couple of hours to kill before my next bus. The bus driver retrieved my heavy backpack and I departed quickly, avoiding the man in the hoodie.

I headed towards the market square. I was hungry and, even though I'd been sitting on and off for hours I was too tired to do lots of walking. So I hunted for somewhere I could sit and eat.

There were plenty of places open but nothing seemed to appeal until I found a rundown café. Its chipped and scarred façade didn't put people off the food if the line out the door was anything to go by. I joined the back of the line and as I made it through the door I glanced up at the chalkboard. Although I'd left England aged two, England had not left me and as I read the first item listed, I knew exactly what I wanted.

"A bacon butty and a hot tea," I said to the buxom woman behind the counter.

"You'll get noffin' but 'ot tea here, love. Four pound, please." She held her hand out for the money. I got the impression I'd offended her but I wasn't really sure how.

As the woman handed me my order, I scanned the café for a free seat. The place overflowed with the lunchtime crowd. There was seating outside too but I was cold so I made my way to the rear to see if a table was free. Heavily

19

shadowed and all tables taken, I eventually spotted one seat right at the back. It would mean sharing with someone else who seemed preoccupied with a newspaper. His back was to me so I virtually had to sit in the spare seat before I caught his attention.

"Is this seat taken?" I asked.

He looked up and I couldn't believe it. It was Mr. Hoodie from the bus.

I could feel my neck and cheeks heating and I tried to smile without appearing too dumbstruck, especially after all the staring I'd done on the bus with him. Then I reminded myself he hadn't actually seen me gawping.

"Hello. Again," he said smiling. That voice: deep, gentle, calming. This time his hoodie was down and his glasses were off. His eyes captured my attention immediately and I struggled to respond to him or even to stop staring…again. A vibrant emerald with slashes of gold appeared almost translucent, reached to the edge, covering nearly the whole of the white of his eyes; the pupils were large, each a black abyss.

"Please, have a seat," he gestured his hand – that hand – towards the empty chair as a way to confirm that the seat was available, and then he quickly returned to reading his paper.

"Thank-you," I mumbled.

I sat quietly, enjoying my tea and sandwich. I really didn't know what to say to this guy but it seemed rude to share a table with someone and not at least say a few words.

"Are you going far?" He asked casually in his eloquent English accent, as if we'd already been conversing. Great minds thought alike – I was grateful he'd started a topic.

"Mablethorpe, a small seaside resort on the east coast." I tried to sound normal but my voice came out as a squeak. This was ridiculous – when had I ever had problems speaking to a guy.

"Yes, I know where Mablethorpe is." He answered. I had stated the obvious. "You're American?" He questioned yet his face told me he knew the answer. Well, maybe he didn't.

"Yes. Well no. Kind of. Well, not really. I live there but I'm originally from here." At least my voiced stopped sounding like someone was strangling a cat, so I continued.

"My parents moved when I was two. I don't have much memory of living here but for some reason it still feels like home." His face showed no surprise and very little interest. I shouldn't have said so much. I should have stuck to my normal answer when asked that question. I should have just said 'yes'.

He returned to reading his paper that lay open on the table. His glossy, virtually black hair fell round his face. Straight except for a slight kink where he tucked it behind his ears. His hair wasn't long per se, just brushed the top of his shoulders. It suited him, matched his eyes and dark olive-colored skin.

I held my mug of tea between my hands and let my focus stay on him. I analyzed the contours of his face, the flicker of his eyes and eyelids as he scanned the newspaper. I watched his hand move and turn a page.

He stared back at me. Just stared.

"Do I have a horn growing out the top of my head or something?" He smirked. I jolted out of my trance. I'd never felt so embarrassed.

"No! No. Sorry." Diverting my eyes rapidly, I

21

concentrated on the hot tea and moved the mug up to my mouth to take a sip.

Why was I acting so juvenile? I needed to gain some control of what I was doing, what I was saying.

I struggled to capture my heart back. It had decided to not only go somersaulting, but take a much needed jog around the room with my blood gushing through my veins at the same rate, pulsating in my neck and wrists. My hands felt hot and clammy, and yet holding the hot mug helped.

"I'm Khal," he offered. I really wished he wouldn't keep smiling like that.

"Abby. Well, Abigail but I don't like Abigail. Actually, I don't like Abby either but I consider it the lesser of two evils." Shit, I was rambling again.

"I wouldn't have expected to find you in a place like this," he said as his eyes scanned the decorations at the back of the café. Rustic was a compliment. The peeling faded floral wallpaper still held the remnants of the old smoking laws, the mismatched tables and chairs had ancient love-hearts etched deep into their history, names past and present.

"Why not?" I asked. At least it matched the outside.

"You don't seem the type. I would have put you more for a modern wine bar, enjoying the young crowds. Or country club."

I couldn't help but screw my face up at the thought of the ostentatious idiots who thought that if you go to a wine bar you were considered important, there to be seen and noticed. And I'd had enough of country clubs to last me a lifetime for the same reason.

Khal laughed at my expression, "Okay. Maybe not then," he added with a giggling sigh and shake of his head.

"There's nothing pretentious about it, no airs and

graces. I love it."

"Yes, me too."

A comfortable quietness descended between us and I finished my tea. Khal read a bit more of his newspaper. He had what looked like a black coffee that had hardly been touched.

"The weather makes it easier for traveling today. We've had a lot of rain over the last few days." Khal was folding up his newspaper.

I burst out laughing.

"What's so funny?" He asked, his eyes dancing with laughter.

"You're talking about the weather. That is such a British thing to do. Doesn't it always rain? This is England after all. If it isn't raining, it's grey, cloudy. Even in the summer."

He was amazingly expressive in his face, in his eyes. He watched me laugh, his eyes dancing, his mouth turning into a full grin.

"Okay," he resigned, pulling his fingers through his hair, something he had done a few times now. "So, where do you live in The States?"

"New York. Well, I'm at college in New York – NYU – but I live in New Jersey. It's a state next to New York City."

"What brings you back here?" Like before, when he asked about my being American, I couldn't quite make out whether he was just making idle conversation or whether he was actually genuinely interested.

"Summer vacation. Job."

"Is accommodation provided? It can be expensive finding somewhere for just a summer job."

"I don't need to." When my parents moved to The

23

States they'd sold the house and bought somewhere smaller near one of mom's friends. Investment and vacations they'd said – we never came for a vacation

"You have a home here?"

"My parents do, yes," I answered hesitantly. "That was a good guess."

"Well..." He looked thoughtful. "You didn't mention family in your reason for being here. So if you're not staying with family, the logical answer was because you have a home here." He smiled as if to dispel my questioning.

It worked. "Ah. I will be seeing family while I'm here. But my cousin is still in school so we're planning on meeting up in London in August."

"Do you come back often then?"

"No. I haven't been back since I left. Eighteen years. Our family normally come over to see us. They like New York, the shopping, the weather. Or sometimes we'll meet up in Florida. But I wanted to come home. I've wanted to come back for a long time. Now that I'm in college I have more flexibility and my mom's friend asked if I'd come and help out. So here I am."

"What are you studying?"

"Art History. I'd planned on being a doctor but couldn't cope with the gory bits. Had a major freaking out session and it brought my whole college route to an abrupt end. Jen and I – my best friend – were waiting in the lab for Jason – her twin brother – to return with our assignment for that lesson. We were chatting about an upcoming test and I didn't pay attention to what was on the agenda until Jason turned up with a fetal pig. At first he wiggled it in front of my face then slapped it down on the tray in front of me. I completely freaked, screaming and jumping around. Quite pathetic really when I think back.

"It wasn't my first over-reaction. I'd fainted a couple of times before, but screaming blue murder with the pig was the last straw. The professor called me in for a conference and encouraged me to look at other options for my future. He said my over-reactions were a trait of someone who shouldn't be going into medicine. I agreed without hesitation. I was still reeling from the dissection class and could understand what he was saying. Anyway, that was the end of my career as a doctor. Art History was already my minor and was a safer bet. Can't really overreact too much with it."

Our conversation stopped there. Or should I say I stopped rambling. He'd been attentive so it wasn't awkward; I just felt as though I'd done almost all of the talking between us. Anyway, I needed to go and catch my bus. I also wanted to go to the newsagents for a magazine. I needed a change from my Kindle. Lots of colorful photographs and short articles sounded very good right now.

"Thanks for sharing your table." I stood up and lifted my heavy backpack onto my shoulders and attached the waist and chest straps. Then undid the chest one – my boobs were already obvious without encouragement. "It was nice meeting you."

"Hope to see you again soon," he said.

Not thinking anything more about his last comment other than it was better than saying 'goodbye,' I left.

Chapter Four

I loved the quaint newsagents. They were like a dampened down, almost childlike version of a corner 7/11. And I knew the minute I walked in I wasn't going to get just a magazine. I opened the rickety door and a little bell rung above my head. The door caught the metal flap that rung the bell and I experienced a sudden flash of memory, a recollection from long ago – mom, me, and a sweetie shop. For the first time I could actually remember something from my life here. I waited for more of the memory to surface. Nothing came. And although the smells in the shop were familiar, I couldn't be certain whether they were provoking the same memory as the bell or reminding me of the times relatives brought the requisite candy when they visited us in the States.

I headed straight for the counter and scanned the rows of jars behind the stooped, gray-haired man. Eeny, meeny, miny, moe... There were so many good choices – some I'd never heard of before. "I'll take 50 grams of Cola Cubes and 50 grams of strawberry BonBons." While my selection was being weighed I headed back to the magazine racks. I picked up two magazines that looked interesting. I knew there would be features in the magazines that I wouldn't have a clue about – the Soap Stars were a given. But the short stories would be readable.

The man finished weighing my candy and placed them into two small white paper bags. I placed the magazines on the counter and paid. Although I'd been lucky to be served quickly when I'd arrived at the shop, it was now bustling with about half a dozen customers waiting after me which made it a struggle when I tried to leave with the huge backpack on my back!

"Excuse me…excuse me." I squeezed my way through as each person squished themselves up to the shelves on the opposite wall.

"Thanks." A kind gentleman held the door open for me and I breathed a sigh of relief as I made it outside.

Now, for the coach. I headed back the way I came, passed the café and towards the bus station. I couldn't decide which candy to pop into my mouth first – both took a long time to eat if you sucked them. I chose a bonbon.

I arrived at the station, my mouth bulging on one side with my piece of candy, and checked the monitors. This final part of my trip was going to be a slow run. It stopped in every village, and there were a lot of them. After collecting my ticket, I walked across to section three where my bus was waiting, and again handed my backpack over to the driver and embarked. The bus was packed and all the seats were taken in the front. I made my way down to the back – the only space left was on the long back bench across the rear.

I was not looking forward to this. I hated travelling in the back of cars. It was the one place I was sure to get travelsick. I just hoped a coach wasn't worse.

I shuffled into the corner so I could keep out of everyone's way. I knew I wouldn't be getting off for quite a while.

Village by village, the coach made its stops, and as people got off some occasionally came on. The coach did appear to be losing more than we were gaining because there

27

were fewer people close to me, but it was hard to tell how empty the front was from where I was sitting. I tried to close my eyes for a short while. I was exhausted. It didn't work for long. Having to stop so often kept me awake; I slept on a coach as well as I did on a plane - never.

I flipped through the magazines to see if there was anything interesting to read. Horoscopes, crosswords, Dear Ann, Dear Doctor, soap opera news – the normal contents of a weekly magazine. I flipped past them to the stories. Real life or fiction, it didn't matter, they were all the same: summer romances! Typical. I gave up and just enjoyed the view of the countryside. It didn't take long for the effects of being on the back bench to take ahold of my stomach and it took all my effort to concentrate on keeping my lunch down.

"Hello." The voice made me jump and I looked quickly to where it came from.

"Khal. What are you doing here?" I was utterly surprised to see him. Pleasantly surprised.

He was wearing his hoodie and dark sunglasses again – and his infectious smile. I couldn't help but smile back as he placed himself next to me on the bench.

"You don't look too well." He seemed genuinely concerned.

"I don't travel too well in the back. I'll be fine, though. It doesn't help that I'm so tired." I didn't want my upset stomach to make Khal run in the opposite direction.

"Wait there." He went away and came back a minute later. "Come on."

I followed him. He walked towards the front of the bus and stopped three rows in. There was a seat free.

"Thank-you." I slid onto the bench and Khal came in next to me.

28

My upset stomach didn't stand a chance with him so close. I had butterflies fluttering like crazy inside, and my heart was skipping along with the rhythm of the engine. Then I soon forgot about my queasy stomach because all I could think about was how good he smelled. Delicious in fact. Almost better than the candy I'd just finished.

Did I really just think that? I was never normally interested in that stuff, never normally noticed the smell of a man unless the idiot had doused himself in cologne or he stank of B.O.

He sat very close but didn't touch. I couldn't look at him. My cheeks were burning and I was sure my neck would be just as crimson. But I felt this uncontrollable desire, need to at least sneak a glance. So I watched his hands on his legs and then occasionally peeked upwards trying to just use my eyes rather than move my head.

"Is that where your family's from? Mablethorpe?" It was obvious he liked to work with his hands; tiny scars were dotted on the back of each one.

"No. Coventry." His hands stroked his thighs. I could feel the heat radiating from his body.

"So why Mablethorpe?" A tingling ran through me as if some type of magnetic force vibrated between us. I tried very hard to ignore it – but it was difficult. Actually, impossible.

"I don't know for sure. I think it was because Mom had a friend who moved there and it was easier to have a property near someone we knew so they could keep an eye on it for us. I think mom planned on coming back either every year for the summer or move back permanently. But it didn't happen." I took in another breath and relished inhaling the smell that was all Khal – man and nature and

29

ruggedness. If he was wearing cologne, it was subtle, organic. And it allowed my mind to wonder for a few minutes.

"What about you? Where do you live?" I asked. Even though our chatting was effortless, relaxed, unforced, I still felt as though I was doing all the talking.

"Not far. Near a village called Alford. We'll be there soon." He noticed my magazines. "Not interesting?"

"No. Trashy holiday romances, and articles on soap stars and I've no clue who they are." Khal laughed at my lack of interest.

I flipped through one of the magazines to show him some of the articles. He explained who the people featured inside were.

We seemed to talk non-stop. I talked non-stop.

Before I knew it, Khal was getting off and I was sorry to see him go.

The rest of my journey, another twenty minutes, took forever and for some reason my excitement at being here dampened. I kicked myself for not asking for his number or something, for not asking him out for a coffee.

My exhaustion came back with a vengeance, only just realizing that for all this time it had abated. I'd been up for almost twenty-seven hours and it was obviously starting to take a toll.

The coach was still pretty full when it was time for my stop. There were about six more people that got off with me: a couple in their sixties and a family. None of them went in the same direction as me. I wasn't even sure if they noticed I existed, they were so caught up in their own world. Good. I didn't want to stop and talk to anyone. I felt talked out.

The coach driver retrieved my backpack from the hold for me. I placed my magazines into my pack, put the pack on my back and fastened the buckles. I tried to stop it from weighing me down by keeping the straps tight. Weary, I told myself it wasn't far to go now.

Unfortunately, it was still a bit of a hike to the house from the drop-off point. I'd checked the map before leaving New York; it was a pretty easy route. I walked as quickly as was humanly possible on the narrow sidewalk. Sand lay along the edge of the roads and felt soft under my sneakers whenever I had to step off the curb to go round people and obstacles. Schools were finished for the day and there were quite a few teenagers hanging around, enjoying the nice weather. Mothers and fathers collected their little ones from school and took them for ice-cream. Yes, there were many clouds, but the sun was warm when it managed to sneak through the gaps. Yet I felt cold.

The front door to the cottage was literally on the sidewalk where the sidewalk narrowed even further, away from the main hub of the town. It was the second in a row of four stone cottages, just before a stable where I could smell the horses. Obviously, being directly on the sidewalk there was no front yard, and from what mom said the back yard was tiny and slabbed, not even big enough to swing a cat round in. Good – no upkeep.

I placed the key in the lock and turned it to open the door. There was a little step up into what used to be a hallway and now was part of the snug living room. I breathed a sigh of relief when I saw that Alice, mom's best friend and my godmother, had taken all the dust covers off and laid a fire ready for a match to light it. I had never seen anything look more inviting.

31

I dropped my things down at the foot of the stairs and collapsed. I had made it. I went through to the kitchen, a door just off the living room. I could hear the fridge humming and there was a box of groceries waiting on the worktop. Inside was a loaf of bread, cereal, tea, coffee, sugar and a bottle of red wine.

I couldn't help laughing to myself thinking I'd just struck gold – *Alice, you're my hero*. The under-counter refrigerator housed the milk, butter, cheese and eggs. She'd thought of everything.

Right, first things first, I needed to call Mom to let her know I'd arrived safely. I hunted for my cell phone in the side pocket of my backpack, and switched it on. It took a few minutes for the phone to recognize the different country and service. I put some coffee on while I waited.

"Mom? It's me. I'm here." I got through first time and wasn't surprised to find mom at home, probably waiting for my call.

"Yes, everything looks fine. Alice has done a wonderful job of making sure everything was ready for me … yeah, she even did some shopping. She thinks of everything…yeah, I'll go upstairs soon." Mom was her normal self and worrying, checking I had everything I needed.

"Tell Ben I'll call him later in the week. Okay. Love you too. Bye." I left my phone in the kitchen and found my charger with adapter and plugged it in.

The house was perfect for just me on my own. Cozy, Mom called it, a two up, two down plus one (the bathroom). There were two rooms downstairs, the kitchen and living room, both of which were smallish and were positioned one behind the other. Then tagged on the back was a tiny utility with washing machine and back door. The stairs were steep and narrow, and led from the corner of the living room to a small platform where there were two bedrooms and a bathroom: the larger bedroom was over the living room at the front of the cottage; the smaller one on the right was over the kitchen; the bathroom was next to the small bedroom, cute and functional.

I didn't waste any time. I took my things upstairs to the front room, unpacked what I needed for now and headed for a shower. A relaxing evening and an early night was in order for sure.

Chapter Five

I woke around midday, feeling groggy. The bottle of wine had aided my sleep well. Too well.

I ventured downstairs to the kitchen, collecting the local newspaper on the way that was lying on the floor under the mail slot in the door. Alice really was determined to have me blending in with the locals if she thought of having a newspaper delivered – I wondered if she expected my accent to change too. I placed it on the kitchen table, switched the radio on, and headed over to the sink. The dishes from last night were piled haphazardly, waiting to be cleaned: a small frying pan that I made an omelet in – one of the very few things I could make – my plate, cutlery and glass. It wasn't a lot, but the sink was small.

Singing along to the radio, as I'd always done since I could remember, I put the coffeepot on, put bread in the toaster, and cleaned the dishes. There was no dishwasher in this kitchen – there wasn't room – so I stood at the sink, looking out of the kitchen window, and washed the few items, enjoying the freedom of singing at the top of my voice without Jason joining in and ruining my fun. I put the last provisions away that were left in the box, and made a quick list of items I needed for the next couple of days.

The kitchen was tiny; enough room for two people. There was a small counter and some old cupboards: two double base units and a small row of wall units. There was a pantry in the corner that ran under the stairs for extra storage. The kitchen table was a little collapsible thing that rested against the only free wall. It was left permanently up, and two small chairs sat opposite each other, ready for use.

My toast was ready and waiting, popped up in the toaster. I spread a small amount of butter on my toast, cut it in two, and poured a coffee. I perched my tush on the edge of the chair next to the table and looked to see what news was being sold today.

News was news, no matter where you lived in the world. Headlines were there to capture the reader, even when the story had little substance. It didn't matter whether it was local, national or international news, as long as it was dramatic, theatrical, or spectacular enough so someone would buy their paper. The gorier or more shocking the better. And today's corny quip was no different:

CAT-ASTROPHE: SIGHTING ALARMS LOCALS

The story told how for years there had been sightings of large cats – wild panthers, leopards – throughout Lincolnshire. Early yesterday evening, a local couple were walking their dog when they spotted what appeared to be a large black cat. Was it the return of the *Lincolnshire Panther*, or the *Lindsay Leopard*? Had the *Beast of Bodmin* ventured north?

The paper dedicated virtually three pages to the story, rehashing past sightings, showing fuzzy photographs, going back decades. Yet, no large creature had ever been caught, so the journalist hinted at the possibility of it being the same cat.

I smiled at how over-the-top the reporters had gone. It was just one sighting, something that didn't happen very often by the sound of it, and would mean that this one cat would be nearly forty years old. I dismissed the hype as I did many stories like it in the States – it was just a local legend that kept resurfacing when there was nothing else to write about. The opinion column, at the end of the three-page spread, basically said the same thing. It was good to see that some people still had the ability to think practically, and live in the real world.

I finished reading the rest of the paper – nothing else was written to amuse me. I had a lot planned for today. Apart from doing a little local exploring and shopping, I needed to go and see Alice at the store. I also needed to get one of the bicycles in the shed checked out if I wanted some transport. Apparently there were a few in there.

My coffee and toast had revitalized my body, my brain. My head felt better and I was raring to go.

I dressed in my jeans and sneakers, grabbed my rain jacket – it looked like it was going to rain – and headed to the shed in the corner of the backyard. It took no more than six steps to reach the shed from the back door. The door creaked as I opened it. Inside were the bicycles lined up with their front wheels away from me.

I kind of looked forward to having the freedom of cycling around the town and out on the quiet country roads. I was normally petrified of riding a bicycle on roads but there were many cyclists here and I was told the drivers were used to bicycles. I needed some easy transport and didn't have a driving license. I'd never learned to drive.

I needed to take one of the bicycles to the local repair shop to give the bicycle an overhaul. I had no idea how long it was since the bicycles had been used and the tires looked like they had disintegrated as bits of rubber fell away as I wheeled the bicycles one by one out of the shed. I picked one that looked in relatively good condition – apart from the tires – and put the rest back.

Above the bicycles were shelves where all the outdoor supplies, bicycle pumps and helmets, and cleaning stuff were kept. I reached for one of the buckets off the shelf, and a sponge.

I filled the bucket with warm soapy water in the kitchen sink and returned to the yard to clean the bicycle. It was covered in thick grease that looked a lot like Vaseline with bits of dust and grit embedded from lack of use. I had to move the bistro table and chairs over to the corner of the patio to make room for the bicycle, bucket and me. Cleaning the bicycle was a quick job, and I was soon finished.

I returned the bucket to the shed and left the sponge on the garden table to dry. I took the bicycle through the back gate to the alleyway that ran behind the cottages so I could wheel it round to the front of the cottage.

I changed my jeans because they were covered in soapy water, and collected my pocket book and my shopping list. After locking the front door I walked the bicycle to town.

The bicycle store was in a direction perpendicular to Alice's shop, down one of the side streets behind High Street.

I dropped the bicycle off. They said it would take two days before they'd have it road-worthy. I wasn't surprised. I was actually grateful they'd be able to get it fixed.

I left the store with my receipt and headed towards Alice's, the other end of town. It was a pleasant walk with just a fine drizzle. I had my yellow jacket on and my hood up. There was a wide variety of stores between the bicycle shop and Alice's shop: pizzeria, fish and chip shop, tacky gift shops, newsagents, grocers, bakers, butchers, cafés, florists, pubs and even a wine bar. Unfortunately, no bank. I needed to find a bank so I could open an account.

I arrived in front of Alice's shop and noticed a bookstore next door. It looked new. It attracted my attention immediately with its name – on a bright blue background, the yellow writing said "Yellowbellies". A strange name for a bookstore but certainly eye catching – I smiled wondering what it was like inside. Small bookstores were a rarity these days. Even the large book stores struggled against their online competitors.

I headed into Alice's store and pulled my hood down. It was a seaside gift shop, not quite as tacky as some could be. If Florida was anything to go by, tourists enjoyed tacky, the tackier the better. However, locally made products were always sought after all year round by everyone, tourists and locals. Alice's store sold everything you could imagine for vacationers and more. She was also one of the few stores that specialized in many local items: pottery, jewelry, lace, wooden ornaments, puzzles, children's toys, homemade candy, preserves. It was a positive hive for someone needing that gift and who couldn't decide what they wanted.

"Hi Alice." Even though she had her back to me, I would recognize her anywhere. She hadn't changed a bit. With Alice being mom's best girlfriend from school, I had known her my whole life. They had been friends since second grade. Mom told me many fun stories about the antics that the two of them got up to. Both didn't have siblings, and bonded immediately, confiding in each other their most intimate secrets. They were also there for each other's joys and sorrows, the best and worst of times: their first crush, their first kiss, their first piercing, their first period. Their first love, their first heartbreak, their first time…

Mom told me how she was the first one to discover Alice was pregnant. A time that turned Alice's life upside down forever. Alice complained of feeling sick a couple of times, nothing drastic. Then turning her nose up at foods that were normally her favorite. Then she missed her period. She was staying over at mom's one night so mom picked up a pregnancy test and persuaded Alice to take it. Alice couldn't look so mom did. It was positive.

When Alice's family found out they kicked her out. She was 17 and moved in with Rob's family until they had enough money to get their own place. Rob and Alice had been together since ninth grade, Rob was in twelfth. Mom said how everyone knew they would stay together. They were inseparable. And they did stay together. Rob supported and cared for Alice through her whole pregnancy and birth. And loved being a father.

With the help of Rob's parents it took Rob and Alice two years to get their own home, and they loved it. Alice finished her high school education at home then continued with some college courses, while being a stay-at-home mom. Rob worked during the day and went to college at night to finish his degree. Their life was perfect…

Until Rob died when Kristen was four. When mom told me the story, she cried. She'd been with Alice through it all. And Rob had remained the love of Alice's life.

A couple of years after Mom told me about Rob and Alice, I found a photograph of the three of them in Mom's treasure box. Mom was out and Alice was looking after me. She came every year to visit and stay. After I found the photograph, I asked her about it. I will never forget the look in her eyes, the way she glowed talking about Rob, came alive with the memories. She loved talking about him, the past. It became our thing to do whenever she visited.

"Abigail!" Alice flung her arms around me and kissed me hard on my cheek. It was wonderful seeing her again. When I was younger, she was like a second mom, especially when mom was pregnant and having my brother, Ben. Mom and Dad had found out that Ben had Downs Syndrome while mom was pregnant, and they took the news hard. Life at home was never the same again. Alice dropped everything, closed her little shop, and came to stay with us to take care of me whenever mom and dad needed her. Alice never had any more children so I became her 'other' daughter. Kristen was a lot older than me, 13 years older, so Alice was flexible with her time. Our time together became important because it was my escape from the pain at home, the pain I saw in my parents' eyes every day. I wasn't old enough to understand what was going on. I was only eight when Ben was born, but I was old enough to know it was something serious, something their marriage never got over, never recovered from. And even though mom and dad remained married on paper, I became aware as time passed that it was in name only, separate beds, then separate homes, then dad with women on the side, then no communication between the two of them apart from anything to do with us children. And no family vacations. Something had died in them both. But Alice was still Alice. My rock when I needed her.

But for the last few years, Alice had been unable to come over, instead making her annual vacation a trip to see her daughter. And I'd missed her.

"Oh, it's so good to see you." Alice took a step back. She kept her hands on my shoulders and looked me up and down. "Goodness you've grown up. You're absolutely beautiful. I always knew you would be." She grinned and a tiny tear fell down her cheek.

"It's good to see you again too. And I'm so pleased I can help out. I bet you're very excited to be seeing Kristen." Kristen had moved to Australia about five years ago, and was now getting married.

"Oh, I can't wait. She sent photos through of where the wedding's going to be. It looks amazing. Miles and miles of white sandy beaches, crystal clear waters. Perfectly romantic."

Yuck.

Alice let go of me and went to go into the back room of the store. I followed.

We all knew how hard Alice had found it when Kristen decided to move to Australia. But Alice knew the importance of letting her daughter go, and never regretted her decision to give Kristen her blessing. Alice had once told me she never wanted Kristen to experience the pain of a parent's rejection as she had.

Alice put the tea kettle on to make a pot of tea and she chatted about Kristen's wedding, and she showed me all the recent photos. I told Alice how mom and Ben were doing, and how Ben was getting on in his new school. I told her about JJ and how college was going – or not going as the case may be. I told her about Mr. Pillow-head on the plane and we laughed together, calling him all the names we could think of and pretending we were phoning his wife to tell her what a slimeball he was. Before we knew it we were both

41

almost rolling on the floor laughing. I was holding my stomach because it hurt so much.

"When do you leave?" I wiped the tears from my cheeks, still giving an occasional giggle.

"In four days, and counting! It's up to you how you want to do the swap over. Do you want to come in for a couple of days?"

"Sure." It sounded like a good idea.

Alice continued to explain the hours her employees worked and where the banking needed to go. "There is a bank at the top of High Street. I have arranged for John, the owner of next door, to take the banking for you on Fridays and Tuesdays. That way you're not walking around with wads of money."

"The bookstore? That place stands out."

"Yes, it does. It's made a huge difference to my business. I get a lot of his customers calling in now. And John's a great help whenever I need some muscle around here."

"Yellowbellies is a funny name. What made him choose that?"

"It's a nickname for people from Lincolnshire."

"Why yellowbellies?"

"No idea. It's totally crazy, but it makes people laugh."

"Talking of banking, I need to open a bank account. Is the one you mentioned the best?"

Alice smiled, "This is a small place. There isn't a lot of choice. There is another one on the other side of town, but I have no idea what it's like."

"I'll stick with the same one then. I'll go there later. Would it be ok to come in on a banking day so I could see what needs to be done?"

"Great idea. And you could take the laptop back with you so you can go over the book-keeping. I'll make sure everything's in order for you. Oh it's good to have you here." Alice was grinning from ear to ear.

"It's good to be here." The last few years melted away as if our time of separation never existed.

Chapter Six

So, dating anyone serious?" Alice poured another cup of tea for the two of us.

"No, not me. A couple of, you know, hook-ups."

Alice looked questioningly at me. "And that's it?"

"I'm not interested. I love my freedom, being able to do what I want to do. You know that. Why?"

"Oh, just wondering. I was thinking that now you knew you weren't going to be a doctor that someone may be on the scene."

"No. I...I don't know what to do. I had everything planned out: college, med school, doctor. Then think about my personal life, settling down. Now all that's changed. I'm enjoying what I'm doing, love living in New York, but I've one more year and I'm finished with my degree. And I don't know what to do. Panicking a bit. The changes hit my confidence a bit but I'm trying not to let it get me down. I plan to use this time away to really think, look at my options. Oh, I don't know. Maybe I should do some travelling."

"Do you know where you'd like to go?"

"No. That's what's so crazy. I have these ideas but nothing concrete anymore. It's as if my life fell apart when I changed my career path. And I can't make a decision. I'd like to travel but I don't know where I want to go. I'm enjoying my art history but I don't know what to do with it. I thought about combining the two, travel and art, but I still get stuck.   Except wanting to be here.   Coming back to England, well, it feels like I've come home."

"I'm sure you'll have an inspiration one day and it'll all come to you. And you never know, you may just meet that man of your dreams." Alice laughed at the face I pulled. She was such a romantic. As bad as Jen.

"Well, I did meet the most gorgeous man in the whole world on the coach. Maybe the love of my life." I exaggerated a swoon making us both laugh, but there was something inside me that jumped when I added that last comment.

"Oooh, tell me more."   Alice always liked to play along. She loved to make up stories for me when I was a little girl, trying to get me interested in fairytales, Prince Charmings, knights in shining armor. I had never been a girly girl, even though Alice tried different techniques – make up, pierced ears, pretty dresses, Disney princess movies – so when we did play our games, I always voted to be the man. And I could never quite get the hang of bridging that gap between it being fiction and really meeting Prince Charming one day and falling in love. To me, they were just stories, and never based on any kind of reality. My only real role models were mom and Alice and just look at what happened to both of them and their *Prince Charmings*.

"I'm sure I won't see him again."   I paused a moment, remembering. "He was mysterious, gothic almost. Not normally my type. But there was just something about him that, well, I don't know. He was…different." I thought about that face again, those eyes, his hands; they weren't something I was going to forget in a hurry.

Alice laughed, "Well, don't forget to let me inspect him if he does turn up."

"I doubt that will happen. Anyway, you never know, I may meet the man of my dreams, right here, in your store and stay here forever." Alice knew I was joking. She knew I'd never believed her romance stories. It never stopped her from telling them, though. And it never stopped her believing that one day it would happen.

We finished our teas and Alice went back to work. I headed up to the bank to transfer my money over from the U.S.

The rain had come and gone and it was now back to a gray drizzle, the type that penetrated deep making me feel cold and soggy. I really didn't want to go anywhere else except back home, but I craved some ravioli for dinner. And I needed to replenish the empty wine bottle.

On the way to the bank I'd passed a deli where I would be able to get everything I wanted. I hated cooking so having things pre-made was a must. I had my hood up on my rain coat and rushed to the deli after the bank, not looking where I was going.

As I opened the door, I ran straight into someone who was carrying a shopping basket. Unfortunately, the basket didn't move.

"Ouch!" I hunched over and grabbed my stomach. That really hurt.

"I am so sorry. Are you okay?" His voice made me stop complaining instantly. It was Khal. Of all the places to bump into him. The raindrops dripped off my hood and ran down my face. I dropped my hood down and tried to dry my face off a little with the back of my hands. I knew I looked a complete mess: my hair would now be uncontrollably frizzy and it was coming loose from my hair-tie; my make-up was smudged if the black, beige and gray marks across the back of my hand were any indication.

"Yes...yes, I'm fine." I lied.

And he knew. I could see it on his face that he knew I was lying.

I kept running my fingers under my eyes and across my cheeks in hopes of removing any residual make-up streaks and tried to change the subject so looked in his basket, "Did I hit anything interesting?"

Everything he had in his basket was what I was wanting – wine, cheese, crackers, ravioli, more wine, sliced peppers, salad, fruit salad, more wine.

"Similar tastes, I see." Teasing him came easily and I didn't find myself feeling flustered or experiencing uncontrollable blushing like I had yesterday. "Did you read my mind?" I was only joking, but Khal was still looking a little upset, and now a little perturbed at my joke.

"I'm okay, you know. I'll live." I reached out to reassure him by touching his arm, but he quickly moved out of my way and went to the counter to pay for his items. Okay then. I backed off.

"Would you like to share?" he said, looking over his shoulder. He had on his shades and a raincoat over his jeans with his hood still up.

"No, you don't have to do that. I was coming in to get some supplies." I was surprised by his offer and really felt awkward now. Yet, I wanted to say 'yes'. I knew it was dangerous to agree to dinner with a total stranger. But... He was incredibly attractive, and so easy to talk to – way too easy. And we obviously had a similar taste in food and wine.

There was also something about him, something that told me I could completely and utterly trust him and he would keep me safe.

"I know. But I want to...if you'll let me."

How could I not. He only had to smile and I forgot about his mood swings.

Khal finished paying for his basket of shopping – I completely forgot to check my list for anything I would need – and we walked casually to the cottage. It never occurred to me we would go anywhere else, and Khal didn't suggest an alternative or show any resistance. In fact, if I actually thought about it, he led and I followed...in the right direction to my cottage.

He asked about my day as we walked side-by-side, and I told him all about having tea with Alice and then going to the bank. And all the time I could feel the buzz of electricity between us and struggled to keep my hands to myself. I was sure he knew the effect he had on me yet he showed no reaction himself. And then there was this incredible response of my body when he smiled, and when he talked. A flutter, deep in my stomach that would jump up to my chest and make my heart beat faster.

I never ever expected to experience such a strong attraction to someone. Oh, I'd heard from friends about the sensuality of meeting someone you are seriously attracted to. Some of them even believed in soulmates – I always put that down to infatuation, obsession of the opposite sex, something that had never interested me, or that I had even thought about until this moment.

Oh for God's sake – soulmate, I didn't even know the man. Not that that had ever stopped me before. No attachments – a quick fling. That's all I was interested in. So what was stopping me just going for it with Khal? I could only put it down to the way he kept a distance from me, just enough that told me not to touch.

No, it was definitely just being here, on vacation, on my own and jetlagged that had my head stumbling over these ridiculous thoughts. I knew the feeling would wear off soon. And I would find something out about him – a disgusting habit, a criminal past – that would put an instant stop to all this. Or I'd just do my normal thing; have sex with him.

Then it would all be over and I could stop thinking about him...

We reached the cottage door and I retrieved my key to open the door. Khal followed behind closing the front door behind him and I headed straight for the kitchen.

Out of habit, I switched the radio on and began to hum to the music.

"Red or white?" Khal held both bottles in front of him.

"Red." I handed Khal the corkscrew and held my hand out for his coat so I could hang it up with mine in the back porch. He quickly removed his hoodie and almost flung it at me. I removed my rain jacket and hung them both up. Then returned to the kitchen and retrieved the cheese board, a knife and a couple of plates then a tray to put everything on. I placed a pan of water on the stove top and once it came to a boil I dropped the ravioli in for a few minutes.

Khal reached for two glasses from the first cupboard he looked in and disappeared into the living room. By the time I came in with the tray he'd cleaned the fireplace out, laid a fire and lit it.

"Wow. You worked fast." It was obvious that Khal had done this many times. The fire was roaring, very different to my attempt the night before.

"It takes me forever to light the fire. I end up using nearly a whole box of matches." Khal didn't answer and I returned to the kitchen to strain the ravioli, placed it in a bowl with butter and parmesan on top, and brought it into the living room.

We both sat on the sofa, one at each end, and I found myself talking non-stop about my family, my life; I'd gone into motormouth mode. Khal only had to ask a simple question and I'd go blabbering on while he listened patiently. I was worse than I had been on the coach.

I eventually asked him questions – I wanted to find out about him, about his life. At least try and show an interest.

He wasn't very forthcoming but I did discover Khal's name was actually Khaldun, an old family name.

"Do you know the meaning behind your name?" I asked him, wondering if he knew.

Just for fun, Jason decided to look into the meanings of our names – mine was 'father's joy' and his was 'healer' – because he thought it'd be really cool to know what our futures would be. At least his was fitting considering he was still determined to become a doctor. I still hadn't figured out what mine had to do with anything.

He looked incredibly uncomfortable for a moment. "Not really sure."

"It sounds Middle Eastern, especially the way you pronounce it."

Khal changed the subject, asking me about my brother, Ben. I was going to have to remember to look his name up.

I did manage to get him to talk about his work...kind of.

"I dabble in different things, website designs and apps, especially ones that pertain to helping the environment. But mainly I work on the farm, where I live."

"I'd love to visit it sometime."

"It's pretty desolate. Nothing there."

"Where is it?"

"It's in the middle of nowhere, not far but difficult to find."

Okay then.

So I asked him more about the area. That's when he talked enthusiastically. He was passionate and knowledgeable about Lincolnshire, the history, and how it was isolated in many ways. "None of the large road systems venture this way. The farmland keeps big businesses away, and large crowds of people. And when the weather's depressing, the Wolds and lowlands become bleak. Non-locals don't like it."

I had seen photographs and video of Lincolnshire at its worst. The dense fog that hounds the lowlands, not allowing you to see your hand in front of your face. The depressing weather where it was non-stop drizzle for days on end. Or the gray clouds that lay heavily in the troposphere, oppressive, making it feel like the sky was falling. With the small country roads, I imagined it made the isolated places creepy. But I had also seen images of the incredible flowers and hedgerows in the spring and summer. The early daffodils and tulips that were grown for the flower festivals and florists. The fields of vegetables, wheat and the vibrant yellow rapeseed. The occasional fields of cows or sheep. And the amazing thing was the view, seeing for miles on a clear day. Standing on the rolling hills of the Wolds, I imagined I would see the world in front of me. After living in the city and suburbs my whole life, I was looking forward to spending time in the country.

As Khal talked, I could really imagine what he was saying. And I loved hearing him talk about the rich history, how the gentry had divided the land. How now, a lot of the land was used for arable farming. And how, placed strategically all over the county were air force bases that had played a huge role during World War II.

I could listen to him talking for hours. His voice was quiet yet commanding, gentle yet firm, deep and definitely sexy. I ran out of questions to ask him so that he would keep talking. I went into the kitchen to fetch the fruit salad and remembered today's newspaper on the table, so decided to bring it through with me. With Khal living here, and knowing so much about the local history, he was sure to know about any legends.

"Did you see the paper today?" I handed it to him. "I'd never heard of England having large wild cats. It was interesting reading how sightings have happened periodically for decades. I've always put these things down to the mind playing tricks on people. But I'd be interested to know if there were any old Lincolnshire legends flying around?"

"You get used to seeing these sensational headlines. They happen every few years." He dismissed the paper to his side and ignored it.

52

"Do you know anything about the sightings? Ever seen anything yourself?"

"Nothing ever comes of these things, and there is never anything to worry about. You are completely safe."

"Oh, I'm not worried," dismissing his uneasiness. "Fascinated maybe. I love cats, big and small. It just wasn't something I expected here."

"I bet there won't be any more reports of sightings. There never are," he grabbed a fork, put a piece of melon on the end, and offered it to me.

There was something extremely flirtatious, almost erotic when a man offered food to a woman. He certainly knew how to get me to forget about what I was saying. And the feeling that I experienced on the bus between our bodies, like a magnetic force vibrating, came back whenever we were close to each other. It was the most incredible thing I had ever felt with a man.

Khal listened to me tell him all about a pet mouse Jason had bought me for my birthday, and how it had died before I was due to fly over here. So Jason, Jen and I decided to hold a funeral for the mouse. That we'd concocted a coffin from a semi-used popcorn box, discarded the last popcorn packet and placed 'Larry the Mouse' inside and sealed the box with blue tape. Then Jason read a passage from the Bible before running down the twelve flights of stairs to the garbage. And how we watched him from the balcony toss the box high and far. It bounced off the side of the dumpster and landed on the floor. The box split open, 'Larry the Mouse' fell out and one of the many stray cats that lived in and around the dumpsters sneaked out from behind said dumpster, grabbed the dead mouse and ran away. Jen and I shouted down that Jason should run after the cat and rescue Larry – he refused. So I told him he had to buy me a new pet.

"What do you want?" Khal topped up my drink.

"A cat. I love cats. When we lived in Coventry, before our move to America, we used to have a cat, a moggy called Willow. She died. Then when we moved we got a couple of cats from the local shelter. We called them Yin and Yang. But I never forgot our first cat. She was special.

"I would like a kitten for the apartment. I think when I get back I'll go and have a look in the animal shelter. You know, your eyes remind me of Willow. She had the most beautiful green eyes, and she would snuggle on my knee and let me tickle her under her chin while she looked up at me." I thought it was a compliment. I didn't mean to hurt his feelings. But the moment I finished talking I could see he looked so hurt and almost offended.

"Sorry. I didn't mean to upset you. I like them, your eyes. They're unique. Incredible."

"That's okay. You haven't," his reassurance didn't sound convincing, didn't look convincing.

The atmosphere tightened, our closeness changed. And I didn't know what to say to bring the fun back. I was having such a great time – and I thought he was too.

We sat quietly for a while, finishing the wine and fruit salad.

"I think I better go. You look exhausted," Khal placed everything on the tray and took it through to the kitchen.

He put his Jacket on and his sunglasses, flipped his hood over his head, turned and smiled, then left.

It had been a magical evening, but when Khal left, he didn't mention anything about meeting up again. And I had no idea how to get in touch with him.

I was left with the feeling that I wouldn't be seeing him again.

Chapter Seven

I cleared the dishes away and decided to go for a walk. It felt strange thinking back to my chatting with Khal, looking in like a fly on a wall, seeing this strange person – me – chatter on and on like verbal diarrhea. I started to wonder what was wrong, what was making me be someone I wasn't.

It was dusk out, the sun faded into the night sky, filtering its last rays behind the homes of the town. The moon was high and the street lights were slowly coming alive, illuminating my steps across the promenade. There were many people around, enjoying the pleasant evening: dog walkers, couples walking hand in hand, and me. I seemed to be the only one alone. I didn't mind, didn't really care. It was just good to be outside, to clear my head.

"A pleasant evening." I physically jumped at the voice behind me. I turned to see a dark shadow walking quickly with a dog.

"Yes, yes it is." My heart raced and as I turned around and saw a tall slender man, it gave another little skip. He was handsome, debonair, and not what I expected with such a dog. I was not a big fan of dogs at the best of times, but this dog looked particularly scary, a cross between one of those fighting dogs and a wild wolf.

"It is not very often we see pretty single ladies walking alone." He slowed his pace to mine. His steps were flawless and it was difficult to make out if he was actually walking or floating.

"Really? You surprise me." God, he was a bit forward and it wasn't the most original of pick-up lines. I supposed there was nothing like jumping in with both feet.

"You are not from here? Your accent?" He showed no inclination that he got my sarcasm at all, something I'd picked up from my dad.

"New York. You?" I wasn't the only one with an accent.

"Lebanon." He had a large mouth and when he smiled the white of his teeth twinkled in the moonlight and under the streetlights. Stunning. His skin was pale white, almost waxen, his hair dark, probably black, and he had incredibly deep blue eyes. Quite beautiful actually and not what I'd expected for someone from Lebanon; maybe his mother was Scandinavian. I could understand now why he saw himself as a charmer. He was obviously used to women swooning over him. Mmm, he was going to be disappointed tonight.

"What's your dog's name?" Considering how scary looking the dog was, it was certainly obedient, hung on every word, every step, of its master.

"Gadreel. He's a wonderful companion. And I am Greg"

"I'm Abby."

We walked along the main hub of the promenade, chatting for a few more minutes. Greg asked me about why I came to Mablethorpe. I just told him I was here to work for the summer. I didn't expand on the family or friend connection, and I didn't mention where I was working either. Instead, I asked him about his home in Lebanon.

"Where in Lebanon are you from?" I knew very little about the country except that it was near Israel.

"Near the border with Syria, on Mount Hermon. It is very old with a rich history that dates back to before biblical times." I'd never been further east than Spain so it was interesting listening to Greg talk about his home. I enjoyed asking him questions and he took great pleasure in answering, describing the mountains and his people, the conflicts and wars that have resided there, and how Israel now has a ski resort not too far away. The more I listened the more I saw his voice as being majestic, eloquent, and I began to wonder where he learnt his perfect English.

Even though he didn't hesitate at answering my questions about his home, he rushed in with his own questions about my life which I veered away from answering. When I didn't give him what he wanted, he continued chatting about such totally random topics that I didn't have a clue what he was going on about. Then he'd throw in compliments telling me how beautiful I looked in this light, that he loved the color of my hair, could fall into the abyss of my eyes, that my skin-tone was exquisite etcetera. Each time he leaned in a little closer. I didn't mind at first. It was in complete contrast to Khal. But I'd heard most of it before, albeit from drunk frat boys trying to get in my pants. I smiled to myself – Greg was probably doing the same, even though he was a good ten plus years older than I.

But I soon felt like puking as he went over the top, showing no sign of stopping, and began to touch me on my arm and shoulder and face. He also didn't get the hint that all his gushing didn't have an effect on me. I wasn't impressed. Although, I did admit to myself his cool hands sent tingles running down my spine. Pleasant tingles.

Having met Greg, I hadn't spent any time on my own. I was tired which probably added to my building annoyance. It had been a long day and I was probably still suffering from jetlag. Well, that was my excuse and I was sticking to it.

"I've got to go. I'm still unpacking. It was nice meeting you." I didn't wait for Greg's response. Instead, I turned away from him and began my walk home...alone. I just needed these moments unaccompanied so I didn't feel forced into having to talk to someone, or to listen to someone else talk. And it wasn't because I was still dwelling on my evening with Khal. Khal's visit was now a distant memory. Honestly, it was. I hadn't forgotten, but I no longer focused on my stupidity, or his strange behavior.

"Will I see you again?" He called behind me.

"I'm sure you will. I'll be here for the summer." I didn't tell him where I was working, or where I was living – I didn't know him. I quickened my step, giving a nonchalant wave over my head as I left.

Chapter Eight

I spent the next couple of days settling into the cottage, unpacking my belongings and enjoying my freedom, not having to answer to anyone or think of another person. It was bliss.

I strolled through the town, checking out all the sights: from the shops to the touristy things. I went to the animal sanctuary, and enjoyed lounging on the beach, especially in the dunes where the air was calm and the sand captured the heat from the sun.

I decided to read the book Jen had said I needed to read. I finished it quickly, speed-reading and skipping some of the more...intimate scenes. And boy there were a lot. The soppy love story was as bad as I thought it would be. After the two lovers departed, they both realized they couldn't live without each other and she went back to their holiday island hoping he would be there waiting. And of course he was – as if that would ever happen in real life...not. And nor did a 'happy ever after' – life just wasn't like that.

JJ were now back home in Florida. We had chatted briefly when I first arrived so they knew I was here but we hadn't really spoken. Now I had finished the book I needed to talk to Jen, to let her know how utterly crap it was.

Firstly, I IM'd my brother telling him about what I'd been up to since I arrived. He loved to hear about the animals in the sanctuary that was on the outskirts of town, and I'd taken some photos so I sent them through to him.

Ben was amazing on the computer, and the practice with typing helped him with his dexterity. But he didn't want to chat long. He was going to the movies with his friends. Dad was taking them.

I said goodbye to Ben and while waiting for Jen to come online I decided to take the time to look up Khal's name. I suddenly remembered how I'd wanted to find out the meaning behind his name. It was an unusual name, one I hadn't heard before. I noticed Jen come online and let her know I was there just as I found out Khaldun was Egyptian meaning 'immortal'. I chuckled to myself thinking how cool it would be to have a name like that. A lot better than mine.

Me: *Hey Jen, how's it going? I've finished the book.*

Jen sent a jumping, summersaulting emoticon.

Me: *Don't get too excited.*

Jen: *You didn't like it, did you?*

Me: *No. It was crap. Just as I'd expected.*

And as we chatted and discussed the intricate details of the book, it became clear very quickly that Jen was not happy I hadn't enjoyed it.

Jen: *You just close your mind off to anything that includes love.*

Me: *No I don't. Love has a place, but summer romances are pathetic and this lived up to every bit of that. There was nothing different about it. The same as any other love story. Romeo and Juliet, here we come. Except at least Romeo and Juliet has some truth to it – no happy ending, unless you believe in life after death…which you know I don't.*

I was just teasing, knowing how much it would wind Jen up. I was sure somewhere in the world there were couples who were still happy – yes, and in love – after being married for a very long time. But looking around, I hadn't seen any.

We compared notes and continued pulling the book to bits, something we regularly did. We were like our own little book club. I said I would bring it back so Jason could put his two pennies worth into the discussion, knowing he would be on my side. The idea of making Jason read a holiday romance made both of us laugh. And I did make her promise that the next book she chose was not to be such a soppy romance.

Me: *It's so far from reality it's a joke.*

Jen: *Abby, you just need to experience true love, enjoy giving yourself to another person. Then you might get something out of these books, see just how close to reality some bits are. Of course there is an element of make-believe, but a good romance gives you that truth factor too, that belief that there is a Mr. Right out there for everyone.*

Jen hit a nerve. And I was so grateful she couldn't see my face because she'd know.

I had always dismissed the idea of finding that one person that I would want to spend the rest of my life with, making excuses that I was too young or too busy with my education and wanted to fulfil my dreams first. But recently I'd started to question myself, what it was I wanted with my life, why I always kept a distance, why I felt my life had fallen apart because of one simple change. And I didn't know anymore, except for the fact that I knew relationships didn't last, they always ended in heartbreak one way or another. Mom and Dad's marriage was a disaster. They were loving, caring parents, but that was it. Alice still held onto the memory of Rob, someone who'd been dead for 30 years. And then JJ's parents divorced when the twins were young and no longer communicated with each other without it being a screaming match – I got an earful of that one once when they decided to have a conference call with JJ at the apartment. I decided I didn't know which was worse: the silent treatment that my parents gave each other, or the screaming communication JJ's parents had. Then not to mention the uncles and aunts who were divorced, parents of friends divorced or dead. The everyday Joe Blogs on the street looking miserable and uncommunicative with the female next to him. Nothing ever lasted – relationships, dreams, ambitions. Nothing.

I finished chatting with Jen, smiling. Jason had been out and I missed him. Jen was great, I loved her, but Jason and I knew each other, understood each other. I wanted to tell Jen about Khal, about Greg, but nothing would come out. For some strange reason I didn't trust myself. And I knew Jen would read more into what I said than was actually there. I knew she'd have me married and pregnant before the day ended.

However, I was sure I'd have said something if Jason had been there. I knew instinctively that Jason would've told me to stop being so soppy about Khal, tell Jen to keep her nose out and encourage me to play the two men off each other. Although I'd never actually done such a thing before – never had the nerve – it was something Jason would do. He and I didn't take relationships with the opposite sex seriously. They were just for fun.

This wasn't like that, though. I knew it wasn't. Both men were incredibly handsome but so completely different, especially in the way I reacted to them. I didn't want anything serious, and if I hadn't met Khal first I'd probably have been more taken with Greg, done what Jen suggested and had a summer fling. After all, he was stunning. Polite, chatty, extrovert, debonair, classy. I was sure he would be great to enjoy an evening out drinking and dancing. And yes, he was probably okay between the sheets too.

If I hadn't met Khal first.

Khal: all I wanted to do was jump his bones. Yet every time he was near I felt flustered and clumsy. I just couldn't understand what it was I was doing wrong with him, and why I kept acting so strangely around him.

And there I went yet again, thinking about him.

For goodness sake, I was supposed to be here to enjoy myself, not worry about men.

Jen and I signed off and I went for a walk again.

It was late, dark out. I was still struggling with adjusting to the time differences – getting up late, going to bed late. However, this was only the second time I'd walked around when it was late and dark. The first time was meeting Greg and guess what, I bumped into Greg again. This time he was lounging on a bench, looking out to sea, without his dog.

"You like this time of night as well?" I joined him on the bench.

"Yes. A place comes alive after dark. Have you not noticed how groups communicate loudly, energetically, people emerge from the woodwork and head to the bars and clubs. Everyone arrives home from work and breathes a sigh of relief. Fascinating. And you? A night bird too?" As he spoke his arm came up behind me and rested across the back of the bench. He didn't touch, but I could feel him there. It wasn't the same chemistry, the magnetic field I felt with Khal but there was definitely a buzz. Maybe a bit of flirting would be fun.

"Time difference. Although I do enjoy staying up late, clubbing, drinking, I also like my bed too much so if I have to be up early I have to go to bed early."

Greg smiled at me and lifted one of his eyebrows at my talking about bed. He didn't say anything, didn't add any innuendoes, and I chickened out.

We stayed silent after that and it felt awkward. I frantically tried to think of an excuse to just leave without it seeming rude, contrived. But the strange thing was he was okay. He didn't show any signs of being uncomfortable or struggling to find something to say like I was. Instead, he looked out across the water and began to fiddle with the ends of my hair.

"Can I interest you in joining me for a drink?" I offered. Just one. Then I could go home.

"That would be most enjoyable. I would like that." Greg took the lead and led me to the wine bar on High Street. I tried to explain that this was not what I'd meant but he wouldn't listen. And then he didn't even allow me to buy him a drink. I felt frustrated and angry. Having to fight my position was not my idea of fun. I was pissed so I kept my distance from him, sitting opposite him at a table.

This man was just going to be too much hard work. First the charm, now the power struggle. Give me a break. It didn't matter which continent you went to, men were all the same.

Then there was the fact that the wine bar was typically showy, classy, and Greg seemed to revel in it. He and I were not on the same planet.

"You like these places?" I asked, knowing full well what his answer would be. I'd been watching him eye the crowd, follow the people – mainly women, but sometimes men – with his eyes.

"Oh yes. It's where all the young people mingle, where the beautiful ladies enjoy coming." I didn't know what to say. Is that all he saw? What about a woman having a brain, the ability to think for herself? So we sat quietly and Greg soon started his constant chatting.

I couldn't wait to finish my drink. I picked up my glass and took a large swallow.

Chapter Nine

Walking home alone was wonderful. All my anxieties disappeared with my own company. I scolded myself, vowing that next time I bumped into Greg I needed to keep it polite and friendly but not stay. He was definitely hot, but just not my type. I had quickly finished my drink, and politely turned down the offer of another one, making the excuse I had to be at work early the next morning. And then left, not giving Greg the opportunity of offering to walk me home.

By the time I arrived at the cottage I was smiling, happy, and ready for a soak in the tub and bed.

I visited Alice again the day before she left. She was almost packed and so excited to be heading off to see her daughter she couldn't sit still. "Kristen calls every day. She's getting nervous about the wedding."

"I'm sure she'll be happy to have you there."

"She can't wait right now. She's made a huge list of all the things she wants me to do!" The excitement in Alice's voice expressed how much she couldn't wait to give her daughter a hand.

"I can't imagine trying to organize a wedding." The idea seemed preposterous, especially if it meant big frilly dresses and fancy cakes. "*If* I were ever to get married, I'd opt for Vegas."

"You make it sound as though you'll never get married."

Alice sounded as though she was questioning me and I really didn't know how to answer her. She already knew my thoughts on romance and happily-ever-after. Why would I want to get married knowing it wouldn't last? "I think I'm just too independent. Weddings, marriage, it just sounds so restricting. Claustrophobic."

Having these few moments chatting with Alice reminded me of my childhood. I could always talk to Alice. She just had this way about her that made me comfortable telling her what I thought. Yet I couldn't believe that for the past couple of days all I'd seemed to talk about, think about was relationships, love, romance and marriage.

So I changed the subject. I let Alice know I'd settled in, unpacked. And we sat quietly for a while, enjoying our tea. Alice was an amazing woman. She knew when to speak and when to stay quiet. And she was the only person who could actually get me to talk, especially about a subject I wouldn't normally voluntarily talk openly about. So before I knew it I was back onto the subject of men again.

"I bumped into Khal. Last time I was here." I really tried hard to sound pleased. But I was disappointed – not that I bumped into Khal but the fact that it hadn't gone too well.

Alice just listened, quietly. "I thought I would be happy to see him. God, who am I kidding? I was happy to see him. Ecstatic. He's incredible, everything you could ever imagine. He came over for dinner. Spontaneous. I've never done that before, brought a man home like that, knowing there was no one else there, at home. It was just a spur of the moment thing and I loved it." I sat and thought for a moment, back to that night. "I thought he did too."

I sipped my tea. Alice joined me and sipped hers. I gave a little giggly smile. "Can you believe I went into chatterbox mode."

"You? Oh dear. You have got it bad. Did I ever tell you that that's what your mother did when she met your dad?"

"You're kidding?"

"Nope. She was talking so much she started to tell him all her deepest darkest secrets and it didn't dawn on her what she'd said until he dropped her off at home. She called me hysterically crying telling me all that she had talked about. From her pet dying to an argument she had had with her mother that morning. Well, he came back and eventually she was able to be herself. Maybe the same will happen with you."

"I don't think so. I can't see him wanting to see me again. I think I said something that made him uncomfortable and he left not saying anything about meeting up again."

I was shocked at how disheartened I felt. Relating what happened to Alice had me going over everything openly and I soon dismissed my disappointment; I wasn't going to let it – or him – affect my vacation. I was determined to make the most of my time, no matter what. And I was resolute in keeping my confidence above ground level.

"Oh, I also met a man on the beach. Well, the boardwalk actually. Greg. He comes from Lebanon. And can you believe it, with him I couldn't think of anything to say. He was hot…really hot…and sexy. Two attractive men in the space of two days – who'd have guessed it? But there was just something about him that made me feel uncomfortable, like he was looking down at me.

Intimidating almost. And can that man talk." Talking about my chatterbox mouth and then my awkwardness with Greg got me thinking. Comparing the two men, they really were like chalk and cheese. And neither were men that I usually dated, or was normally attracted to.

"There are a lot of foreigners here now. Many come over to work on the farms and learn English. He's probably one of them."

"I doubt it." I thought for a moment. "His English sounded virtually flawless, eloquent. He just had an accent with it. And he certainly wasn't a farmer. His hands were too perfect: no calluses or scratches, and immaculate fingernails."

I paused again, thinking of what possible work Greg could do. And then I remembered how Khal said he worked with computers and software and wondered if Greg might do the same thing. Yet Khal's hands were working-man's hands. Strong, rugged. I began to wonder what they'd feel like. Would I like that roughness on my skin? I needed to change the subject. I didn't want to talk about this...them anymore. And Alice needed to make sure I had everything in order before she left.

She gave me all the other ins and outs of the shop that she hadn't told me before. Then she took me to meet John in his bookstore.

Wow! What a hunk. Just my type. And so easy to talk to. He didn't look that much older than me and had a great sense of humor. The first thing he did was make fun of my accent. We hit it off straight away. And he put my mind at ease, telling me that he was happy to help me whenever I needed it. It was reassuring knowing I'd have John there. Actually, who was I kidding. This was a man I could easily flirt with. He was the whole package – sexy, easy to talk and joke with – I couldn't wait to see him again.

I left Alice letting her know I would be there in the morning to say goodbye. And as I left, Alice gave me a knowing grin; she knew exactly what I was thinking regarding John.

Bright and early the next day, I went over to Alice's home so I could see her off. She had organized for a car to take her to the airport. Her bags were packed, ready and waiting by the front door.

"Have you got your tickets, your passport, insurance documents?" I began listing.

"Yes. My dollars, my outfit, and my shoes."

"Toiletries, swimming costume, underwear?" I added.

"Yes, yes and yes. So that's it." Alice paced nervously, waiting for her ride.

"Did you cancel your mail? Paper?"

"I cancelled the paper but I had the mail redirected to the store."

I couldn't think of other essentials. Alice didn't look like she wanted to talk so we stood quietly in the living room, waiting, impatiently.

We heard a knock at the door. The car had arrived. I helped Alice with her bags and gave her a hug. "Enjoy yourself and don't worry about a thing. I'll call if I have any problems. Promise."

"I know you will. So, see you when I get back." Alice was grinning from ear to ear, and climbed into the car. I closed the door to her home and left for the cottage. It was too early to open the store yet.

This was it; I was on my own. I was more nervous than I expected, petrified of making a serious mistake.

It was still very early, the sun rising majestically over the horizon, gleaming its pure white rays across the incoming tide. There was a smattering of clouds in the sky – that would change later. More clouds would form and the sun would begin its daily battle as if struggling for power in the skies.

As I opened the front door to the cottage, the paperboy arrived with the daily paper.

"Thank-you." He handed it to me rather than squeezing it through the tiny slot in the door.

I hadn't had a drink at Alice's – I hadn't wanted to create any dishes that needed to be cleaned – so I switched the coffeepot on as soon as I walked through to the kitchen. Then I reached for the radio, and sat at the table to read the paper, singing along as I read.

ANIMALS MUTILATED, FARMERS ANGRY

Two local farmers lost valuable animals last night in a vicious attack. Is there a connection to the cat sightings?

Wow. It was one thing to joke around chalking the cat sightings up to the figment of someone's imagination; it was another when something like this happened. I read ardently. The details were specific but in a practical, non-gory way. And there was a thorough rehashing of previous reports with extra details. There were photographs this time – including images of the slaughtered animals to show the extent of the damage. Mom would worry. She'd read about this online and start imagining the worst. I shook my head – sometimes I wondered where I ever got my sanity from.

Experts were unsure as to what type of animal created the carnage, except to say it was large and brutal. The farm animals had been ripped apart, flesh torn with what looked like sharp and very large teeth. When asked if it could have been a fox, it was unanimous that it was not.

I finished my coffee and took the paper to the store with me. It was still early so there was little to do. The town was quiet, some people rushing off to work for the day, others taking their children to school. And it was rare now, even after just this short time, that I was able to walk anywhere without someone saying 'hi'. It was all very different to New York City where it was always busy and everyone kept themselves to themselves, went about their day without a care or concern about the person next to them.

Unfortunately, once I arrived at the store, problems began. The drawer jammed on the register and I couldn't get to the money. That was my first call to John. He was already at work and a great help. He came over, found the issue and fixed it. Then the power went out and I couldn't find the trip switches. Back I went to John. It felt like I was running to John every hour with something new. And I hadn't created these problems on purpose...honest.

By the end of the day he no longer waited for me to go to him – he came over with cookies in hand and asked for a coffee to go with them.

"Listen, if I'm going to be spending so much time here, I might as well make it worth my while." John made a good point, one I was happy to accommodate.

John was a joker and it became obvious very quickly that he was an astute businessman. His store was always busy, even when the town wasn't. His incredible sense of humor worked well with his intelligence and ability to balance life.

We flirted together. And while I gave a few hints that I'd like it to be more, John kept it all friendly: an arm on my shoulder, a bear hug, a smooch on the cheek. And crazily, I loved it.

My first few days flew past. Early mornings, late evenings, it all mingled together among the important tasks of filling orders, emptying boxes, banking and book keeping, with the jokes and laughter between the two stores. I became used to John teasing me over my accent and I was intrigued when he came over looking distraught.

"Your accent. It is, no more." John acted out his disappointment as if he were in a Shakespeare play.

"You're crazy." He was, and I couldn't helping falling just a little bit more enamored by it...by him.

"Well, how can I tell American jokes if you no longer sound American," he light heartedly complained.

"Get me some Americans and I will listen to them talk. Then it will come back." I was joking. My accent hadn't really gone but I was beginning to pick up some of the local lingo when I talked to customers: trainers instead of sneakers; biscuits instead of cookies; chips instead of fries.

"Is that all you need, to hear Americans talk?"

"Pretty much." He ran out the store and disappeared. When he came back he handed me a DVD.

I laughed so hard my stomach hurt. "I can't believe you did this! *Grease!*"

"Well, you did say you needed to hear the American accent to copy. And even after all these years, the music is still pretty cool."

"I hope you're prepared to sit through this with me."

And then an inspiration hit me. "I know, why don't we make a night of it? See if any of the staff and other shop

74

owners want to join us. You have a DVD player in your store. I can bring the popcorn."

His store was a great place to hang out. He'd built it for the purpose of being flexible. His bookshelves moved on wheels, he had a variety of comfy chairs and sofas strategically placed so customers could relax and enjoy a book, and there was a huge TV screen that regularly played the latest DVDs.

John readily agreed and we invited all the staff from our two stores and the others along the block. And what a night we had. Dancing and singing, laughing and joking.

We all vowed to do it again. The movie did not help my accent one bit – what a surprise.

By day four I felt more confident with the store. But John was such a great person to have a conversation with that we still got together whenever we both had a free moment. We no longer focused on what I needed to know; instead we enjoyed talking about non-work related issues. I soon discovered John loved the controversial stuff, the more controversial the better. So when he brought up the large cat sightings one day, and the brutal attacks, I wasn't surprised.

"I don't blame the farmers for being worried. Did you read how some farmers are talking conspiracy? They think it's a large consortium trying to take over their land, running them off. I can't imagine that somehow, but I'm sure the farmers are desperate to find an answer." John almost seemed excited when he talked about juicy topics.

"I read that the vets who inspected the slaughtered animals don't see the attacking animal as a type of cat. They're calling in a zoologist to make sure. But from what they can tell, it looks more like a dog attack. It must have been a pretty large dog to take down all those animals in one night." The idea of a vicious dog on the loose was not good – this was when I really hated dogs. A totally irrational fear because I'd never been attacked by a dog or anything, but it was still there, and very real.

"A huge, vicious dog. Maybe even rabid. Whoever owns that dog better watch out – those farmers are going to be after blood." John was right, they were.

"Did you also see that there have been two more cat sightings? We haven't had so much excitement in this neck of the woods for…well…forever. Coming from New York, I suppose you're used to this?"

"No, not really. We do have to be more vigilant, more aware of our surroundings, but New York is quite safe." I never felt unsafe living in the city. But then, I never travelled anywhere on my own without it being by taxi or limousine.

"I've become more vigilant around here. And I've started carrying my camera around with me so that if I do see something I can take a picture." John sounded more excited over the opportunity of snapping a photograph than the fact that a wild animal was on the loose.

"Do you really think you'll see something?"

"No. But if I do, I could photograph it and sell it in my store." His logic did make me laugh.

"I must admit, though, I'm surprised that if this is something that has happened before, how there's so little known about it. Some customers were talking about old legends, but that appears to be vague." I said.

"Oh, there are some books on it all, both for cats across the whole of the U.K. and other phenomena in this area."

He brought over a couple of books that had been written on the subject, thinking I might enjoy reading what the 'experts' had to say without all the media hype. I was ecstatic. I couldn't wait to spend some time delving into what the books had to say.

I went home that evening and read well into the night. It became clear, on reading the books, that Lincolnshire was not the only county with a possible wild cat. In fact, one book had whole sections on the *Beast of Bodmin*, the *Beast of Exmoor*, and other large cat sightings from various other places across Britain. And there had been cases of farm animal attacks too, similar to the ones recently. Large cat sightings, and other strange happenings like U.F.O.s, were not unusual here, especially in Lincolnshire with the flat land. Official records had been kept since the late 1800s.

Like always many sightings – both U.F.O. and cat – were explained by other issues: more fighter aircraft in the area; laws banning the ownership of large cats without a special license. Logic was a wonderful thing when reporters weren't involved.

I couldn't wait to tell John about all that I'd read.

Chapter Ten

I arrived at work early again. John was on the late shift today. The morning went by quickly. I was used to the regulars now, enjoyed helping them choose gifts, chatting about their day. Some of the mothers liked to come in when they dropped their older children off at school. They would bring their younger children, their pre-schoolers, to see the toys, maybe treat them to some candy before going next door to the bookstore for story-time.

It was a quiet day for me with no deliveries, no banking, and no John for coffee. So I helped Barbara restock some of the candy, and took out the trash. And then out of the blue, Khal walked in.

I hadn't seen Khal for what felt like a lifetime, since that night of awkwardness. I'd resigned myself to the possibility that I wouldn't see him again. And I was okay with that. Disappointed, but okay. John had been a good distraction...and easier to talk to.

Yet, now that Khal had turned up at the store and asked how I was enjoying being a local, I felt flustered and wanted to giggle like a stupid teenager. My heart tumbled around in my chest and started pounding, trying to escape, and my whole body vibrated with involuntary attraction.

"I...I'm enjoying it. Thanks. How...how are you?" I tripped over my own tongue talking to him. And I felt hopelessly desperate, desperate to not scare him off again. It

78

was ridiculous – I tried very hard not to chatter on but my mouth wanted to get going at full speed.

And I couldn't fathom his sudden appearance. Maybe things had gone better the last time we were together than I'd thought. He certainly seemed at ease, especially compared to the way I was feeling.

"I'm well thank-you." He wondered round the store, looking at all the merchandise.

"Would you like help with anything?" He was looking at the jewelry. My heart sank; the only men who looked at jewelry were men who had a woman to buy something for.

"No. I was just looking. These really are not to my taste." Khal moved along to the other trinkets, jewelry boxes, shell boxes, shell ornaments.

"What is to your taste?" I asked, although I wasn't sure I wanted to know the answer.

He remained quiet for a moment. "It would have to mean something, have a purpose. Something that signified truth, honesty." He smiled and my whole body melted into a pile of mush.

He just stared at me, not moving, capturing my attention. He had me rooted to the spot, to his face. I completely understood what he saying, knew what he meant, the idea of value, the point of a gift or purchase. But I couldn't talk for ages.

I heard my name being called as more customers came into the store.

"I…err…better go…and help someone." I didn't really want to move. And after Khal left I completely forgot about John's books and what I'd read. Forgot about anything and everything that I'd planned to do, and just walked around the whole day in a haze, wondering why Khal had suddenly turned up at the store.

Khal came again, and again, sometimes twice a day. He never bought anything, just looked around, asked me how I was. I asked him to stay for coffee, but he turned me down. Said he had to get back. I presumed to work. I felt rejected, dispirited. Why was he coming so often all of a sudden if he wasn't interested in me? Why had he stayed away for so long? And if he was interested, why didn't he take up my offer of coffee. Okay, a week wasn't that long – it'd just felt like a lifetime.

I also couldn't understand why my heart was doing somersaults every time I saw him? And why did my stomach have butterflies while I waited for him to arrive?

Whenever he left after his brief visits, my disappointment was obvious to the others. And all I was left with was confusion and questions.

I found that the days he came over I was restless when I got home. Walking helped, but when the rain came, I ended up at the movies.

I didn't mind going to the movies on my own. And I didn't mind if it was a movie I'd already seen. Sometimes just having the chance to organize my thoughts – or switch off my churning brain – was comforting.

This time it was a new movie: *World War Z.* I picked up a bucket of popcorn and a large soda from the kiosk, and headed to my seat. I found a vacant row approximately half way down and settled in for the movie to start.

"Hello. Nice to see you again." Greg was behind me, climbing over the back of the next seat.

"Hi. Didn't expect to see you here. You on your own?" I offered Greg my popcorn bucket but he shook his head. I returned my popcorn to my lap and took a handful.

"I believe it would not be a good idea for me to bring Gad. Being a wolf she would probably eat everyone here." I gave a false laugh at Greg's joke.

"Poor taste, Greg. Especially after all the newspaper hype on the animal killings in the area."

"Oh. Yes. Of course." It appeared he really hadn't thought about what he'd said. Well, I was glad he hadn't brought his dog.

Greg sat next to me the whole evening, spreading his arm out behind me again and keeping it there. And it didn't take him long before he began to play with my hair, then the sleeve of my shirt. I didn't mind; there was something quite comforting about feeling his hand on me, albeit a cold hand. I smiled to myself. He should be pleased we weren't in the US where movie theaters were freezing in the summer.

After the movie, I walked slowly home, Greg accompanying me. We chatted about the movie. It'd been good but not that good. Greg disagreed. We laughed and argued the good and bad points, how realistic and unrealistic it was, and before I knew it I was home. This was the first time I actually felt as though I'd had a decent conversation with the man, not all one sided. And it'd been good. Really good.

And he hadn't hesitated when we left the theater – he held my hand all the way.

"Thank-you for walking me home." I considered inviting him in for coffee, but I just couldn't bring myself to say the words. I couldn't put my finger on it but there was a barrier that prevented me from going that far. A prickly feeling crept up the back of my neck.

So I just said 'goodnight' and turned to open my door.

"Please will you allow me the honor of accompanying you to the movies again?" He hadn't taken me to the movies this time, but I did agree.

He moved in close to me and wrapped his arm around my waist. He wasn't pulling me to him, but he wasn't letting go either.

Then he leaned in closer and…sniffed. I froze. That was too weird to even try and figure out.

"Maybe next week. I'll meet you there." I pulled away, gave a tentative smile, and closed the cottage door leaving him on the outside.

The night after the movies Khal came over to the store and stayed for coffee.

Chapter Eleven

May slipped by quickly and June began with a heatwave. The store pretty much ran itself, with the employees' shifts balancing the opening hours well. John and I held one more movie night which attracted even more local shop-owners and their staff. To cover John's costs, a small donation was asked for. Everyone obliged willingly.

I came into the store regularly but I didn't need to be there every day. Khal continued coming over for coffee during the day when I was at work, and I met up with Greg twice more at the movies – the movies seemed to be the one place we actually gelled together, enjoying each other's company.

He became more physical. Instead of taking the slow route of lounging an arm across the back of my chair he would take my hand or place an arm around my waist or shoulders. And even ventured to kiss me. I gave him my cheek. His hands were always cold but his lips on my skin felt warm, sensual. I felt a slight pull inside of me, wondering if I should turn my head towards him so our lips touched. I'd never hesitated before when a man showed an interest in kissing me, and I found him attractive. Why was I this time?

I agreed to have dinner with him. He was charming, as usual, and instead of sitting opposite me, he sat in a chair next to me and held my hand throughout dinner, feeding me little titbits. Then leaning in to kiss me: again I gave him my cheek. He was a lot of fun when he wasn't being pompous or overly gushy.

I enjoyed the time I spent with all three men for very different reasons. John kept our relationship at just friendship, although I wasn't quite sure why because we had so much in common and really seemed to enjoy each other's company. Well, I loved his and he kept coming back for more.

Greg was more than just a friend. But for some reason I couldn't bring myself to move forward with him, I couldn't take the next step. I was the one keeping a distance, not Greg. He pushed and I pulled back. He was insistent and persistent about our time together, and I often got the impression that if I allowed his charm to get the better of me he wouldn't hesitate to dive in. I shouldn't have been surprised because that was me all over; I didn't like being pursued so overtly. I never brought him back to the cottage and I was sure Greg was annoyed by this. I didn't care. I was in control and I intended for it to stay that way.

Khal, on the other hand, was…well…different. And I definitely had no control over anything related to him…and us. He was a friend, but I wanted more. My cravings grew worse, more intense, every time I saw him. Yet he kept a quiet distance between us, an obvious distance that screamed at me 'keep your hands off'. Khal began to arrive at the store after I finished work, and I loved it. The first time he brought me a small bunch of flowers, not saying anything when he abruptly laid them on the counter rather than handing them to me. Then he walked me home.

I enjoyed these moments with him, sometimes talking sometimes not, and I began to try and stretch my time out with him by walking slower and slower, preventing my reaching home too soon. I'd stopped cycling to work just so I could walk home with him hoping he'd hold my hand or place an arm across my shoulder like Greg. He never did. However, I didn't make my previous mistake – I didn't invite him in again. He left when I was home and never seemed to expect anything else.

Then one day, my time with Khal changed…

It was my day off from work, a day I normally had to myself, and I decided to enjoy the wonderful weather and have a walk along the beach. The beach went on for miles, and the tide retreated a long way. Much to my disappointment, I hadn't been to the beach in days. I'd been too busy with other things. So today all I wanted was to go over the road and feel the sand on my bare feet, sit in the dunes and read my Kindle, or wade in the water, the sea or the residual pools.

There were steps to the beach strategically placed on the sidewalk opposite the cottage. I was excited, couldn't wait to enjoy the sand between my toes, the cold water on my feet, the freedom to reflect, contemplate my time with Khal – and why I allowed my mind to become consumed with images of him.

I hadn't slept well since Khal came back. I dreamed about him, woke in the morning thinking about him, went to sleep with a vision of him galvanized to my brain. And I couldn't function properly. His image flooded my mind even when Greg or John was around. Yet when I was with Khal I never thought of anyone else but him.

This wasn't me. I was a practical person, irrational at times, over dramatic too, but not when it came to guys. I needed to get my head out of the clouds, stop living in this fantasy world, and enjoy my time here. I knew it would be over all too quickly.

I spoke to JJ online again last night and Khal was the first person I told them about. Not John, not Greg, Khal. Jen was incredible, listened patiently. And suggested I be kind to myself:

Just think of yourself for now. Do what it was you went there to do – chill out on your own. Get a book, walk along the beach. And if the opportunity presents itself where you want more then go for it; you have nothing to lose.

And she was right. Even Jason agreed with Jen which was a first and something I didn't expect. I began to wonder if there was a conspiracy going on between the two of them. I also told them about Greg and John. But every time I mentioned anything about either one I either reverted back to talking about Khal, or compared them to Khal. It was ridiculous.

The stupid thing was that if I could have nothing more than friendship with Khal I would be happy. Although, I wasn't sure if I was trying to convince myself of this or whether I truly believed it.

Anyway, I took up JJ's idea of chilling on the beach and put on my white Capri pants and pale blue shirt with a bright pink bra underneath and was ready to head over the road. I slipped my flip flops on, picked up my keys and closed the front door behind me.

And there he was, waiting at the foot of the steps. Even with his face almost completely covered by his hoodie and glasses, I would recognize him anywhere. I didn't know how he knew what my plans were, but I didn't care.

All my thoughts slipped away – my conversation with Jen, my time with John, with Greg – at this heavenly sight. I skipped across the road, being careful to avoid being hit by the oncoming traffic.

He smiled. I grinned.

We said nothing more than 'hi' to each other and it felt comfortable. I slipped my hands into my pockets and walked by his side. As soon as I stepped off the wooden planks onto the sand, I removed my flip flops and bent down to pick them up.

My feet sank into the soft sand and made walking difficult, but I didn't care. I watched where I put my feet so the grass spears didn't cut them. I remembered how much that hurt. And I put my arms out for balance; I really didn't want to fall flat on my butt.

Khal was wearing jeans and sneakers, as usual, and didn't attempt to even take his sneakers off on the sand. He must have had a pile of sand filling his sneakers by now.

"You don't like to walk barefoot on the sand?" I asked him, trying to keep my balance as I toddled over the high mounds.

"I don't mind." He looked down at my feet and chuckled at my bungled walk.

It was a lot easier walking on wet sand so I headed down to where the tide had left. The sand was cool and it squelched between my toes. My feet sank leaving behind tiny puddles of salty water as I moved.

Occasionally there was a tide pool which I dared to venture in, running through it, jumping in it, splashing the sun-warmed water up my legs. There was a large tide pool further away from the dunes. I waded in carefully; I wanted to check to see if any fish had been left behind.

Khal watched, keeping a distance. But I could see him smiling, laughing quietly at me. I kept glancing over, trying to encourage him to come and join me. But he never did. So I continued on with my exploration. This was my day off and I wanted to do what I wanted to do. Spontaneous and fun. I didn't want to have to deal with this unsure feeling inside of me.

Alice had been right – give it time and I would be myself with Khal. And I was. This was me. I had no idea if Khal was being himself or not, but I'd come to the conclusion I didn't care; I was just grateful he was here, even if it was at a distance.

Yet I also wanted more. I'd heard many of my friends call it animal magnetism – I just called it severe sexual attraction that turned my brain into a pile of mashed potato. Whenever I was attracted to a man, I acted on it. But how could I with Khal?

I was still very aware that Khal had placed a rigid boundary between us. I wanted to break it down. I wasn't completely sure why or even how. I knew I wasn't interested in anything serious and so I wondered why I wanted to bother at all? I couldn't answer that question because I didn't know. But his huge brick wall that appeared virtually impenetrable bothered me. And challenged me.

"Can I ask you something?" I returned to the dry sand and stopped in front of Khal because I wanted him to see I was genuinely interested.

He didn't answer me but did stop walking, planting his hands firmly into his jeans pockets, his legs slightly apart, and always keeping a distance between us.

"Why don't you take your glasses or hoodie off when you're outside? Even when you're inside sometimes. Your eyes are amazing…incredible." I bit my bottom lip, unsure if my question would have him running in the opposite direction again.

He didn't run. Instead he smiled and walked round me to continue our walk along the beach. He didn't look at me for a moment, looking down at his feet, tensing his arms and hands. I could see the rippling in his jeans pockets of his clenched fists, the bulging of his biceps inside his jacket. Eventually he answered.

"Because I don't like the bright light." And left it at that.

Thankfully, what appeared to be a personal question, hadn't deterred Khal from spending time with me. He answered, with what seemed a genuine answer, albeit vague. That was a start. He hadn't turned away, or said 'bye'. Instead, we laughed and joked around; I told Khal some of the jokes John had shared with me.

We must have slowly walked and talked for a few hours because the tide was on its way back. So I ran into the frigid water chasing the rushing ripples. It was so childish but I loved it, laughing and giggling. Khal laughed and shook his head. I tried to splash him, kicking my legs hard and high in the water. Every time I tried though, he made sure he was far enough away.

"You don't like the water?" I teased.

"No, I don't like the water," He cheerfully answered and ran up to the dunes to hide.

It was lovely to have him accept my more personal questions a little more readily, even if he didn't want to answer them with more than one short statement. He no longer took offense, nor seemed off handed in his replies. But I also didn't push my luck by asking more.

Khal went hiding in the Dunes, sneaking off then appearing to see if I had found him. I hadn't played hide and seek since I was a kid. I loved it, loved being with Khal in such a relaxed way. And we laughed until I hurt.

Khal spotted a couple of dragonflies among the tall dune grasses. "Shhh, come here. Look. Just there." He came up very close to me and it was there, that incredible force that trembled between us again. I was more interested in his closeness than I was the dragonflies.

We sat on the dunes for a while and watched the seagulls scavenge for scraps washing up on the beach. I read for a bit and then we walked along the beach again.

By late afternoon I was exhausted, and hungry. Khal noticed I was tired and suggested we head back. He was the first man I knew to ever be that observant. We left the beach and walked along the sidewalk instead. Khal ran ahead for a moment heading toward the chip shop.

I put my flip flops back on and continued to walk – I just didn't have the energy to run and catch him up. By the time I was opposite the chip shop, he had some fries and was perched on the back of a bench, waiting for me.

"I don't know where you get the energy. I'm pooped." I slumped down onto the bench seat, and Khal carefully handed me the tray of fries, keeping the distance there.

I heard him try to stifle a giggle.

"What's so funny?" I had no idea what I'd done that had him giggling quietly.

"That is such an American saying," he glanced my way and the side of his mouth curved upwards. "Your accent has definitely changed, mellowed, and you've picked up a lot of the lingo but then you come out with these adages that almost seem out of place."

I smiled between my bites of a fry, enjoying the taste of the salt and vinegar on my tongue.

"Don't you want any?" I asked him concerned he hadn't had anything to eat either.

"I may have one later. I knew you were hungry so I got them for you. I put salt and vinegar on." I was hungry, and was grateful to not have to think about it.

"Mmm, I know," I licked my lips to show him my approval of the salty tangy taste, and we both laughed. I sighed in appreciation as I ate another fry…chip.

Khal chatted away about the last time he'd been to the beach. He looked relaxed and happy to talk to me. I told him about the beaches in New Jersey and New York, the differences compared to how things were here. "It's also really hot there in the summer. Many families spend the full 10 weeks of the school vacation at the shore."

"Do you?"

"No. We would sometimes go for a day, maybe two. Long Island beaches or New Jersey: we did both. And depending on visiting family we would sometimes go down to Florida. But we mainly stayed at home and Ben and I did the summer camps. Ben's my brother."

"Did your brother mind staying at home?"

"No. He was happy to be able to be with his friends. And his school's open all year so he gained more benefits from being there than going away for long periods of time."

Before I realized it I had completely finished all the fries. I must have looked like a complete pig!

"Don't worry. I don't mind. You enjoyed them," he smiled and laughed at the same time.

I grinned too, as I tried to wipe the salt and vinegar and grease from my face with the back of my hand.

"I need a drink now," I said absentmindedly.

Khal went to get up and I was sure he was going to get me one when I stopped him.

"No, don't go." I tried to think fast – I loved talking with him, just spending time with him.

Timidly Khal asked, "Would you rather go home?"

My smile, my face said it all.

Chapter Twelve

We walked back, enjoying the warm sunshine that had continued to bathe the day in heat.

When we reached the cottage, Khal was right behind me and followed me into the kitchen.

I put the coffee pot on and slipped my flip flops off. There were bits of sand stuck to my toes and ankles. And I felt salt covering every – and I mean every – part of my body.

"I don't mind if you want to take a shower," Khal casually offered as he reached for two mugs and the cream.

"Great. Thanks." I was puzzled at how he knew what I was thinking. I probably looked a complete mess and he was being polite, letting me know subtly that I needed to do something about it.

I wasn't long. I just needed to rinse off. I nipped upstairs and headed straight for the bathroom.

Unfortunately, after I finished in the shower, I noticed I had caught the sun and burnt. I had tanned also but my skin did look a little red.

When I came downstairs in clean jeans and t-shirt, Khal noticed the redness immediately.

"Oh. You've caught the sun. Do you have any lotion on?" He seemed genuinely concerned. Caring.

"Yeah, I put some on after the shower. It doesn't hurt." That seemed to satisfy his question and he handed me my coffee – cream, one sugar. He had also noticed that too.

We took our coffees into the living room and continued chatting.

"Your mom teaches?"

"Yeah, she teaches math. She thought I would follow in her footsteps." It made me smile when I thought back to my high school math class.

"Maths not your thing then?"

"Well, no. I was okay with it, but I'm much better at the sciences. Well, I was. What about you?"

"Sciences for me too. But you're studying Art History now, right?"

"Yeah."

"So tell me, are you a Renaissance fan or modern abstract?"

I laughed and gave detailed descriptions of the periods and pieces I liked: from Ancient Egyptian and Mesopotamian antiquities to Native American and Aborigine pieces; paintings to hang on a wall and Pulitzer prize-winning photographs. There was not one favorite artist, just many incredible pieces that spoke of a history or a conflict. It wasn't just pictures that painted a thousand words, it was every piece of art that told a story.

We chatted on and on, generic topics, easy subjects, until Khal caught a glimpse of the pile of newspapers I'd been collecting – all related to the cat sightings – and the two books John had given me.

"Are you still reading about the Lincolnshire cat sightings?" He asked.

I hadn't actually picked up the books again since Khal came back. For some reason the whole subject had taken a back seat. Now Khal brought it up I was unsure how much to say. After what happened last time, I hesitated.

Well, I told myself after a moment's thought, he had broached the subject so maybe I should just answer it as honestly as I would normally.

"It's fascinating, apart from that one night of savagery – that was just horrendous. I can't imagine how those farmers must have felt finding their animals like that." It really did make me feel sick just thinking about it.

"Different sightings have been reported on and off for a while now. I found out from the books that John gave me, these sightings don't just happen in Lincolnshire." I stopped for a bit to see Khal's reaction. I was surprised; he actually appeared to be interested. I picked one of the books up to show him some of the photos taken of the mysterious sightings. I didn't know if that was a good idea or not but it felt right.

"Yes, I've read both of these." Khal flipped through the book nonchalantly. "So, do you believe in these sightings?"

"I think it's hard to not believe something after the official reports on those farm animals. It would be hard to see this being done by anything other than a wild animal." I stopped for a moment, thinking. "But I'm someone who sees the news and journalists as things that are there to sell stories. I don't want to dismiss people's concerns but the slaughters only happened one night. I'm hoping it stays that way, and these *things* that people think they see turn out to be nothing more than shadows fueled by myths."

"Do you believe in myths?" Khal put the book down having gotten to the end.

I thought for a while, wondering how to answer but decided to go with what I'd always believed. "Myths are just that, myths."

Before I knew it Khal and I were having a serious conversation about the idea of myths, legends and reality actually having a connection. It was interesting talking to Khal about an in depth subject that I had a strong opinion on and one that Khal seemed keen on, and knowledgeable.

"There is often a reality to a myth or legend somewhere. But it doesn't have to be the creepy, frightening descriptions that people hype some things up to be. And these large cat sightings could be harmless. Nothing more than a misunderstanding of what people are actually seeing," he said.

"There are often very logical explanations for such things. But to think that there is a reality to a myth is going a bit far, don't you think. I mean, surely that is why such creatures, such legends are called myths, isn't it – they aren't real."

"But if Lincolnshire has these myths, and then there are sightings to support the myths, surely that puts some reality to it? And the fact that there is obviously some reality to this, does it excuse the posse mentality of going hunting for this...creature, even when no one really knows what it is?" He seemed genuinely perturbed by the groups of people that talked about hunting down the creature, or creatures.

"No animal should be hunted down like that, no. There are always alternatives somewhere." I couldn't agree with him more on the thought of a hunting group. Animals didn't deserve to be hunted in such a manner, especially if there were some unanswered questions. "But that doesn't take away the fact that a myth is unreal, nothing more than a figment of someone's imagination and a way to validate a phenomena that has no explanation."

It was fascinating listening to Khal talk. But I struggled to see why he was interested in this now, when before he seemed so annoyed with me for even mentioning it.

I dismissed my question as just one of those things. Like many questions I had that related to Khal. It had obviously taken Khal time to feel that he could talk to me.

Our evening was wonderful. Relaxed, happy, extremely comfortable.

"I better go. I'll see you tomorrow." I walked Khal to the door, giving him a small wave goodbye and then closed the door.

That was the first time Khal made a *date*, albeit a loosely labeled one. I didn't care. I had a huge grin on my face that felt no rush to disappear anytime soon.

Khal continued to be a regular visitor to the store during the day. Some days he would come for coffee, others he just came to chat. The other shop assistants had grown used to his presence, laughing and joking with him. It was a different side to Khal that shone through his austere persona. And he became a permanent fixture after I finished work, sometimes just to walk me home, sometimes to take me out for a drink after work. And then he began to come back for dinner. We found a variety of subjects to while away the evening hours, including silence, watching the fire or reading a book. We just enjoyed each other's company, chatting when we wanted to. It was like having Jason here...but different. I'd never been attracted to Jason.

Of course it did mean I never saw Greg during all this time. And although John came into the store and would see Khal there, even chatted with him, I rarely hung out with John during the day and hadn't seen him after work since our last movie night.

My time with Khal was fun, special so I didn't notice the absence of John or Greg that much. And Khal and I became regulars at the local pub, enjoying one of the quiet tables in the back. We took it in turns to buy the drinks; he seemed happy to support equality. And it was my turn tonight.

Khal went to our usual table and I went to the bar to order our drinks. "A pint of Tetley and a bottle of Bud," I said to the barman as he came to take my order. It was late. I should be exhausted having worked both the early and late shift at the store. But I wasn't. I was on an adrenaline rush, looking forward to spending my evening with Khal.

"Hello." Greg arrived at my side, looking his normal dignified, ghostly self. Dressing in black did not help. Whenever I saw him he never wore normal clothes: jeans and sneakers; shorts and t-shirts. I wondered if he was always just coming from work, but I still had no idea what he did. I tried not to laugh as a sudden thought came to mind; I wondered if he was a mortician. Well, it would explain the look.

"Hi. I haven't seen you around." Even though I made this statement, I knew it was me that had been absent from the beach and movies recently.

"I have been watching, looking out for you. I thought I might have seen you at the cinema the other night. There was a new French film playing. I thought it would have been your type of thing." Greg looked questioningly, and I felt guilty. I couldn't ignore his inquiry.

"Oh, I hadn't noticed. I'll have to pay more attention to the showings. I've been busy…with work." I thought as quickly as I could to explain my absence. And then wondered why I was. What I did with my time was my business. Okay, so we'd begun getting close, but we certainly weren't exclusive or anything.

"Would you join me next week? I would like to take you to the theatre and for dinner, again." Greg pulled me into his cold body and leaned in closer, licking his lips.

"I don't know." I glanced over my shoulder. I couldn't see Khal at our table and wondered where he was.

"I don't know, Greg." I pulled away and gave him a hesitant smile. Maybe I should. We were friends...kind of. I was friends with Khal...kind of. It couldn't hurt arranging an evening with a...friend? But it felt wrong, almost deceitful...almost.

"If I do, I'll see you there, but I won't be available for dinner." There, that felt more...friend-oriented. Dinner was too couple-ish.

The bartender handed me my two drinks and I paid.

"You are not alone." Greg sounded angry and grabbed my wrist before I lifted the drinks. Well, I wasn't having that.

"No, I'm not. We're just round the corner."

Greg pushed himself off the bar with force, flung my wrist from his grip and left without saying another word. Yep, definitely angry.

Well, fuck him. I headed back to Khal. Whatever Greg's problem was, he'd get over it.

When I reached our table, Khal was back from wherever he'd disappeared to and was agitated. And his sweaty appearance gave me the distinct impression he hadn't visited the bathroom but instead had been running for miles.

"Sorry the drinks took so long. I bumped into a friend. And the bar's busy. Are you okay?"

"Yes, of course. I...I just didn't notice the time." I glanced at him as he looked around. He genuinely seemed surprised by the number of people there. But as he continued to scan the crowd, I started to ask him who he was looking for but then thought better of it, in case he was looking for Greg and would start asking questions.

After taking a good long drink of his beer, Khal looked calmer. My evening with him flew past as usual. He still had an incredible effect on my body and my mind, a buzz that became stronger the closer we were to each other. But I treasured his friendship, our talking. Controlling my feelings for him, though, was becoming harder as we spent more time together. I felt sex-deprived; BOB and self-gratification just weren't cutting it anymore.

If Khal showed just the slightest interest in more, if he asked me out on an actual date, I would jump up and scream 'yes' over and over. It was strange. I had one man who seemed overly keen to ask me out, getting angry at my being with someone else. And I have one who never asks, seems only interested in being friends and I wished there was more. One side of me was disappointed – the other didn't mind. Typical. Since leaving home for college, and losing my virginity, I couldn't think of one man I'd wanted to have regular sex with and wanted to spend time getting to know. Not one...until now. Because the rare times Khal didn't come over, didn't show up at work or after work, I was heartily disappointed and felt lost on what to do with my time.

A thought suddenly occurred to me: why had I never asked him out? I didn't have an answer. I'd approached men before, offered to buy them drinks while in a bar, asked them to dance when in a club. I even asked one guy out on a date...once. But with Khal, for some reason, I hadn't even tried. And I didn't rectify the situation either.

I put it down to Khal's distance, my reason for never asking. There was the physical distance he constantly kept in check, never touching, never brushing up against me. And then there was the other distance he kept. There appeared to be some subjects that were completely out of bounds: he never talked about his family, and never asked me back to his place. And there was always some part of him he kept back. I didn't know what but there was something.

I was beginning to read his expressions extremely well, especially when he wasn't wearing his glasses. I began to know what topics were off limits and what weren't. This distance kept my feelings at bay – I convinced myself that there was no way I could have more than a friendship with someone if they weren't prepared to be open about their life. It didn't always work, but I kept trying to convince myself. And it was obvious from the physical distance he kept, I wasn't going to get anywhere close for this to be a one-nighter. So either way, I was frustrated.

I should be grateful. I should be pleased my feelings were being kept in check because I didn't want more. I didn't.

Chapter Thirteen

Now that I was no longer cycling to work, I actually began to miss the freedom of it. There was something quite refreshing about feeling the wind through my hair, the cool air flowing across my body. My cycle helmet restricted its flow a little but I didn't mind.

I used my days off, the days Khal wasn't around, to cycle around the neighborhood, venturing further and further away from home. It was fun and cleared my head. I enjoyed the peace and not having to answer to anyone.

Today was one of my days off again. I was up later than usual so I took the opportunity to lounge around the cottage for the morning, reading the paper and drinking my coffee. I couldn't get through my day without my coffee; it was my sustenance...and my addiction.

I hadn't been able to read the paper for a few days. Work was getting really busy. It was approaching the heart of the summer season even though the schools wouldn't be out for another month. The reporters were obviously getting fed up with repeating themselves regarding the sightings of the cat because their stories no longer captured my cynical side. Except there was one crazy report that had a large cat and massive dog sighted together. It was so obscure that even the reporter joked about the ludicrousness of it.

I checked my e-mails. There were two from home – Ben and mom – then one from Alice, and lastly one from Jason. It took a while to reply to them all, but the one that caught my eye was Jason's. He asked how things were going with Khal, Greg and John.   He was being soppy and emotional, telling me how much he loved me and wanted me to be happy. Apparently, I needed to make the first move with Khal if he meant that much to me, and I should tell Greg to *fuck off* and leave me alone.

Jason added at the end of his very long e-mail: *When someone makes you feel that good you need to tell them, and when someone annoys you that much you need to tell them too. And I want to tell you I love you and want you to be happy. If these guys can't make you happy then come home to me. I'll make you happy, Abby. I'll love you the way you deserve to be loved, Abby.*

Where did all this come from? This was not like Jason. He'd never given any inclination that he felt anything more than friendship for me...unless he'd been drinking.

I sent a one line reply back: *Jason, are you drunk?*

And walked away from the computer smiling and shaking my head. Typical. There I was, thinking something was wrong with Jason, something had happened, and then the light bulb went off in my head, and it registered what he'd done. He must have been out on the town last night.

By the time I finished with everything I wanted to get done it was lunchtime and I was hungry, but when I scoured the fridge there was little in. I sighed realizing I would have to leave the house earlier than I'd planned. I'd forgotten I hadn't been shopping for a few days.

I took a shower and dressed in my denim shorts and bright yellow t-shirt. I enjoyed wearing bright colors on my bicycle. It made me feel safer; there was no way a car could miss canary yellow. By the time I was ready to leave the house I had decided to just grab a banana and ride my bicycle to the seal sanctuary as planned and then go to the store on my way home.

I loved visiting the sanctuary. The seal pups were cute, wanting attention and food. The birds of prey were incredible to just look at and amazingly impressive during the show times. Even though this place opened all year round helping wounded animals, it attracted more tourists during the summer months so the shows were packed. I bought a season pass on my first visit so I could go anytime during my more-than-three-month stay. I hadn't gone as often as I'd wanted so today was a wonderful chance. And every time I did go, I took photographs to send through to Ben, just so he knew I was still visiting. Today, I decided to miss the shows and instead offered to help with the animals. I was handed a shovel and bucket with a smile and a grateful 'thanks'.

It was late when I left and I was exhausted. It was a good exhausted, though. By the time I got to the store the sun was below the horizon, setting off an assortment of oranges and reds across the drifting clouds. I parked and locked my bicycle on the side of the building and watched the array of colors span the distant sky. I smiled; there was something quite enticing, mesmerizing about a setting sun. I sighed and went into the store. I collected a basket from the stack by the door and walked along the refrigerators to the milk.

"Hello again. On your own?" Greg didn't waste any time annoying me. Or making me jump out of my skin.

"Nice to see you again too." Yes, I was being sarcastic. I hadn't forgotten that last time I'd seen him – he'd taken off so angrily when he'd found out I was with another person that he was lucky I was still willing to talk to him. God, sometimes men were so stupid.

Whether I was on my own or not should not affect him or result in him going off in a huff.

"I have upset you."

"I wonder what makes you think that?" I moved on to the cheese counter and picked up some cheddar. Then continued onto the bread.

"Are you meeting anyone later?"

"My plans are not normally something I broadcast." I began to wonder what Greg wanted. God, I was too exhausted for a confrontation tonight.

He soon made his intent clear when he leaned in and brushed his lips over my hair. "You smell divine."

"Greg. I'm still mad at your for last time. Don't push your luck." I moved out of his reach and carried on with my shopping by collecting some packaged cakes. My personal life was my own business. I didn't like people inquiring about it as if they had a right to know. So I used that thought to help me keep my distance and to keep my anger at him in place.

But a part of me wanted to stay close to him. I couldn't deny I was attracted to him and although he annoyed me, he was cute when he knew he had to suck up to me.

He followed me round the store, not really saying anything. And it didn't take him long to move in close again until he was almost breathing down my neck. I shivered and moved away. My anger transferred from being aimed at him to myself as my libido heated up.

I swore he moved in even closer and I heard him take another sniff, long and deep this time. Now that was just too creepy. I'd been out all day and probably stank of fish and sweat.

I went to pay for my shopping and hopped out of the store. Greg never left my side and began chatting away about how much busier it was in town, how a particular store was having a sale, and what was playing at the movies.

I should have paid more attention, but I didn't. Next to my bicycle was Gadreel, waiting patiently.

I stopped, dead. Gad didn't growl at me or do anything that made me think he would hurt me in any way. But he did watch me, looked up into my eyes and stared following my every move as I placed my shopping in the paniers. After fastening the clips I turned to unlock my bicycle but couldn't reach the tumblers to put my combination in.

"Would you mind moving Gadreel so I can get to my bicycle."

Greg moved right up to me and took my hands in his, intertwining our fingers, stroking the back of my hands. "He's not hurting anything."

"Greg. I'm tired."

"I know you are, darling. Let me help you. I could rub your feet...wash your back." He began to kiss the side of my head and slowly let his lips move down to my cheek then to my neck. It felt so good that I moved my head over to feel more.

But as his lips came up to my mouth and he began to caress my back with one of his hands, all I could think of, all I could see in my head was Khal.

Greg licked his tongue over my lips, asking for an invite. I just couldn't do it. And I knew it was because of Khal.

106

I gave Greg a little push with my hands. "Greg. Please. Not tonight. I'm tired and I'm hungry. I smell awful because I've been working at the sanctuary, helping clean out some of the enclosures. I need to get home."

Greg didn't argue and he did stop his advances which surprised me. He ran his hand down my face, cupped my chin and leaned in for a chaste kiss. There was no doubt in my mind he was a good kisser and knew what he was doing. There was also no doubt in my mind that I'd made the right decision no matter what the rest of my body was craving.

Greg snapped his fingers and Gad moved to his side and sat obediently at Greg's feet.

I took a deep breath and returned to my bicycle to remove my lock and place it in a panier. Then I maneuvered my bicycle so I could climb on it. But Greg and Gad stayed by my side. I didn't want to be rude so when Greg began walking in my direction I politely walked too.

Greg never stopped talking the whole way. He held my hand and rubbed his thumb in circles across my wrist, over and over. Yet all the time he talked and did the circle thing I couldn't get Khal out of my head. What would he do if he knew another man was attracted to me...and I was attracted to him? I couldn't deny my reaction to Greg; that would be stupid. But I was even more attracted to Khal...wasn't I?

Even though my mind was struggling to clear and organize my thoughts, when I got to the cottage I didn't want to go round the back on my own – or with Greg. It was dark and something was telling me not to trust Greg. So I left my bicycle under the front window, removed my shopping and opened the door.

"If you have no plans for tonight, I would enjoy having dinner with you?" Greg was smiling his radiant smile, his dark eyes in complete contrast. In the moonlight his skin looked translucent, silky, his lips a vibrant red. There was no doubt about it – he was strikingly attractive. And my blood began to warm my insides up to the idea of his hands on my body.

His demeanor was more relaxed than usual, almost provocative. But did I want him to come in? Did I want to encourage him?

Being asked out like this and accepting the invite would encourage Greg with our relationship. I was sure it would give him the green light. And I didn't want that. Not yet anyway.

I remembered Jason's polite words: *tell him to fuck off.*

I had to stifle my sniggering. I couldn't say that to Greg. At the very least he was still a friend.

"No thanks. Maybe another time." I gave Greg a smile and closed the door behind me, happy to be on my own.

Chapter Fourteen

It was another couple of days before I had a day off to do my own thing again. I hadn't forgotten my encounter with Greg and really didn't want another day like it. Since then, I'd avoided being out late as that seemed to be the only time I saw him. The weather continued to stay warm and dry. I looked at the local maps to see if there was anything further afield that I would enjoy visiting. There was a nature reserve west of town. It was a good distance away – the furthest I would have cycled – but I had all day. If I got up early, gave myself a full day out, I also wouldn't need to go walking around at night, on my own. The idea appealed greatly.

I was still a little nervous about the cars while on my bicycle, but I was getting used to the amount of traffic around. The roads weren't as quiet as I'd hoped. But I knew the drivers here were used to people on bicycles; they knew how to give a wide birth – so far anyway. All I needed to do was relax and trust them. Riiight.

I also needed to make sure I didn't ride too close to the ridge, a join between the tarmac and grass that continued into a drop which appeared to contain ditches of stagnant water. If a car whizzed past too fast, I had a tendency to wobble. I had caught my wheel in the ridge once and I couldn't control my fall. Thankfully, there was no ditch and I only fell onto grass. It would just make my day if I wasn't as lucky this time.

I packed a picnic: just a sandwich, apple, and drink. Then some breadcrumbs for the ducks and the map I needed. It was an Ordinance Survey map. These maps were great for exploring and finding the best walkways and footpaths. I had studied the map before leaving and knew where I wanted to head. There were two small rivers that met near a tiny village, west of Mablethorpe. Apparently – according to *Wikipedia* – it was a popular fishing spot. I wasn't interested in fishing today…or ever for that matter. I hated the slimy worms and then having to take a flapping fish off the hook. Yucky. I would much rather enjoy the natural environment of the countryside and find a meadow or something to relax in and read my Kindle or write in my journal.

I packed my Kindle, my journal and pen, and a blanket with my picnic in the panniers. I made sure I put a long-sleeved shirt on so that I didn't burn again. It would also protect me if I fell…hopefully.

I got on my way.

Now and again a cyclist or two would fly by; obviously the riders were used to getting from A to B as quickly as possible. I wasn't in any hurry and just sauntered along, enjoying the warm breeze. Some farmers were out ploughing the fields. Others were harvesting vegetables. The occasional home I passed had fresh washing hanging out on long washing lines. Propped up by a large wooden pole, sheets, shirts and pants billowed with the rhythm of the wind. It was fascinating, something you don't see in New York City…or even in the suburbs.

I became completely oblivious to the tractors, cars and other cyclists that passed me by so I didn't notice how one cyclist had caught me up but didn't overtake. Instead it steadily pulled up alongside me.

It took me a second or two to register the bicycle was not moving on. I started to slow down to give it chance to overtake. I didn't think we were going up a hill or anything, something that might have caused the rider to struggle to get passed me. But the bicycle slowed down with me. So I slowed down a little more, and a little more. The cyclist wasn't going anywhere, and I could feel a pair of eyes looking at me.

Trying to steady my grip on the handlebars, I took a quick glimpse to my right to see what the problem was and came face to face with that irresistible smile. Khal.

I came to a sudden halt before I tumbled off my bicycle from losing my balance.

"What are you doing here?" I was shocked. Happy – as my skpping heart could attest to – but shocked. This was the last place I expected to see him.

"I just thought I would join you. I can go away if you want." He tried to look hurt, but that was impossible; his smile gave too much away. I may not be able to see his eyes – he was wearing his dark glasses and hoodie again – but what I could see spoke volumes. He wanted to be here.

"Where's your helmet? And how did you know where I'd be?" My fake annoyance didn't work. He confused me but I was too thrilled to see him. I enjoyed his company, enjoyed having him close by. Everything else in my life disappeared when he was around. My heart was enjoying its somersault trick, and the current that flowed over the space between us went wild.

Yet I knew I hadn't told him I was planning a bicycle ride today. I didn't even know myself until last night, after he'd left.

"All these questions. Aren't you pleased to have some company?" He put his foot on his pedal, ready to push off again, and gave me a crooked, one-sided smiling glance. It was a clear indication that he wanted me to join him.

I couldn't answer him. Of course I wanted his company. Of course I wanted him with me. Who wouldn't?

Khal rode on the outside, making the cars move out of the way when they overtook. I felt safer, more in control with Khal there. We didn't talk. I really began to enjoy the ride through the countryside, appreciating the day. I occasionally caught him looking my way. He looked relaxed and I couldn't be happier. This was going to be a perfect day.

We arrived in the village late morning. There was a pub and parish church in the heart of the village, and at the T-junction there was the footpath to the rivers. The whole area was part of a natural conservation area and the original bridleways had been cleared for the public to use. The tall wooden signs indicating direction were placed at a crossroads and there was one that pointed towards the rivers.

We left our bicycles next to the stile, the gateway to the public thoroughfare. Khal had a backpack of his own and automatically went to empty my panniers. He placed my picnic, book and journal into his pack and carried the blanket. I took my helmet off and placed it into one of the panniers and locked it and our bicycles.

We walked quietly for a while. I needed to mull over Khal's appearance. I ought to, needed to at least try and take control of what was happening to me. But I didn't know where to start, or what to do.

We didn't rush along. Whatever pace I set, Khal matched. There was no awkwardness, no forced conversation, nothing.   Just two people enjoying the countryside, together.

The hedgerows along the path were so thick with a variety of vibrant green leaves that it was impossible to see the fields behind them.   In front, along the edge of the walkway, were an abundance of colorful wild flowers. Bees were gathering their much needed supplies of pollen from the newly emerged sprays along the ground and the tiny white bramble blossoms in the hedges. Some brambles were still in flower, other stems had fruit growing. None were ripe yet.

The multitude of butterflies quietly rested in the sunshine enjoying the best part of the day. They were joined by some spiders, waiting patiently in the center of their traps. A ladybird crawled up a stalk of grass heading towards a web. Khal put his finger out so the ladybug would transfer to his hand, preventing it from being caught and depriving the spider of its lunch. Khal moved it to a leaf, further away. My heartbeat gave a hop and skip in approval.

Tall grasses peeked out from inside the prickly brambles and other thriving vines and saplings. Dandelions interspersed with the other wild flowers along the ground, some with their yellow blooms and some with their white fluffy headed stems waiting for the wind to carry their seeds. I remembered them as a child: dandelion clocks. Mom showed me how to blow and count the clock. I enjoyed reminiscing and went to pick one.

I leaned forward to reach the stem, but Khal's hand grabbed my shirt sleeve around my wrist and pulled my hand away quickly.

I was astonished, alarmed by his action. I felt like a scolded child and showed my anger at his interference of my childhood memories by scowling at him.

"Be careful," he let go quickly. "You could be stung." I frowned at what he'd said. I knew dandelion clocks weren't dangerous.

"You hadn't noticed the nettles."

"Nettles?" I looked to where I had put my hand and growing among the flowers and wispy dandelion clocks were stalks of soft green leaves, some small, some larger. There appeared to be tiny flowing buds but it was hard to tell.

I looked questioningly at Khal, no longer angry at him.

"They sting," he explained. "Here." He picked a dandelion clock away from the nettles. "Just watch where you put your hands. Those leaves hurt." He came in close and carefully, quietly handed me my clock. His nearness caught me off guard, the tiny currents firing their cannons in every direction from my body to his and back again as if trying to reach across the gap between us, and I was wondering if he could feel it too, if he could hear my heart bouncing around inside my rib cage, beating a wild tattoo.

I reached out slowly to take the stem. "Thank-you," I stuttered. My hand brushed his and a shot of electricity exploded through my body, making me jump visibly.

Ouch, that hurt. And...it was just like at the bus depot. And I felt the same reaction through my body. I was instantly aroused.

"Sorry," Khal said, and swiftly moved his hand away from my touch giving me the dandelion.

I looked up at Khal wondering if it had made him jump as much as it had me. There was definitely something written on his face, but it didn't look like shock. Was he aroused from it too? I glanced at his pants but couldn't see a telltale bulge. I returned my eyes to his face; he looked in pain, almost agonizing. And so tense as if he were trying to control an unwanted emotion. Was he trying to stop his desire showing? He would have to have amazing control if that was what he was doing.

I lost interest in the dandelion. I held it limply in between my fingers, not really remembering what I wanted it for. It fell to the ground and I watched some of the seeds fall and catch the breeze.

Khal picked it up and blew the clock. "One O'clock...two O'clock...three O'clock."

His pain vanished, his tension eased.

"Come on," he said and smiled as we began walking again, quicker this time, Khal setting the pace, and the larger distance between us.

The moment was lost and I was...what? What was I wanting? What was I thinking? I didn't know, except that the closer Khal came, the more I wanted him to stay there.

Chapter Fifteen

The pathway brought us to a well-trodden trail that ran along the edge of the river. The brush was thick and I considered the two directions presented. I wanted a meadow, a field or something, somewhere where I could put the blanket down and enjoy the surrounding natural beauty, read my book.

"This way," Khal went right, and within a few minutes we arrived at a magnificent grassy slope, covered with an abundance of daisies and buttercups.

Like a hand of God, the sun peaked through a slight gap in the scattered powder-puffed clouds, and gently laid its fingertips along the petals of the tiny meadow flowers, stroking the grasses like a soft pillow.

"Khal! How did you know?" It was perfect.

"Just a hunch." Khal laid the blanket on the ground in a spot away from everyone else who'd had the same idea as me and emptied his backpack. He rested, leaning back on one elbow. I switched my Kindle on and leaned back to read.

We must have stayed like that for over an hour, not saying a word to each other.

I soon realized I was hungry so opened up my picnic and took a bite of my sandwich. I offered some to him but he wasn't interested, so I placed it back in its bag, grabbed the bag of breadcrumbs for the ducks and headed down to the river.

The shrubbery was thick along the embankment, the waters calm. Willow trees dipped their long branches, allowing their leaves to suck the fresh water. Little inlets were created from the thriving plants and a family of ducks floated close by. I opened my bag of crumbs and scattered a handful. The youngsters scrambled around hunting for each piece, their parents holding back, waiting for the morsels their children missed.

I peered back at Khal. He was watching, I thought. I wasn't completely sure. It was difficult to tell with his glasses covering his eyes and hoodie covering his face.

Coming back to the blanket, I sat on the edge near a small cluster of daisies. Khal didn't move. Didn't talk. Just stayed put. I was happy. I enjoyed the tranquility, the peacefulness of just watching the birds, listening to the water. And I enjoyed not being alone. I never thought I would see the day where I was pleased to think that. I'd always enjoyed my own company, my own space. But Khal's presence blended with my own that I couldn't imagine him not being here. I glanced in his direction a couple of times, watched the virtually invisible movement of his breathing. I smiled to myself, completely relaxed.

I picked a daisy, poked a hole in the lower part of the stem with my thumb nail, picked another daisy and threaded the stalk through the hole. Poked a hole in the new daisy and picked another one, threading the stem through the hole. I hadn't made a daisy chain in years. Quietly I worked, enjoying the warm breeze on my hair, the sun on my back.

A group of ramblers walked by and waved hello. A couple and their dog went past in the opposite direction but were deep in conversation, not acknowledging our presence or anyone else's.

"Here." I'd finished my chain and turned to put it round Khal's neck. He sat up and held out his hand to take it but I wanted to put it in place. I reach out to take his hoodie down so I could place the fragile daisy chain over his head.

"No!" Khal grabbed my wrists over my shirt and pushed me. He jumped up to his feet in one swift fluid move and walked away. I didn't understand. What had I done that was so wrong?

"It's only a daisy chain." I couldn't believe his reaction. It was completely over-the-top. "It's not going to kill you!"

I felt hurt, rejected. The daisy chain went to waste on the ground and I sat, cross-legged and head down. Tears stung my eyes but I refused to let them fall. For God's sake, I thought I'd really got to know the man. My barriers of stopping a man reaching my heart were finally dissolving and he appeared more relaxed with me, seemed to enjoy my company. But now? My tears, no matter how hard I tried to stop them, toppled over my bottom eyelashes.

It was ridiculous. Why was I allowing my emotions to control me like this? Why didn't I just get up and leave?

I hadn't heard him come back; his footsteps were always so quiet.

"I...I'm sorry." Khal crouch next to me. He didn't touch: so close and yet so far. He never made that final stretch to close the gap, and it was killing me that he didn't. I was beginning to feel like a leper.

Even crouched he still towered above me, his broad shoulders dwarfed my own yet I wasn't a small woman by any stretch of the imagination. I looked up, tried to read his face. It was confusing, full of pain and yet soft, gentle.

"Why?" It was all I could think of to say. I needed answers. Khal turned up at the most unexpected times, unexpected places, like today. I hadn't wanted someone to be a part of my life but he was. He made me laugh...and now he had made me cry. But he continued to keep a distance, sometimes so small it was virtually unnoticeable, and sometimes a chasm like now.

"Why. What did I do that was so bad? They were only daisies. I made it for you." There were many other questions I had but this one hurt right now. I'd never experienced such passion for another person before, and I needed to know he wasn't rejecting me. And I needed to know why.

And the tears kept trickling.

Khal didn't move, didn't say anything for what felt like eternity. Just stayed close, looking down. I may not be able to see his eyes, but I could feel them boring deep into my soul. I searched his face for answers, but nothing had changed.

He took a deep breath and let it out slowly, sighing as if resigned to an inevitability. But I had no idea what the inevitability was.

He rested back on his haunches, kneeling on the blanket. "Because it will hurt you. I don't want to hurt you."

"What you do mean, it will hurt me? Don't you think this is hurting right now?"

"I'm sorry I hurt your feelings. I never meant to upset you. But I wasn't meaning your feelings being hurt. I was talking about a physical pain, like the one earlier."

I was confused, frightened. My mind was working overtime, irrational thoughts went whizzing around my head, imagining all kinds of crazy things. And I felt my confidence plummet and a multitude of questions ran through my brain.

"You're always so damn mysterious. First the eyes, now this."

"My eyes?"

"Yes, your eyes. You always keep them covered…concealed. It's unsettling as if you're trying to hide more than just your face. What are you hiding, Khal?"

"You want to see my eyes. Is that what all this is about? Because I won't expose them to daylight for you?"

"Yes, I want to see your eyes. I want to see you. I want to see you how you see me."

"Fine." His disheartened face scared me. It was as if he'd resigned himself to my reaction, knew I would reject him.

But I'd seen them before – why was he making such a big deal of this. Khal took a deep breath, held it, then he slowly but surely reached up to his hood and let it fall behind him. Then placed his hand on his shades; he hesitated before taking them off.

Chapter Sixteen

His eyes were closed.

I watched his face, enjoyed the freedom presented in front of me, of being able to see him properly without the obstruction of his hood and shades. As he opened his eyes, I waited to see the green and gold pigment, the translucent emerald color slashed with a vibrant yellow that surrounded a black chasm that never failed to melt my heart. And at first they were just as I remembered.

But then it happened – in a heartbeat they quickly changed. The gold overtook the green and was structured with a strange haughty look. The black void virtually disappeared, leaving a thin trace like a fold in the center of the gold and emerald, just like a cat's eyes.

And he didn't blink, not once. I tried very hard not to react, not to show any shock. They were going to take some getting used to. But they captivated me, drew me into him even more.

The way I saw it, there were worse things in this world to worry about. Having Ben as a brother had always shown me that people come in all varieties and nothing was beyond imagination. Even though I'd never heard of this particular genetic abnormality, stranger things had happened. As long as a person was healthy, kind and happy that's all that mattered. Khal was here, alive and well, and he always appeared kind and caring. Just…different. His differences made him unique, and were worth treasuring.

Khal was quiet.

"Did you think I would have a problem with them? Did you think I would mind?"

"Abby, you make it sound so simple. But life isn't like that."

"Okay, so life isn't simple. Your eyes are different. I've known that for a while now and I don't believe I've ever given you the impression that it bothers me. In fact, I like them. I'm sorry if that disappoints you. But that doesn't explain your reaction earlier with the daisies and why you think I'll get hurt." My tears abated but the hurt didn't.

"One step at a time. Do you have any idea how difficult this is for me to show you, explain to you? Or even just how embarrassing this is?" He looked extremely uncomfortable.

"Look, if you're not attracted to me, you only have to say. I'll understand." I tried so hard to not sound rejected. Oh, I didn't want to give him a hard time. It was obvious he was doing that to himself. But I needed to know what the problem was. He couldn't just keep turning up like this and not expect me to react.

"No!" Khal retorted. "No, it never occurred to me that was what you'd think. I thought my being here, coming to see you was evident that I enjoyed your company."

It was true. It was. That's why this was confusing. He seemed to enjoy coming over but always kept a distance, a barrier. You didn't do that when a physical attraction was present.

"I can see why you would be confused. It isn't just static, Abby, that you've felt. I know you've noticed the trembling that happens between us. I know you've felt...something. I feel that all the time. And I've never known for someone else, someone like you, to feel it too. It's strange. Unusual. I would even go as far as to say it's unique. And I don't know how to react."

"You're going to have to stop there and backtrack a bit – I haven't a clue what you're talking about."

"Okay, my senses are extremely heightened that whenever I come into contact with someone I have tiny but strong impulses that fly through my body, traverse through my nerves and cause multiple jolts. Normally it's only me who feels them and the other person – you – is unaware. Unfortunately, for some reason, you're feeling them too."

"Okay, so it's something unusual. I get that. But why are you blushing? What's so terrible about them?" Khal looked so uncomfortable and, if it wasn't for his skin-tone, I was sure his face would be beetroot.

"Well," Khal gave a little nervous cough. "The only way I feel them – and you when you're with me – is if we have skin-to-skin contact."

"Oh...OH. So you're saying this wouldn't be just a one off? What I felt before – that wouldn't be it? It's going to happen again?"

Khal shook his head. "It does die down, after a few seconds, maybe longer. Well, it does for me anyway; I'm presuming it'll be the same for you. But it's painful for those seconds. Then it goes into a kind of tingling or dull throb. But it's always there. It never goes away completely. It just gets easier the more contact you have. The less time we have together the more it will come back."

I was flabbergasted. This had to be one of the weirdest things I'd ever heard.

"Khal, why me?"

"Well, I don't know. Maybe...well...have you ever experienced anything like this before?"

"No. Never. But then I don't normally..." I stopped. I didn't want to go into any details of what I did with other men, especially the fact that I rarely spent time getting to know any on a long term basis. Jason was a rare example.

"Could it be because you're...you know...attracted to me?" He bit his bottom lip, waiting for me to say something. But what could I say; it was true, I was attracted to him. I couldn't deny that one.

"Yes, I know. I've been trying to get you to see that one. You mean to tell me you've only just figured that out."

"No, Abby. Of course I've always known that. I'm not talking about what you think it is. This isn't just libidinous. I'm trying to tell you it's more than that. Look, we've both had other...partners. You're not my first, just as I'm not yours. But this...there's a chemistry. You enchant me; I'm enamored by you. And, even though I know you're not going to admit it, it's the same for you too."

"Admit to what? I'm attracted to you, end of story. But that's it." I was putting a stop to this now. He could think what he liked. He was sexually attractive, but nothing else. I wanted to touch him but I certainly didn't want a commitment, if that was his intention.

"If that's how you want to play it, then fine." Khal turned to sit down next to me, and didn't move.

I needed to calm down. I didn't like the direction he'd taken this and refused to either continue or justify my feelings. I looked at him, expecting to see him sulking but surprisingly he appeared calm and was...smiling.

"So what does this mean? I can't touch you, ever?" I couldn't imagine that. No matter how much I denied what Khal said about our being together, I couldn't ignore my desperate need to have him hold me in his arms. I'd never ached so much with this deep necessity in my life before.

"No, I'm not saying that. All I'm saying is, it'll hurt you for a few seconds if you touch me. I'm used to it. I know how to control my reactions."

"How? How do you control? When my hand touched yours earlier, I saw the anguish in your face. If that's you controlling it…" That image continued to haunt me, that painful look.

"Oh, that wasn't because…no, I wasn't in pain from the shock. I can camouflage my sensitivity quite easily. No, that was your pain. Look, I know that sounds bizarre, but I feel your pain, and saw you jump back in shock. I…I expected you to keep your distance, suppress your desires, not come closer, not forge ahead.

"Look, Abby. I can suppress my yearnings so you don't have to ruminate over my wanting a commitment. I'm happy to just have this time with you, like this. But you always seem to want to push for more.   I'm besotted with you, but if I tell you that are you going to run in the opposite direction?"

Did I want this? I'd avoided this for so long, kept away from men so they didn't become attached…so that I didn't. My independence was of paramount importance to me and I was determined no one would ever dictate how I should live my life. Having a boyfriend, another person to think of, always seemed to be a restriction I shunned.

And yet here I was, with Khal, listening to him inform me of his infatuation, and I loved it. He was like a drug I craved.

We sat quietly for a while. "No I won't run in the opposite direction."

"But you won't admit to there being more between us? Even though I know you feel it too?"

"More between us? No way. You're definitely wrong on that count." God, I knew I was attracted to him but that was all. What if he was right? What if there was more? I dismissed these thoughts and questions abruptly but his proximity on the blanket was killing me. I needed him.

"How do you control the shock?" I wanted to know. I was behaving like a complete lovesick teenager, but I didn't want to change this course I was on.

"I just hang on. I don't let go."

We were silent again.

"Can we try?"

Khal hesitated. I wasn't sure if he was just contemplating the idea or contriving a valid excuse for denying my request.

"Are you sure this is what you want?"

"Yes. Yes, I'm sure." I was sure. Completely sure. I needed to know if I could do this. I needed to know if I could manage the pain, the shock. I needed to know if he was wrong and that what happened earlier was just as I predicted: a coincidence and normal static electricity.

I dreaded the thought of inflicting pain on him just because I had this insatiable desire to touch him. And I normally cowered away from pain, especially self-inflicted, but for some idiotic reason, I didn't mind this time. I just needed to know Khal wasn't suffering because of me. Seeing

126

his eyes helped. Seeing him seeing me was a comfort, my safety net.

Khal extended his hand out. I looked at it for a moment, then looked up at his face for reassurance. I took my time; didn't want to rush. And Khal didn't move.

Slowly, very slowly, I reached out with my hand to touch his. The energy between us was noticeable, powerful as I neared. The force intensified as my palm came within inches of Khal's. I was surprised I couldn't see bolts of static jump between our palms. I hesitated; was I frightened? I didn't feel frightened.

I closed the gap, but the force of the shock threw my hand back. And it hurt. My body reacted as if I'd burned myself.

I took a deep breath so I could calm my heart down and I tried again, instructing my brain on the urgency of this matter. But my nervousness hindered my attempt. Now, I knew this was going to hurt. I inhaled deeply again to try and calm my nerves. It didn't work.

At that moment Khal seized my hand and refused to let go. The jolt from both the contact and the suddenness of his action had me jumping and shaking, and sent my heart skipping erratically, pounding violently in my chest. Was I going to have a heart attack? My breath was rapid as it tried to get a grip on reality. And the pain I could see on his face was heartbreaking, mirroring what I was experiencing. It hurt, immeasurably, beyond anything I'd ever experienced before. But at the same time I also felt my desire building.

There was nothing I could do. He wouldn't let go. I tried to pull away, instinctively wanting to retract my hand. But he gripped tightly. He was so much more physically powerful than me that I couldn't fight it. This gentle, quiet man was determined and so sure.

I held my breath as a way of trying to relieve the pain...and to fight the stimulation that was occurring between my legs. Then I blew it out through clenched teeth to only hold it again.

"Breathe, Abby. Come on, just breathe through it."

I tried. God, I tried. Slowly but surely the seconds passed and the pain eased. It was replaced by a tender throb on my nerve-endings. The pulsation that ran up my arm vanished.

Little by little he released my hand, but his face still exhibited remnants of pain even though I wasn't hurting. Well, not as much anyway.

"Don't...don't let go," I pleaded with him. Everything he'd mentioned before vanished in that moment. I didn't care what he thought, I didn't care that he'd been right; I loved the feel of his skin, loved moving my hand around so I could hold his properly. And I came closer, kneeled in front of him. I felt energized...and my arousal intensified.

Khal came up on his knees too, towering above me. Copying his previous move, I reached for his other hand, just grabbed hold, and coped with the initial shock. This time I breathed through it as Khal had suggested. It all subsided quickly.

I knew what to expect now. I was prepared each time I moved, each time I reached out to touch his wrist, his arm, his face. And for the first time I could move my hands over his scars, feel the ripples in his skin, fondle his huge fingers.

"You look worn out." His concern was comforting.

"I'm fine. It does take some getting used to, doesn't it? I can't imagine how you do this every time you touch someone, a woman. Is that why you keep away from people, keep covered up?"

"Yes." He smiled but it was obvious that while I'd found it difficult, Khal had suffered more.

"I'm pleased you explained. I can understand why you found it hard to say anything before. No regrets." I linked my fingers with his.

"Definitely no regrets."

Chapter Seventeen

Our afternoon was blissful. Khal replaced his sunglasses and came to feed the ducks with me, and we had a little walk along the footpath, enjoying the sunshine, fingers intertwined. Our contact felt normal, relaxed, and I loved it.

Our chatting was more relaxed too.

"What's Ben like?" He asked. I knew what he was asking and normally I didn't like talking about Ben. He was just a brother to me. After the revelation that Khal had just gone through, it never occurred to me to do anything but be open with him about Ben.

"He's wonderful. Kind, innocent, naïve. I think I've already told you he was born with Downs Syndrome. I remember being very young and seeing the anguish in mom and dad. They've always tried to make life as normal as possible for both of us, be there as parents, but it was rough on them. Their marriage has fallen apart – I don't understand why they're still together to be honest. They don't talk to each other. They don't even live together anymore. Ben, though, well, he's just Ben, my kid brother. If we got into trouble as siblings do, we were both disciplined. I wasn't expected to be the 'big sister' and look after him..." I stopped for a moment, though, remembering.

"What happened?" Khal had his arm across my shoulder as a protective gesture.

"Some kids at school. They started calling Ben names: retard, mental, psychotic. I didn't understand what

130

they were saying, except I knew it was bad." It broke my heart to think back to that time. My first realization of how cruel the world was.

"Kids can be so cruel."

"Yes, they can. But they hear it from the adults around them."

"How did Ben cope?"

"He was oblivious. Too young to understand. Mom was great. Even though Ben had a lot of problems and mom and dad had a lot of worries ahead of them, mom eventually noticed that I was struggling too. She started to give talks at my school to help the students understand how words can hurt, that gossiping about a person was cruel. And she invited the neighborhood kids over for pizza and a movie, just to hang out. She always believed that you should never shy away from life just because an obstacle was placed in your way. She wanted people to understand his strengths and not concentrate on his disabilities. Everyone came to love Ben and I no longer had children in school calling my brother names."

"You said Ben had a lot of problems?"

"Well, having Downs does have both physical and mental challenges: walking and talking and many other things. But the biggest one Ben had to face was his heart. Downs children are sometimes born with heart defects. There was doubt that Ben would survive. They operated on him within hours of his birth but there were still problems, long term problems. They eventually operated again when there were no other options left, and they saved his life...for now. He still has issues, and always will. He won't live into old age but for now he's really well. How did you cope with the issues you have, growing up?" Khal tensed, removing his arm and placing his hands in his pockets.

"I didn't grow up with it. It was something that happened later." He didn't expand, acting dismissive, and I didn't dare ask. His wall came back, blocking me from intruding. I wondered what it would take for him, or me, to break it down. Would he ever really trust me? I decided I was grateful for the small piece of progress we'd made today and didn't say or ask anymore.

As we slowly walked back, I spotted some dandelion clocks again. This time I was careful to look out for the nettles. I picked one and began to blow.

"One O'clock…two O'clock."

Khal playfully went to reach for the dandelion but I moved it out of his way, laughing.

"Three O'clock." I giggled while blowing. My blows became pathetic attempts mixed in with my laughter. And Khal grabbed for the dandelion again.

I held it over my head but realized he could reach there. Then I swapped it from one hand to the other. He kept up with me and I couldn't stop laughing, dodging him, sneaking it behind my back.

I was about to back away, keeping it out of his reach when his long arms reached behind me from both sides to snatch the flower. But the sudden closeness froze me, stopped me from moving.

My heart was racing from the fun we were having, my breathing turbulent. Remaining frozen to the spot hadn't slowed any of that down. Khal hovered, not moving his arms from around my waist, searching for my hands.

And I gave them to him, placing my hands in his, but he kept them behind my back. He hesitated, just for a moment, then moved his face closer to mine. His aromatic breath warmed my face, my lips begging for relief.

"I want to kiss you." He whispered coming in a little closer. I didn't stop him; I wanted him to know that I wanted this too.

"Are you ready?" I couldn't answer him, my lungs wedged in my throat, but I'd never been more sure of anything in my life.

He came in closer still, until the power overwhelmed me, overwhelmed him. Oh, there was static, painful stinging, almost torturous agony that flowed through my veins, to every point in my body, from my lips down to my toes, but it didn't matter. I didn't care.

His lips were perfect, hot, sumptuous. I couldn't get enough of him, couldn't get enough of the taste, the smell, the touch. It was exquisite. Our lips, our tongues smarted from the contact. And I knew I had to press tight, not let go...and then it happened. I suddenly, unexpectedly, reached a peak in my desire for him. I orgasmed.

Chapter Eighteen

Ha, got it." I blinked. What?
Khal pulled away and had hold of the dandelion clock.

"Four O'clock…five O'clock." His face full of mischief.

"That was cheating." It was difficult to bring myself down from what had just happened. I felt hot, flushed. And while I couldn't be sure Khal hadn't seen or registered what had happened to me, I was willing to play along with his ignorance all the same. Well, there was no way I was going to say anything. This was too embarrassing…way too embarrassing.

Oh, I'd had plenty of orgasms, mainly from my own hand – and BOB – but I'd never experienced one as wild as this, nor without hand – or machine – stimulation.

I took a few deep breaths to help calm my racing heart and cool my skin.

"Cheat? Moi?" Khal put a hand up to his chest acting shocked, and walked backwards, ducking out of my reach then grabbing me round the waist.

I struggled to keep a straight face with his cavorting. He may have caused my overload, but he was also a good distraction.

As we approached the blanket, Khal casually placed his arm across my shoulder again. It was lovely and I took a glance up at Khal, moving my hair away from my face. He was a different person: young, fun, alive.

134

"You have beautiful hair. Can I touch?"

"Sure." I wasn't used to a man asking before just doing what he wanted. Normally they just touched, take first and suffer the consequences of their actions. I hated spending my time with men fighting them off – probably why I never took them seriously and repelled their attractions to me unless there was something in it for me. This difference, this change in control, was incredibly invigorating. I felt like a woman to be respected, rather than a slab of meat to be devoured.

Khal reached and very gently brushed my hair down with his hand. There was a lot of static tingling between the contact, but my hair was thick enough to protect us.

"Did you know your hair changes color in the sun. It has streaks of a dark red, almost mahogany running through it." I didn't really pay attention to the color of my hair. It wasn't something that interested me. It was just there.

"Do you like straightening your hair?"

"Oh. It's just something I do when the mood takes me. If I leave it curly I have to wet it every morning, otherwise a bird's nest grows at the back. If I straighten it, I can go two or three days without having to do anything else but brush it. Why?" This was definitely another first – I'd never had a man ask me that. I rarely got them to notice that my hair was naturally curly.

"No reason. I was just wondering. Your hair looks beautiful straight and curly. Now I have felt it when it is straight, I'd love to know what it feels like when it is curly." Khal kissed the top of my head as he took his hand away.

"Was it you? At the bus terminal in Victoria Station? Before getting on the bus? I went to the ticket office. And touched the door. I felt this shooting pain of static shock. But by the time it dawned on me what had happened you'd gone. It was you, wasn't it? A man, with a hoodie, and a hand that was olive-skinned." After I finished I looked at him and waited. I knew my question had come out of nowhere but once it came into my head, I had to ask.

I wasn't sure how long it took Khal to answer me but I waited, expecting an answer. "Yes. It was me."

I nodded. There was nothing else to say on the matter. Now I knew it hadn't been my imagination. Now I knew.

He affectionately gazed down. "You look tired. Want to start heading back?"

"I suppose we better." I reluctantly went to pack our things. Khal placed everything in his backpack and folded the blanket.

We sauntered back to the bicycles. There were more people around now, appreciating the scenery and each other's company. The whole place felt romantic and I pleasantly enjoyed being a part of it.

The bicycles were awaiting our arrival. I placed the blanket back into the pannier and retrieved my helmet. Khal kept everything else in his backpack. He moved his pack from his shoulder to secure it across his back properly. I went to mount my bicycle when I felt Khal behind me. I looked round wondering if there was a problem or if he needed anything.

"Ready?" I had my helmet in my hand, ready to put on my head.

"Yeah." Khal took hold of my free hand and twiddled with my fingers. I didn't object at all. The tingling shot up my arm making me take in a quick breath of air.

I swallowed, unusually nervous, apprehensive as Khal held my face in his hands and kissed me. His walls may still be intact, but mine were tumbling down…fast.

Chapter Nineteen

I was exhausted by the time we arrived home.

"I'll put your bicycle away. Why don't you go and have a soaking bath." The offer sounded tempting, but I was unsure. It was one thing having him close, having had such a special day. It was another knowing I was going to be naked and him being nearby after what'd happened.

He came up to me, close, and whispered, "I promise I won't look." How did he know what I was thinking? Wait...that wasn't the first time he instinctively knew what I was thinking...or wanting. I brushed my questions aside and went upstairs. I was too tired – and too aroused – to think straight.

The bath felt amazingly relaxing but all I could do was think of Khal, and I became even more sexually heightened by the thought of him waiting downstairs. So after my bath I put on my jogging pants and t-shirt – unsexy.

After dressing, I came down to an amazing smell emanating from the kitchen. There were logs burning on the fire and two glasses with an open bottle of zinfandel, nestled on the side table. Khal was in the kitchen – I could hear him clattering around.

"Are you hungry?" he asked as I came through.

"Ravenous."

"I hope you don't mind but I found some chicken and veggies in the fridge and made a stir fry with them," and he casually tipped the hot food onto two plates then placed the plates on the tray. We took them into the living room, in front of the fire, and enjoyed the company, the food, the wine.

"This is amazing." I wolfed down a piece of chicken with pepper and onion.

"Aren't you hungry?" I asked Khal as I noticed he didn't have any chicken on his plate and only a few pieces of stir fry vegetables. "Are you vegetarian?"

He laughed. "No and no."

"Can I ask you something?" I asked.

"Yes." He looked away, playing with his glass of wine between his hands.

"You don't eat much do you? Or is it my imagination?" I'd noticed his lack of interest in food before.

"No." He looked intently into my eyes but said nothing more.

"Should I be worried?"

"No." Khal took a sip of wine and gave a little smile, and moved his stare away from me. The moment dissipated.

I cleared up the dishes, leaving them in the kitchen to wash later.

"So, what's your favorite color?" It was the first thing Khal asked me when I came back.

"Red. What's yours?"

"Red."

"You're kidding!" What a coincidence.

"No. Honest. Deep earthy red."

"Me too! What's your favorite board game?" I was game to continue with the twenty questions.

"Chess. And you?"

"Checkers. Quicker to play. I lose my patience too quickly with chess." I screwed my face up; I also wasn't very good at playing chess.

"Favorite day of the week?"

"Haven't a clue. Probably Fridays. What about you?"

"Don't have a favorite but I do avoid that Monday morning feeling as much as possible. Okay, what about your favorite novel?" Khal had pulled one of his legs up onto the sofa and had slipped his foot under the knee of his other leg.

"Any of the *Jack Reacher* ones."

We continued with the questions and when I couldn't make up my mind on my favorite movie, Khal couldn't stop giggling.

"Sorry. There are a lot. I love movies. I love books too."

"Yeah, me too."

We kept coming up with new movies, new books, different genres. I discovered that reading was a passion of Khal's. He'd read some incredible pieces of literature – I was astounded; he must spend his every waking moment reading.

The wine took effect and I slouched into Khal feeling sleepy. We snuggled in front of the fire, watching an old Hitchcock movie on the TV. The fire died down and my head slumped on Khal's chest; I couldn't keep my eyes open.

"Come on, I better go." Khal kissed me and left.

And I went to bed, falling asleep dreaming of him.

Khal came over every day from then on. He occasionally came for coffee during the day while I was at work, and always waited for me after work. And on my days off, he either turned up with his bicycle or with a car and we went out for the day, come rain or shine. We varied where we went from nature reserves to historical buildings, theme parks, to other seaside resorts, and we even went to Peterborough to see the Cathedral. I loved seeing the sights, enjoyed the history, but the best part for me by far was being with Khal.

He was not as daring, not as keen to embarrass himself, more reserved than I was but happy to watch me splash in the fountains, dribble ice-cream down my chin or join in with any street dancers. I did get him to experience some scary rides at the theme parks we visited, and he convinced me to hold creepy crawlies, and dead things. No screaming, no fainting, just complete trust.

Khal also enjoyed taking me to the local pubs, especially the ones with a homey atmosphere. We managed to go to at least one new one every few days, north, west and south of Mablethorpe. And the best ones were in the tiniest of villages.

Many of them had amazing histories behind them stemming back to the crusades and various pilgrimages. And Khal was fascinating to listen to when he talked about the local history. His was a wealth of knowledge, an encyclopedia on two legs, a wiki for a brain.

There were also many open markets, open air shows and carnivals around the area too. We combined the shows with a visit to something else to make the most of my days off. But by the time we arrived back at the cottage after our many outings, I was often so exhausted I could do little else but eat and sleep.

And during this time together we never advanced past the kissing stage. Occasionally Khal stroked my back, teasing me, or him – I wasn't quite sure who suffered the

141

most – by caressing the sides of my ribs, near my breasts. But he never touched. Yet I had never experienced so many orgasms in my life; BOB had been put to rest.

I, on one occasion, plucked up the courage to touch the front of his jeans, wanting to feel his erection growing. But no sooner had my hand got there that Khal was moving it away, firmly. I never got to feel him but I actually didn't mind. It had become a game; how much could I distract him before trying to cop a feel – I always lost.

Chapter Twenty

By July I felt as though I'd seen the whole of Lincolnshire. And every carnival and parade going. There was another carnival coming up in one of the seaside resorts. I was pleased it wasn't too far away; I was too tired and needed a quiet night in. Working and then spending all my free days gallivanting round was exhausting. As was my contact with Khal; the bolts of electricity running through my body may not be as violent but they were still energy-draining that I often fell asleep immediately after a large bout of bodily contact.

I'd arranged for Khal to come over late morning. I wanted a sleep in and to get some washing done. I had the radio blaring out music as usual and I was singing along, enjoying the beat. He arrived just as I was eating my breakfast.

I opened the door to Khal and went back to the kitchen to finish my toast and coffee, and carried on singing.

"Want some?" I held out my toast as an offering. I was catching up with the paper and trying to wake myself up.

"No thanks." Khal sat opposite me at the small kitchen table and watched me.

I crunched on my slice and looked up from the paper, humming. "What?"

"Nothing." Khal smiled and kept staring. He looked with his beautiful eyes, and didn't stop gazing, unblinking.

143

His rare blinking had taken some getting used to. Now, I hardly thought about it, until he did something like this.

I finished my toast and took a sip of my hot coffee. I tried not to think of him watching me but it was disconcerting. He didn't normally sit and stare so obviously.

"What?" I nervously laughed.

"Nothing. Honest."

"I'm beginning to wonder if I've a horn growing out of my head." I said to him, repeating his retort from our first day. Khal let out an infectious chuckle that I couldn't help but join in with.

"I was just enjoying listening to your singing. You do it all the time, don't you?"

"Well, you know what they say – sing like nobody's listening."

"Mark Twain."

"You know it."

"Of course. Dance like nobody's watching; love like you're never been hurt. Sing like nobody's listening; live like it's heaven on earth." Khal still chortled as we both recited the lines together. But there was something in his eyes that prevented me from moving, just watching him watching me.

"I'll do those." Khal came over to me, gave me a torrid kiss, making my knees turn to jelly, and then took my dishes to the sink as if nothing had just happened. I ascended the stairs to brush my teeth wondering what had just transpired.

We left soon after and arrived at the carnival just in time to see the parade. The crowd lined the main street, and the decorated floats from the local clubs and schools passed by. The theme this year was cartoon characters. From Garfield to Winnie the Pooh, it was obvious the adults

144

enjoyed dressing up, pretending to be their favorite characters as much as the children. And Khal's excitement was infectious as he pointed some of them out.

There were some marquees set up in one of the fields where a variety of foods were available from local vendors. And some farmers brought their award winning animals for everyone to see.

It wasn't very often I teased Khal for his poor appetite, but I couldn't resist it today. Some of the foods on display were so incredibly tasty that I'd take a piece and waft it in front of his nose and mouth before popping it into mine. Then kiss him with my sticky, greasy lips so he just got the tiniest of tastes. He played along and actually surprised me by occasionally whipping the food into his mouth before I could take a bite. Meat pies, pork pies, fruit pies, Cornish pasties, Lincolnshire sausage rolls, scotch eggs, hotdogs, burgers, cotton candy and cupcakes (or as the stalls labeled them: candy floss and fairy cakes); the list was endless.

There were two competitions available for all to join in – the pig race and the pony race. I hadn't ridden a horse for a few years, but with all the excitement surrounding me, I couldn't resist. I didn't care if I made a fool of myself, it looked fun.

Khal expressed his concern, but even though I detested pain, I couldn't allow his trepidation to make me hesitate; I'd lose my nerve. So I tried to encourage Khal to join in with the pig race; no such luck.

My race wasn't until later in the afternoon, so we bided our time, walking along the promenade, watching the children compete in the sandcastle competitions. There was also an adult competition where experts built magnificent

145

sand models. Unless you were an artist, you wouldn't stand a chance.

I leaned over the promenade's sea wall, to watch the competitors' meticulous work. Khal played with my hair, something he loved to do. I had left it curly today as I had been too tired to wash and straighten it last night, so showered this morning instead.

"Khal!" A voice came from the beach and I snapped around, wondering who was calling him. I was so used to Khal being virtually invisible to other people, that it was easy to forget that he'd actually know someone.

But Khal didn't respond to the artist who was calling him apart from his initial glance. The man on the beach, hidden behind his glasses and hoodie – just like Khal – appeared a few inches shorter than Khal, maybe ten years older, not as broad looking, yet still looked incredibly strong with robust legs.

"Don't you want to go and say hi?" The guy was obviously a friend.

They both looked intently at each other before they carried on as if nothing had happened. Khal began to walk away from me along the promenade, and the artist continued his work, never glancing back up to see where Khal was.

"Khal. What's going on?" I was confused at how he could dismiss someone like that without saying anything. To ignore someone like that seemed churlish.

"Khal. Don't ignore me." His utter disrespect, his lack of ability to even talk to me just added to my incense.

He stopped walking and turned around. "He's just an acquaintance. No one important."

"Okay, so what's his name?" I asked, exasperated by his rejection of my interest in his life. We were having such a beautiful day. And then this happened and it was as if everything else just faded into the background.

Didn't he want me to be a part of his life? Did *I* want to be a part of it? "You know, it's none of my business. Sorry. Forget I asked." I'd overstepped the mark...again.

I really didn't understand what was wrong with me. I hated it when people nosed into my life. People's lives were their own business. I made no sense at all, not even to myself. Khal gave me a little bit more of himself and I expected to have it all. He obviously wanted to keep that barrier there, didn't want me to be part of his world. And I had to learn to accept that.

"No. Don't be sorry." He watched his foot play with a stone, sighed, then raised his face to meet mine.

"It's me who needs to be sorry. I shouldn't dismiss your interests like that." Khal was holding something back, biting his lip.

"He isn't no one. He's actually someone very important to me. I just didn't know..."

Khal stopped talking and turned to look down the beach. I followed his gaze.

The artist had stopped working, stayed crouched in an incredibly well-balanced pose, and met Khal's gaze.

"Come." Khal put his arm over my shoulder, kissed my head and led me down some steps to the beach.

We carefully walked passed the other artists at work, making sure we didn't disturb their masterpieces.

We reached the man who knew Khal. He stood as if expecting us, but said nothing until Khal talked.

"Abby. I'd like you to meet Chaf. Chaf...he's my...he's a very close...friend."

147

"Hi." I held my hand out to shake Chaf's. But he just glanced at it, not accepting the gesture.

"Hello Abby." He gave a half-hearted smile before staring at Khal.

I put my hand down, awkwardly, and waited for a minute or two. No one spoke. The two men just stood awkwardly and I wasn't sure if they were even looking at each other. Either Chaf was annoyed with Khal, or vice versa, but the silence was getting a bit too much, and I began to wonder why I was there.

"You're an amazing artist, Chaf. Tom and Jerry was my Dad's favorite cartoon. I watched it a lot as a kid." I couldn't stand the silence any longer.

Chaf turned away from Khal and softened his demeanor instantly, smiling. "Thanks. They're my favorite too."

We chatted about some of the antics Tom and Jerry would get up to – how Jerry always came out on top. Jerry was a smart mouse, Tom a dumb cat; but there were times when Tom outsmarted Jerry and when the cards were down and Jerry was caught in a trap, Tom became just an old softy and let Jerry go. We even started to laugh when we remembered the same cartoons, and both agreed, without a shadow of a doubt, that our all-time favorite was 'The Night Before Christmas.'

"You remember the bit where Jerry convinces Tom to kiss him under the mistletoe and Jerry kicks him? And Tom is so mad that when Jerry runs outdoors Tom blockades the door." I laughed at the memory.

"Yeah. And Tom feels so bad leaving Jerry out there that he has to go and get him back and defrost him by the fire." Chaf laughed too.

Khal stood quietly.

"I hope you win."

"Thanks. We're going to the pub later. Why don't you two come and join us?"

"I'd like that," I said enthusiastically. I thought Khal was going to object – I felt him tense up next to me. But he never said a word.

Chaf had seen it too because our conversation came to a quick stop and Chaf no longer smiled as he looked at Khal.

"I'd better get back to work. I only have half an hour left before judging time. Hope I see you later, Abby." Chaf returned to his sculpture and we strolled back to the promenade.

"Khal, can I ask you a question?" It felt strange asking such a ridiculous question. Telepathy was fictional, something that happened in the movies, not in real life. But there was just something about the way he and Chaf interacted with each other. And I remembered the times where I thought about something and Khal answered me without me actually saying a word. I'd never broached the subject before, dismissing it as just coincidence, a quirky thing that I just imagined.

But Khal froze.

Chapter Twenty-One

Y ou heard me?"

"Yes." He didn't move, didn't elaborate. Nothing.

"Okay. And you were 'talking' to Chaf before?" I air-quoted the 'talking'.

"Yes."

"Well, at least I know. Are you going to tell me what about? Why you were being so secretive about it?"

"We weren't being secretive. It's just…habit."

"Okay?" He'd already shut me down once today so I wasn't going to force him.

Khal didn't say anything more until we were nearly back at the field.

"Chaf was asking me what I was doing here. And why…how serious you and I are." Khal didn't expand or add anymore. He just left it at that.

There had obviously been more to it than that, but he knew where I stood on that subject. And that just added to the already tense, strained atmosphere between the two of us.

It was nearly time for my pony race, and I quickly forgot about Chaf and Khal's uneasiness. I ignored Khal's strange behavior; he needed time obviously to come around. And if he didn't…well, maybe I needed to think twice about our time together.

Although I was extremely rusty, I relished the challenge of the tough race, even though it had been a few years since I'd last mounted a horse. I'd learned to ride as a kid, and I'd kept it up as a hobby. But I hadn't done competition riding for many years, and I hadn't jumped with a horse since my last competition.

I was the third rider. I chose my pony and spent valuable time with her before my race. A couple of jumps had been erected in the far corner of the field, away from the crowds. I enjoyed the excitement of the horse, enjoyed the horse beneath me as we eased over the jumps. Khal watched me practice but looked nervous. I tried reassuring him to no avail, so ignored him, putting my annoyance down to my still stewing over what happened earlier. Anything Khal said or did right now made me wonder what his ulterior motive was, why the concern, the caring.

My turn came. I walked the horse, Frenchie, to the start and mounted her.

"Ready?" The Starter asked. I nodded and waited for the 'go' flag to descend.

Once I get over that first jump I'll be fine, I said to reassure myself. It was always the first and last jumps that were problematic, and I'd quickly learned to only ever concentrate on the first one, knowing the rest would just happen. I got through the slalom of jumps without knocking over too many bars, until the final jump.

I was overconfident, and too hastily tried to get the pony round for the right angle on the last jump. I failed, miserably. The pony stopped short, refusing to jump, and I continued, kept going right into the pool of water.

Thank God the sludgy, muddy water was there to break my fall.

"Ugh." I landed smack on my back. The wind knocked right out of me and my head swam with stars and fog. I didn't move; I needed to catch my breath, make sure I hadn't broken anything, make sure I hadn't actually hit my head on anything.

Khal flew over the fence and across the arena, looking agonizingly worried. He splashed into the water and squatted next to me, fear and pain ravaged his face.

"I'm okay...I'm okay," I grunted as I considered the idea of moving before actually following through.

Every bone in my body writhed from the impact, my wobbly legs faltered as they tried to bear my weight.

"I don't believe it. The stupid horse is laughing at me." I tried to see the funny side but even smiling hurt.

I grimaced as I took a step, spasms besieging my back. Khal didn't hesitate and picked me up with ease, carrying me over to the first aid station.

I was sure I hadn't broken anything. I'd fractured my leg and arm before, falling off a horse and this wasn't the same. I'd been winded, that was all. The first aid guys agreed.

"Let's get you home."

"No. I don't want to go home. I want to go to the pub." I pleaded with Khal, virtually begging him to not take me home.

"How about we just go to the pub for an hour? Then I'll let you take me home." Khal's expression softened in contemplation. "Ten minutes, then."

He giggled as I sneakily used my female ways to win him over. All my frustrations from Khal's reticence had vanished, the hostility gone.

"Okay. Okay. Ten minutes...but you do need to go home and get changed first." He gave me the once up and down, chuckling to himself.

I looked down and saw what Khal saw; I was caked in mud. In my agony I was oblivious to the cold water or heavy mud stuck to my clothes. It was everywhere, my hands, my hair.

"Oh!" A deep hue of red covered my face in seconds.

"Come on. Let's get you home."

The journey home was wretched. Once home, Khal helped me out of the car. But sitting for just that short journey, I had stiffened considerably.

"Ouch!" I struggled to move.

Khal placed his arm under my knees, the other across my back and carried me to the house effortlessly. He never asked, he just took over instinctively. I handed him the keys so he could open the door. He walked over the threshold with me still in his arms and I was petrified of him putting me down. He closed the door behind us, sat on the stairs, flipped my sneakers off with ease, and then continued up the stairs, not saying a word, not faltering or wondering if I would mind.

He took me to the bathroom and placed me on the seat of the toilet. He switched the shower on, then asked after deliberating this predicament, "Can you lift your arms up?"

I throbbed in places I never dreamed possible, and just trying to lift my arms sent shockwaves rippling through my body. I was not eight years old anymore.

"Don't move. Just stay still." Khal dashed out the door. He was back quickly with a pair of scissors in his hand.

"No! You can't do that!"

"Well, it's either I cut your top off or you bear the pain. Your choice," and he stood in front of me holding the scissors, with a business-like expression across his face.

153

"No, I'll try to move." He was not cutting my top…

Chapter Twenty-Two

I stifled the moans, suffered in silence, as Khal helped get my arms through my t-shirt. Between the shocks of his touch on my arms, and the pain in my muscles, I didn't know which way to turn. I was in complete and utter agony, but I refused to let any tears fall.

I breathed a sigh of relief when my second arm was through and it was just a simple case of lifting my t-shirt over my head.

Khal carefully undid the two buttons on the front of my t-shirt and lifted my shirt over my head, hesitantly.

He advanced to my jeans, undoing the button and zip and sliding them down my legs carefully, trying to prevent his hands touching my legs. They caught a couple of times, making me flinch.

"Sorry," he responded, knowing how much it hurt. One by one I lifted my legs out, leaning into Khal as I did, my cleavage at his eyelevel.

There I was virtually naked in front of the man, and he was not responding. I had been waiting for this moment since the day I met him. But for some inexplicable reason, I was unsure of myself. Men were creatures I bedded with ease, without a second thought. Khal...was different. I desired him, craved his touching hands, and yet being lascivious with Khal seemed inappropriate.

Khal continued silently. He stood up in front of me and took his shirt and jeans off, leaving his snug boxers just where my eyes rested.

I didn't know what I expected but this wasn't one of the options that ran through my head. My lust was breaching its barriers as I desperately tried not to stare straight ahead. I focused my eyes upwards, believing this might actually help my body's lechery – it didn't. His physique was defined by his labor: taut. Hercules, here we come. His chest was well defined with a small black tattoo slightly hidden by his abundance of dark chest hair. I wanted a closer look but didn't trust myself. A chain hung to just below the top of his sternum with what looked like some type of charm or talisman attached. In a strange way it looked slightly familiar, and became a much needed and good distraction to help alleviate this hankering inside that kept telling me to jump on him. God, I hoped I didn't orgasm when he touched me again.

"Your chain. What is it of? It looks old?"

"It's nothing." Khal was dismissive as usual with anything remotely personal and continued with his mission. "This will hurt – but you've grown quite used to the feeling of my touching you. Are you ready?" I just nodded. I had never considered the dynamics of this.

Khal lifted me into his arms and waited a few seconds until the jolts of his touch dissipated.

He carefully stood me up in the shower, coming in behind me. The piping hot water ran over every inch of my body, soothing my aches, slowing down the spasms that shot through my back and legs. My muscles loosened and I relaxed into the water as I lifted my hands to my face and hair, and Khal's presence virtually vanished for that moment.

156

But his gentle hands as he drizzled shampoo into my hair stroked my erotic fantasies again. God I wished I didn't hurt so much.

I needed a distraction.

"You don't like water." I remembered our time on the beach, his resistance to being splashed.

"No, I don't." He didn't elaborate or explain again. He just carried on. I wasn't interested anyway – I just wanted his body. But how was he able to control, restrain himself so efficiently? I was dying. His detachment was frigid; I needed to break his impenetrable sexual wall down. Then he may be more open with other aspects of his life.

I rinsed my hair and Khal covered the sponge in soap, rubbing it over my back and legs. The water washed the suds away and he leaned over me to turn the shower off, stepped out and grabbed two towels. One for him that he put round his waist immediately, and one for me that he wrapped round my shoulders and helped my now more flexible body step out of the shower.

"I'll bring you some clean clothes through." He didn't ask, or give me chance to object. He turned me round and unfastened my bra, then suggested I take off my wet underwear while he was gone.

Khal grabbed his clothes off the floor and left. Dressed in clean jeans, t-shirt and jacket, he returned with a clean pair of jeans, t-shirt, and underwear for me. "I'll come back to give you a hand after you've dressed." Then left again with my dirty clothes.

I was slow, hurting with every movement. By the time Khal returned, I'd only managed to get my underwear and jeans on. I had been unable to fasten the button and zip on my jeans, and couldn't fasten my bra.

"Here." Upon his return, he turned me around and fastened my bra. Then turned me back to fasten my jeans. Finally, he picked up my t-shirt and slipped it over my head and arms.

"Thanks." My confidence tumbled, unsure how to react to his coldness. We'd just shared the most intimate of moments. Yet he'd been robotic, automated, unemotional. I began to wonder if I'd imagined that amorous kiss this morning.

Khal went to fasten the two buttons up on my shirt. As he fastened the second button, I watched his hands. I loved those hands, worker's hands, sturdy, large, masculine.

"How are you feeling?" He asked after he'd finished the button.

"Better. Thanks." It was true. I was feeling better. Didn't hurt as much, physically.

But my heart was aching. And I felt my self-confidence fall as Khal kept an emotional and physical distance. Touch me. Hold me.

He smiled and kissed me ever so gently. "Come on, let's get you something for the pain."

I didn't want to leave yet. I couldn't contain my desire any longer. I grabbed his arm, leaned up and kissed him provocatively, my body unable to restrain its response to the intimacy of the shower, of his hands undressing me.

I wrapped my arms round his waist, gave myself to him. I wanted my passion to take hold, rage through my veins. And I could feel Khal reciprocate. I hadn't imagined this morning.

His hands caressed my face, moved down to my neck, stroked my back.

As his intensity rose, his hands and arms embraced me, squeezing harder, tighter.

"Aagh," I moaned in agony. God, why did I have to hurt so much.

Khal suddenly stopped and pulled away.

"Sorry." My self-confidence plummeted even further. He was obviously annoyed by my lack of restraint.

"No. My fault. I shouldn't have taken advantage...come on. Do you still feel up to going to the pub?"

I wanted to stay in, spend the night with Khal, but it was clear he didn't feel the same. So what choice did I have? I wanted to meet his friends, be a part of his life. I'd never felt the need for another human being so acutely and I was confused. And I was willing to agree to almost anything Khal suggested just to be with him.

Khal grabbed a towel. "Turn around."

I did as I was told, wincing as I moved. He dried my hair, took the spray conditioner I handed him and sprayed my hair, then gave it a brush, pulling it all to the back and letting it fall down. He put the brush down and swiftly braided all my strands together. I handed him the tie from the sink and he placed it on the end of the braid.

"There."

"Thanks." I turned to smile at him but he was already collecting the wet towels to take them downstairs.

"Come on." He held out an arm as an assistance. His face expressionless.

I took some painkillers with a glass of water and Khal put the washing machine on with my dirty clothes, his jeans and jacket, and the wet towels in.

"Are you ready?"

"Yes, I'm ready."

Chapter Twenty-Three

Silently, half an hour later we arrived at the pub. It was already quite late, the sun fading from the sky, reaching up its last rays, waving goodbye. Its descent felt like my heart, sinking rapidly.

It was an old quaint pub in one of the small villages nearby. As usual, there was quite a crowd around the bar. Khal led me to a small crowded table near the back of the pub. Khal removed his hoodie and glasses, and because no one else wore a hoodie or glasses I couldn't make out which man at the table was Chaf. There were three men apart from Khal and a couple of them could have been Chaf: two of the men were very similar in age and looks, and the other man while obviously younger, had an uncanny resemblance to Khal. I wondered if they were brothers. There were two women: one older, possibly early thirties, tall; the other petit, possibly in her mid-twenties. No one looked up to say 'Hi' or registered that we were there. In fact there was no talking among any of them.

Khal pulled a chair up for me. He went to the bar for two drinks: a half and a wine cooler. He sat on the chair next to me and handed me my bottle. His initial distance with me was back, and still no one spoke.

While everyone remained silent, I continued to observe them. One pair, a man and woman in the far corner, were obviously together but everyone else seemed just friends. There was one thing that was striking about them all

161

–their eyes. Although they were slightly different colors, all a variant of brown unlike Khal's, they all had that translucent look about them, and I was beginning to wonder if they looked the same as Khal's in daylight.

The woman to our right, the small, pretty brunette, suddenly turned in my direction glaring at me. "You showed her!" I was going to describe her as angelic looking...until she opened her mouth.

Astounded, I glanced up at Khal. What had just happened? She continued to scowl at me, and my already rock-bottom confidence just took another nosedive.

Everyone else looked at Khal, then glanced at me. I didn't know what to think. I didn't know if I could take any more emotional turmoil today. And then it hit me...

Oh my God – it wasn't just their eyes they had in common.

It didn't bother me that their eyes were similar. I was fascinated, intrigued. But to have them all be able to delve into my thoughts, read what I was thinking...feeling extremely uneasy, panicky, I had a choice – let my awaiting tears fall, or be angry.

The brunette spoke again. "We're not a fascination for you to study." Her daggers exposed, and I grimaced back – how dare she speak to me like that. But I couldn't think of how to respond to her. All I could think of was Khal and how I couldn't endure his rejection too if I said the wrong thing.

"Leave her alone, Lisa." Khal, for the first time this evening, he pulled me in close to him, protecting me from the group.

"Come on. Let's go." He was serious.

"I'm sorry. I didn't mean to upset anyone." I didn't want to just leave like this, but I also didn't want to be read like an open book. Having my private thoughts intruded upon was frustrating. These were my personal things and were only made available to those I wanted to know. To have someone else peer into them without my permission was unnerving.

"You have nothing to be sorry for." Khal came in closer still, trying to reassure me. "I should have warned you, but you're right, you shouldn't have to watch what you're thinking. It's no one else's business but yours."

"Come on everyone. Abby is Khal's friend. She should feel welcomed, not bullied. Lisa, give her a break. She's more nervous than we are." I recognized Chaf's voice immediately.

"Yes, Abby, I'm Chaf. And this is Lisa, Wali, Rose and Dru."

Chaf went round the table in order.

Everything went deathly quiet again; they were all looking at each other, moving from one face to another.

"No, I'll not stay if you continue with this," Khal quietly muttered. I couldn't tell to whom.

"And I won't stay if Abby's unwelcome." Khal looked mad.

"Yes, you can trust her." He became extremely irritated. "I wouldn't have agreed with Chaf to bring her if there was any doubt. I knew this wouldn't work. Why do you think I never said anything before, why do you think I never bother...it's up to you. I didn't want this, wasn't interested. Look, Lisa, lay off will you."

I had never felt so unwanted and just wanted to leave.

163

Khal looked at me and for the first time since our encounter with Chaf this morning, he smiled. "No, it's fine. Don't worry. They're naturally cautious of people they don't know. We've lived here a long time, kept ourselves to ourselves and no one bothers us. We're not a cause for curiosity with anyone, even if people do ask themselves questions about us. Having someone else join our 'clique' is hard, especially for some of us." It was obvious Khal was referring to Lisa.

"It's something that everyone will get used to. They just need time." He never let go of me, making it very obvious to everyone there that he meant for the two of us to stay together, at least for now. And my elation from this sudden show of affection bolstered my spirits.

"I'm sorry, Abby. I didn't mean to make you feel unwelcome. I'm pleased to meet you." Wali was the first to speak up, and one by one everyone else followed, Lisa being the last and quietest. I got the distinct impression she was reluctant and only obliged to save face.

Occasionally it all went quiet but more open talking went on as each person remembered that I couldn't 'hear' them.

Khal told them about my tumble off the pony. There was genuine concern. Chaf talked about his second place in the sandcastle competition. I was surprised he hadn't won because his artistry was amazing.

"I never win," Chaf answered my thoughts. "To be honest, I don't like winning. I prefer to get second or third...it was a good idea, though, wasn't it." He winked at me, smiling.

164

Slowly each member of the group relaxed a little, allowing me to see a little bit of them. Except for Lisa – she continued to keep her distance as if she didn't like me.

I ignored her.

I discovered they all lived and worked together on the farm, leading a very simple life, enjoying each other's company. And while Khal didn't say an awful lot, it became very clear that he was close to both Chaf and Wali.

We ended up staying over an hour. I started to hurt a lot by the time we left, very stiff. But I was sorry to be going.

Khal helped me out to the car by keeping his arm round me and holding my hand. I wasn't sure how much it did help but I needed his contact. The pub was still busy and it was difficult leaving through the crowds. I scanned the room and I caught a glimpse of a face I recognized: Greg.

Chapter Twenty-Four

I stopped for a moment, thinking I should go over and say 'Hi' to him. But the look on his face told me I'd be ill-advised to venture that way. He was in his normal black from head to toe and his eyes glared in my direction. No, more than glared – they appeared to glow with a tinge of red to them. Boy, was he angry.

Had he seen Khal? Would he realize this was the same person as last time? Probably. I felt a sense of fear – Greg's gaze penetrated, bored deeply. Maybe I should go and speak to him. I still considered him a friend.

Khal grabbed me tightly around my waist, stopping me from moving. I turned round to Khal to see what the issue was, then looked back in Greg's direction. Khal just stared towards Greg, but there was hatred across Greg's eyes, a viciousness that I'd never seen before. Then before I knew it – and I honestly did no more than blink – he disappeared.

Khal squeezed harder.

"Ouch, Khal that hurts." I tried to pry his hand off but it was fastened tightly.

"Sorry. Do you know him?" The pain had distracted me from Greg's reaction, but Khal's tone was disconcerting and I didn't know what to make of it.

"Oh. Just someone I met on the beach. We went to the movies a few times but I haven't seen him in a while...until tonight." I wasn't used to talking to one man about another. I didn't have anything to hide from Khal. I wasn't interested in Greg anymore. But Khal's interest gave me hope, and I wondered if he was jealous.

"Do you still see him?"

"No, why?"

Khal didn't answer me. We continued to walk out of the pub and Khal drove me back home, quietly.

"What can you see in my head?"

"I can only see what you're thinking at that time. And I can't be too far away."

"Doesn't it feel like you're intruding?"

"I've never really thought about it until you. Although we can 'see' what people are thinking around us, we don't make a point of looking or prying. We just shut the images off. But when we get close to someone, like I am with you, the images become more intense, more clear. And Lisa was just being nosy, not trusting."

We arrived back at the cottage. The car journey left me sore and exhausted.

Khal helped me into the house again, and straight up the stairs into my bedroom.

"Come on, let's get you into your pj's." Khal began to undo my t-shirt. It didn't matter how much I ached at that particular moment, I needed to know that I hadn't imagined his interest, his reactions. I reached up to kiss him.

He laughed, "No. We're going to get you ready for bed."

Khal pulled my t-shirt off and undid my jeans. I reached up to kiss him again, turning the heat up.

He laughed again, "No. Behave yourself." And he gently sat me down on the bed and pulled my jeans off.

Khal reached for my pajama top and was about to put it on when I kissed him again, fuelling the fire burning inside me even more.

And Khal responded, caressing my lips with his, searching my mouth with his tongue, embracing my desire.

I really did hurt terribly, but loved having him here, so close. I needed to feed my desire, and there was only Khal who could satisfy this insatiable thirst. I wanted to feel his skin again, watch his arms, his muscles flexing. I started to pull at his t-shirt.

"No. Come on. Pj's on." Khal stopped kissing me. He wasn't laughing this time, wasn't even smiling, and held out my top for me to put my head into.

"What's wrong? I know I hurt but..." I tried not to sound offended. I was prepared to bear the pain if it meant that Khal stayed close. If I could feel his naked body next to mine.

I kissed him again, voraciously pushing myself on him.

"No!" He backed off immediately.

I'd never put myself in such a vulnerable, provocative situation like this before. And I'd never been rejected so readily.

"I don't get it. You were the one who said there was an attraction between us. Yet right now I'm questioning if you even feel any desire towards me. What am I doing wrong? What do you want from me?" Tonight he was so protective, kind and loving – was I just imagining it all? This rollercoaster ride was getting out of hand and I was getting whiplash. I honestly didn't know what to do and my emotions really couldn't cope with much more. I needed reassurance from him. I needed to know...what?

"I'll leave you to put your pj's on yourself." Khal went to leave the room.

"No. Don't go. I'm sorry if I've offended you. Please, don't go." Begging? Now I really sounded pathetic.

"You haven't. I'll wait downstairs," and he closed the door behind him.

I waited awhile to compose myself before joining Khal downstairs.

The fire was roaring and there was a tray with a chicken salad waiting on it. Two glasses with a bottle of wine, stood next to the tray.

And Khal was reading a book on the sofa. He had his back to me, quietly turning a page.

Why was I always so against holiday romances? Maybe that was the problem. Maybe it wasn't Khal sending out mixed signals. Maybe it was me.

It'd been two months since I first met Khal and the intensity of our time together strengthened, deepened every time he was here. I was really struggling to control my sexual desire for him. I felt desperate. Dangerously out of control. But there was also something else there. No, I wasn't going there.

I joined Khal on the sofa. He poured the wine and handed me a glass. "Cheers," and he clinked his glass on mine.

I ate my salad quietly. He continued reading the book; it was a book from the bookshelf that was next to the fireplace.

I finished my salad and I started to get up off the sofa so I could take the tray back into the kitchen.

"Here. I'll do it. Coffee?" Khal was already on his feet with the tray in his hand.

169

"No, I'm fine."

We never talked about what happened upstairs. I didn't know what to say and Khal never brought it up. And when he returned to the sofa, he reached out for me, wanting me to cuddle into him, wanting to kiss me. Our evening was quiet. We read, snuggling together on the sofa together in front of the dampened fire. But my desires never dampened. I just had to keep them under control. If Khal was interested it was up to him to show me now because I didn't know what else to do.

I woke up in the morning confused, the sun streaming through a gap in the drapes. I was in bed. How had I gotten there? I tried to think back to the night before but there seemed to be a piece missing.

At that moment, though, I didn't care because the bed felt wonderful on my body, and the aching wasn't too bad until…I tried to move. I was so stiff.

A memory abruptly flashed through my head; Khal had carried me upstairs.

Then another feeling came over me; I wasn't alone.

I slowly rolled over to look behind me; Khal was lying next to me, watching me.

"Hi," he smiled.

"You stayed?" I was surprised. I grinned from ear to ear.

Chapter Twenty-Five

Khal stayed every night.

I left for work, he was there. I finished work, he was there. On my day off, he was there.

It felt comfortable, so ordinary having him there all the time, to hold, to caress, to kiss. But there was little more. The time in the shower was a one off. The uncontrolled moments never happened again.

My aches, pains and bruises slowly improved. I went to the doctor to get some stronger pain medication and muscle relaxers, and they'd worked wonders. I could move more easily immediately as long as I didn't over-extend myself. Some huge bruises had appeared on my back, arms and legs but were now fading to a pale yellow. At first, I used my pain as an excuse for Khal's distance. Now, that didn't work. I was fine, inside and out, but Khal never touched me beyond holding my hand or laying his arm across my shoulder. And he never kissed me *that* way again.

He also never explained why. I was at a loss regarding how he had such amazing control – I was dying. I began to wonder if the charisma was a one-way street, that I was the only one who felt it. And yet, I relished our time together just as it was.

We met up with Khal's 'farm family' – as I referred to them – again. I'd now met them all – eight in total plus Khal – and they seemed used to my being there with them. They became conscious of how their telepathic conversations left me out. I soon began to notice that it upset them if they forgot. Like Khal, they were all extremely sensitive to other people's feelings: a child fell over and everyone jumped and cringed; a woman with no hair and everyone looked desolate. Did she have cancer? I didn't ask. However, Khal was the introvert among them all – well, when I was there he was and no one ever made his reticence seem unusual.

We all went bowling and while I was a terrible bowler, I was as competitive as Zeb and Wali. The two men occasionally joined in with my wild side, my crazy outbursts of irrational behavior, and then left me alone in my quietness. In fact, they just accepted me for me. And I loved them all for it. But there was something about Wali – his energy reverberated through the whole group. When Wali was there, everyone came alive. And he always made a point of dragging me into his games, his competitions, trying to get me to side with him. Khal never joined in as easily, holding himself back, yet never seemed to mind Wali's enthusiasm for encouraging me. Wali and I bantered regularly as if the connection between Khal and Wali, their warmth and understanding of each other, transferred over to me.

We also went to the movies together, sometimes just a couple came with Khal and I, sometimes everyone. None of the animosity that surfaced on our first meeting came back. I understood very quickly what Khal meant about their initial reaction being cautious of a new person among them. And while I never felt completely comfortable around them all – I was still an outsider, not one of them – as they got to know me they all began to accept my presence even if they weren't happy about it...except Lisa. Lisa never spoke to me and always kept her distance. I got the distinct impression she was waiting for me to trip up, waiting for me to expose my agenda. She would have a long wait.

I soon discovered each of them did a lot for the poor, working in local shelters and soup kitchens. They also volunteered to help other farmers fix fences or tractors. I wondered how they had the time with their own farm but they never questioned what they did; it was obvious they got so much out of helping others.

And then I found out some of them had other jobs too. I already knew Khal worked with computers designing apps and other things; I wasn't a computer expert so didn't really know the ins and outs. Dru worked in law enforcement, Lisa wrote and illustrated children's books, and Rose was a nurse. I wasn't sure about the rest. Like Khal, they were all reticent about their personal lives.

Khal and I still spent a lot of time just the two of us as well. Whenever I wasn't working, and we hadn't arranged to go out with his farm family, it was just us.

It was my day off from work and Khal took me out for lunch to a charming inn out of town. This was the first clear day all week: warm, pleasant, with the occasional cloud floating by. A beautiful summer's day. We walked round to the beer garden so we could enjoy the sunshine. But all the tables were taken.

I began to turn around disgruntled that we would have to go inside when I heard my name being called.

"Abby. Come. Join us." It was John. This was the first time I'd seen John outside of work.

I skipped over and Khal sauntered behind. I didn't consult him at all – it never occurred to me that I would need to.

John and I continued to share a coffee when we got the chance. He was the sanity in my life, the stability for my emotions. But after our initial flirtation and John showing no more interest in me than that, I'd backed off. Then Khal and Greg had taken up most of my time and my attraction to John had amounted to nothing.

There'd been no more movie nights at his store; we hadn't had time. However, John did say he would start it up again later in the year, after the summer holidays, and probably do things like a teenage night. It was such a great idea that I was sorry I would miss it.

"Hi, John. Your one day off and you still can't get away from me." I smiled at him and gave him a quick hug. Then turned around and introduced myself to the gentleman he was with.

"Hi. I'm Abby. I work next door to John."

"I'm David." John had mentioned a friend called David. But looking at the two of them holding hands I'd never put two and two together. I grinned at them both as the penny dropped; no wonder John hadn't been interested in me.

I sat down opposite John at the picnic table. David was to my right.

"David. It's great to meet you. This is Khal." Khal said a quiet 'hi' and stayed behind me.

After our initial introductions and pleasantries Khal went inside to get us both drinks, checking if John or David would like anything before leaving.

I enjoyed chatting with John and David, and when Khal came back he sat quietly, listening. I found out John and David had been together for eight years and it was Alice who'd introduced David to John before John bought the bookstore. Apparently Alice and David were on the town committee together.

I considered involving Khal in some of our conversations but I got the impression very quickly that Khal didn't want to talk. He held my hand under the table and whenever I thought about asking him a question, he squeezed my hand as if to say 'no'. It quickly became a secret code. He did chat when asked anything by John or David, but he seemed to prefer to stay quiet and just laughed along with the joking.

David was a great guy. I could certainly see why John had fallen in love with him. He was as crazy as John, telling jokes, laughing. And when we mentioned the store, chatting about how the two stores together worked so well, David was obviously very proud of John.

"His first of many," David grinned, encouraging John with the idea of expanding.

David helped with the business by keeping the accounts and researching books and other bookstores. He also explained how he did the accounts for other local businesses, and the self-employed. He enjoyed it, kept him busy, and allowed him to keep in touch with the local community and people. David had grown up in the area.

When David enquired about my accent, John told David that I lived in New York City so David asked me many questions about my life there, what I did. He also enquired if I'd heard from Alice and how the wedding had gone. Although Alice wasn't a bit fan of social media sites, she did have a *Facebook* page. However, she hadn't been on since leaving for Australia; I imagined she didn't have time.

"She's great. Having the time of her life. While Kristen went on her honeymoon, Alice went on a tour of the outback. I can't wait to see the photos. I'd love to go some day." The idea of that had never appealed before, but the more I thought about it, the more I contemplated that going to Australia would be a great idea when I finished college.

"John and I went to Australia a few years ago: to Sydney. We loved it."

"Oh, it was great fun, but hot. I think next time I'd like to go to New Zealand."

Khal and I finished our drinks. We weren't planning on staying long because we were meeting Rose, Tali and Sim at the movies.

"David, it's been wonderful meeting you. I hope I get to spend some more time with you both soon. Come into the store next time you're around. I don't have much longer there, but I make a mean cup of coffee." John laughed nodding his head at my comment.

"I'll see you at work, John."

Khal and I walked back to the car. This first time meeting David was unexpected but lovely. I was sorry to be leaving but our encounter was unplanned and I didn't feel right taking up David and John's time together. I knew they wouldn't get much with the hours John worked.

I contemplated our time with John and David on our way back to Mablethorpe. I'd never expected to bump into the two of them like that. Who was I kidding – I never expected to discover John was gay. But what a lovely couple they made. I thought I'd hit it off well with John but now that I'd met David I wouldn't be able to choose who I'd have more fun hanging out with.

I did smile a little, thinking of what a great day it was, but remembered Khal's quietness. Khal was a quiet man anyway, but today he seemed a little distant too. This time together would've also been great for Khal to get to know John, but the two men barely talked.

And Khal had stayed quiet when we left the two men. He seemed deep in thought. I was never quite sure what was going on when he stayed silent like this.

"I'm so pleased I've met David."

Khal remained uncommunicative, just kept driving.

"Khal, do you have a problem with John and David?"

He seemed perturbed by my question, "Of course not."

"So, what's going on?" I knew something was wrong.

Khal didn't answer immediately. I could tell he was contemplating his answer. He did this when he wanted to be careful how he worded something.

"You know I can feel emotions?"

"Yes...I know you feel mine. And I've seen the way you react to other people. Can you feel everyone's?"

"Not as strongly as yours but yes."

"So you could feel David and John's emotions?"

"More John's than David's. He worries about David. And it was...painful to feel it so strongly. Did he tell you about David's illness?" I didn't expect this. What did Khal know?

"No...do you know something?" Of course he did. What a stupid question. "Don't tell me. I don't want to know...that's not true. I want to know but only if John or David tells me. It has to be their choice. This is their private life and John obviously had his reasons for not saying anything about David and his life with David. I know you can see things in people's heads but I can't. And it isn't right that you tell me."

Having someone pry into your life just because you exhibit a physical difference is just plain arrogance. Someone who's in a wheelchair deserves the same privacy and non-questioning about their appearance, as I did having an extra toe! Okay, so I didn't actually have an extra toe. It was the principle of the matter.

Khal had said nothing more about it, but he suddenly grinned when I thought of my analogy. If nothing else it had taken some of Khal's tension away.

We arrived back in Mablethorpe at the movie theatre, and Khal came round to open my door. My aches and pains were virtually gone now but Khal continued to pamper me. I thought I'd find this annoying, preferring my independence. But I felt treasured by the way Khal performed his gentlemanly acts and so I'd quite gotten used to indulging him.

He held out a hand for me to hold. He looked down at me and held me close.

I loved it, but I was confused by the sudden show of emotion, such strong affection. Khal wasn't normally so open in public. PDA was definitely not his style.

"So, what did I do to deserve this?"

Khal place a hand on my neck and kissed me gently, "For just being you. Your honesty, your understanding, your compassion."

I wasn't quite following.

"The way you don't want to know about David unless John wants to tell you. Your acceptance of others on their terms. You're an incredible person." And he kissed me again, different to anything he'd done before: deeper more passionate.

"Hey, you two." Sim came up behind us and made me jump. Tali and Rose were hysterically laughing – I wasn't quite sure if it was at my reaction, or having caught Khal in a compromising position. Either way, I was starting on my emotional rollercoaster ride again.

Chapter Twenty-Six

We all walked into the movie theatre together, got our tickets and Khal picked up a small bucket of popcorn and a drink. Everyone enjoyed the movie: *Monsters University*. And because it was a Disney movie there were a lot of children and the theater wasn't very quiet. So we chatted comfortably about nothing in particular. It was as if we'd all been friends for years.

It wasn't that late when the movie finished but Khal said something to the others and we parted. I thought we were planning on going to the pub together. Obviously the plans had been changed. I didn't mind. I enjoyed everyone's company, but I was also extremely selfish when it came to my time with Khal.

We took the car down to the cottage and decided to have a pleasant stroll along the beach. The sun fell over the dunes, trailing its last rays along the rippling tide. There were quite a few people out enjoying the warm breeze but it wasn't crowded.

The schools still had another week before they were off for the summer. That was when this place would become really busy. So it was nice to still be able to enjoy the relative solitude. Not that I would've noticed more people. It was strange – whenever I was with Khal, I rarely noticed anyone else around us.

The light was fading fast and the moon fought with the high cloud coverage to give our walk some light.

It was beautiful. The picturesque setting, the soothing sound of the lapping water, and the man of my dreams. This was paradise. I didn't need a tropical island to experience this, to experience what I was feeling.

Khal stayed close, even when I ventured toward the water. He never let go of my hand unless he had his arm over my shoulder. I watched him. He'd changed in so many ways. More relaxed, more willing to let me into his life. He was still reserved though. I didn't mind as much as I used to. I think I must have mellowed too.

I gazed at him for a moment longer and a sudden realization struck me, taking the wind right out of my sails; beyond a shadow of a doubt, I loved him with all my heart and soul.

I never thought I'd see the day that all those bricks in the walls I'd built would come tumbling down at the hands of just one man, where I would feel so utterly encapsulated, that just the idea of him not being here, with me, was too frightening to consider.

Khal froze next to me, suddenly stopping near the water. He stared intently down at me. "It took you long enough. You always said you weren't interested, but I knew. I knew."

"Sorry?" I was confused.

"You said you weren't interested. In love. But I knew, given time, you'd admit what I already knew. You really shouldn't, though. You really shouldn't have fallen for me." His eyes followed mine. The shadowing moon circled his head, creating an aura of light, a halo round his face.

"You were listening!" I didn't know whether to be pleased or angry. "You told me you didn't listen when you knew I was thinking of personal things?" I searched his face for answers.

"I lied," and he kissed me, gently like a butterfly brushing over my mouth, with the little tingles I'd grown so used to that I barely noticed them anymore. But they were a part of us and I couldn't imagine life without those little electric currents being there.

"Why?"

"Why what?" He held me close wrapping his arms round my waist, and pulling me into him. My heart was racing; so was his. My blood screamed, my breathing erratic, and his close contact rekindled my need to know as much about Khal as possible, to know everything.

"Why shouldn't I...I love you?" It felt so strange voicing these words aloud.

Khal looked at me intently and I began to wonder what the problem was. "Because you don't know me. Because you said you wouldn't. You don't fall in love with men. But God, Abby, this wasn't supposed to happen. I knew it was going to happen but it wasn't supposed to."

"But I do know you. I know you well enough to know what I'm feeling's real. And don't forget you were the one who said this was always more than just a simple attraction."

"But Abigail. What if you find out something about me that you don't like? I *will* hurt you, and I don't see how you could cope with that. But you telling me you love me changes things. I can't continue to control myself if you do this. I won't be able to keep my distance."

"I don't want you to keep your distance. Don't you know that? Unless you're telling me you don't love *me*. And I'm fine with that. I'm not trying to put you on the spot. But you delve into my head like that and you're going to see how I feel. Surely you already have before. I've even tried to show you I want you, but you rebuffed my advances." I was fumbling now, not sure what to say. Grappling for my words to try and make sense of what he was trying to tell me. What I was trying to tell him.

My heart was buffeting against its cage, frightened that he would reject me...again.

"You have no idea how hard this has been for me. But always having you maintain that you didn't want any attachments, and you aren't into holiday romances helped me keep that distance in place. But now...I can't guarantee what the future will be for you."

"Why do we even need to consider the future? What about the here and now?"

"Oh Abigail. You need to be so sure about this."

"Why? I think I am. But you questioning me like this. I don't know. I just know I've never felt like this with anyone before. I don't understand what the problem is."

Khal placed a hand behind my neck and gently moved my head so he could kiss me. He knew just how to make my knees turn to jelly, how to make my stomach quiver. And how to heat my inner core until it burned hot and ready.

I forgot my doubts, forgot what we were saying. I trusted him, trusted him with my life. How could I not love him, completely and utterly.

"Come on, it's getting late. We better get back." Khal snapped me out of my trance and we walked arm-in-arm slowly across the dunes, returning home.

Yes, it was home, for both of us. It was our retreat.

I opened the door and Khal closed it behind us.

I was about to walk into the living room when Khal grabbed my arm and pulled me to him.

His kiss was passionate, deep, intense.

I had to come up for a breath, needed to replenish the oxygen my lungs craved. And when I did, Khal swept me up into his arms and carried me upstairs, effortlessly taking the steps two-at-a-time.

He didn't utter a single word. I didn't want to spoil the moment, hoping he would take me into the shower again, like last time. I wanted that closeness back, the intimacy that'd been missing.

But he didn't. He headed straight for the bedroom and closed the door behind us.

Chapter Twenty-Seven

Like déjà vu, Khal unbuttoned my shirt and took it off, unzipped my skort and let it fall to the ground and I stood in front of him in my bra and panties, again.

His amorous kisses felt wet, succulent, as he caressed my mouth with his lips, stroking his tongue with mine. He moved his mouth down to my neck constantly kissing, deftly using his tongue to entice me.

I was scared. What if he spurned me again? I didn't want to face that kind of rejection anymore.

He moved away slightly and looked down, "Loving me is not a good idea...but I won't push you away. Are you sure this is what you want? There's no turning back."

"I'm sure." I'd never been so sure of anything before.

"Oh, Abby, I love you. I've loved you from the first moment I saw you." Khal lifted me up in his arms and kissed me like never before.

Every inch of my body came alive, inside and out. My skin tingled – both the places that he touched and the places he wasn't.

This time, he allowed me to take his t-shirt off. I let my hands rest on his chest, the hairs crawling between my fingers, dark like his head, soft, comforting, and I played with his chain, having forgotten about its presence, but not really interested in that or his tattoo right now. His hands wrapped around my neck, caressing gently, moving down to my shoulders. His fingers slipped under my bra straps letting

185

them fall. I cuddled in close, running my hands up his back, enjoying the suppleness of his muscles.

Khal unfastened my bra and moved me away from him to let it fall to the ground.

Would he like them? Were they what he expected? I felt so unsure of myself, especially after last time when we didn't quite get this far. I was extremely conscious that I could disappoint him. And I couldn't believe I was actually having these crazy thoughts; I usually never cared what a man thought. In fact, I couldn't remember a time where I'd been completely naked in front of a man before.

"Oh Abby, how could you ever disappoint me? You are perfect in every way," and he pulled me in close again, resuming his kissing. My nipples peaked instantly and my breasts vibrated as shots of electricity zapped through them when they made contact with Khal's chest.

The heat between us intensified, my whole body was on fire, burning, flaring. Khal's torrid touch was hot and felt desperate. His hands stroked my breasts, our fingers playing with each other's nipples. He bent down and licked tantalizingly, circling, softly sucking, tormenting my soul, and I couldn't help but respond, groaning in ecstasy. I could feel my lust building quickly; God, I was going to orgasm.

Khal held me as I shuddered. Obviously this time he was completely aware of what had happened, and I'd never felt so embarrassed in my life.

"Abigail. You will get used to this. I promise. And the effect I have on you will dampen in time. Don't be embarrassed. Please. You are exquisite when you peak."

Khal began kissing me again, following on the train of the path he'd begun to forge. There slowly became no points on our bodies that had not been touched between us except two: his and mine.

Khal still had his boxers on, I my panties. His arousal was evident. Mine was eagerly building yet again. But I didn't touch, and neither did he.

For some unconscious reason I didn't move to change that situation. My instinct told me that if I made the move, Khal would back off. Why, I wasn't sure. He'd said he wouldn't, and I knew he could hear my thoughts, knew what was going through my mind.

Khal lifted me onto the bed and we lay in each other's arms, enjoying the stroking, the touching, the kissing.

I lay my head in the crook of his arm, enjoyed tracing patterns in the hairs on his chest, enjoyed my breasts rubbing against his bare skin. And slowly I was able to keep my libido in check while we enjoyed this quiet intimacy.

I played with his chain. The keepsake that was attached lay flat against his body, and I tried to remember where I'd seen something like it before. Ornate, with a mixture of colored metals. Its interwoven pattern of shapes seemed to depict some kind of bird and another animal, both separated by what appeared to be an oval, an eye. I wondered if it was an elaboration of something associated with his cat's eyes. It was hard to tell. And it definitely appeared to be very old.

"This is incredible."

"Thank-you."

"It seems familiar."

Khal played with my hair and never commented on where I might have seen this object before, just kissed me occasionally on my forehead. And neither of us said anything else for what seemed like eternity.

Then Khal broke the silence, moving me away from him slightly but still stroking my hair, my body. "You haven't forgotten, have you?"

"Forgotten what."

Khal stopped moving his hand. "Abby, I know you've gotten used to our contact, but we haven't been here before. Surely you're not going to make me explain all this to you…are you?" Khal was silent for a minute.

I stared up at him. "Explain what?"

"This has never occurred to you, has it? You're an intelligent woman. Figure it out, Abby." I couldn't make out if he was annoyed, angry or just frustrated.

I lay still, contemplating what he'd said, trying to understand what he was getting at.

"Oh my God!" It suddenly came to me. "The electricity, the pain, on untouched territory! This is going to hurt, isn't it?"

I swallowed hard. It never occurred to me that there would be a problem, an issue. I'd grown accustomed to the tingling, the tiny shocks that still happened. The occasionally painful contact. And the quickly building orgasms – although I wasn't sure I'd ever really get used to those without blushing.

But all these areas weren't our most sensitive, hyper-responsive to certain touches. That's why he'd stopped, why he wasn't going any further.

Khal flipped a small square packet in his hand looking sheepish. "I'm hoping this will give at least some relief."

I didn't know what to say. Utterly speechless. But I hadn't moved. I didn't want to move. I loved this man and wanted to experience that single space phenomenon.

Physicists may have decided that two masses cannot occupy the same space at the same time, but I was prepared to prove them wrong. I'd heard it was possible. Now, I wanted to corroborate it for myself.

Khal kissed me.

Are you listening again?

He nodded, and his ardent kisses had my heart turn to mush.

"Are you sure?" He asked.

"Yes. I'm sure." I'd never been so sure about anything else in my whole life.

Khal's hand moved across my breasts, manipulating, caressing. His mouth joined his fingers, searching out my nipples, one by one. And he slowly, cautiously made his way down my already enticed body.

The heat rose out of every pore, and I couldn't control my inner sexual rage any longer. If he didn't take me now, I would truly die.

Chapter Twenty-Eight

Yes, it hurt beyond my imagination. I stifled my cries, not wanting Khal to stop.

But I could see the pain on his face – he knew. He also read my mind, and I knew I had to get past our first time.

I felt like a virgin, that first painful time that ripped through my body. No, it was worse. The poker hot pain tore through my core, felt like a deep tear. But it had to be overcome. I knew this. So that future experiences were the deep pleasure that they should be.

And our first time was pleasurable. A conscientious lover, Khal's maneuvers were slow, his voice reassuring, all the time making sure I was okay. And I desired more, and more, and more.

But I just couldn't go through that again...yet. I felt euphoric but raw.

I took a shower thinking the water may be soothing, and it did help a little. I washed away the little blood that had appeared. It hadn't been bad. Khal fretted, worried he'd hurt me, and after my shower he held me close in his arms, never letting go as I fell asleep.

I woke sometime during the early hours, wanting him again, insatiably needing him inside me. Khal hesitated but I was determined, reminding him the importance of our contact. Even though I still never understood why his heightened sensitivity affected my nerve endings too, I enjoyed using it as a good excuse to have him make love to me.

I was tender, felt bruised, but the shooting sparks and heat were dampened. Khal's enamor caressed, stimulated my inner soul. And I loved him with everything I had.

We lay spent, and I must have fallen asleep again because before I knew it the sun was glaring through the window.

Khal moved and I rolled onto my back. "Good morning."

"Good morning." I smiled thinking of how precious this moment was, lying in the arms of the man I loved.

"So, did we fulfil your experiment?" It took me a few seconds to recall what Khal was referring to.

"Oh, the occupying of one space!" I giggled as I wrapped my arms round him.

"Yes, I believe so." I wanted to do it again, and kissed him zealously. There was no hesitation from Khal this time, nothing but pure ecstasy. He was an ardent and skilled lover, amorous in every way imaginable. I'd never been with someone so adept at love-making, his attention to detail captivated my heart over and over again.

Our morning disappeared in a cloud of enchantment, and I savored every moment.

I didn't want to move. I wanted to stay like this for eternity.

I enjoyed the feel of him, loved just being there with him, and rested my hand on his chest, just where his tattoo was, as I lay at his side. I played with the hairs on his chest, traced the black tattoo with my fingers, and felt a raised bump sitting underneath it. Having two small tattoos myself,

I found his fascinating. I propped myself up on my elbow, putting my hand under the side of my head, and looked down to see if I could see it properly.

Khal hadn't objected so I didn't expect him to mind. A scar, small but definitely there, lay horizontal along his left breast. It was only about four inches long and appeared to be very old. The hairs on his chest covered it well.

I put my fingers back up to his tattoo and suddenly realized from this angle what it was. "God, it's a scarab. You have a tattoo of a scarab."

I jumped up onto my knees, fascinated that he would have an Egyptian artefact tattooed onto his chest like that. A sudden lightbulb moment hit me.

"Your pendant is Egyptian too isn't it? An amulet. The eye of Horus. Your name. They're all Egyptian." I grinned at him, surprised by how I could've missed it before. His olive skin, dark hair. It all fit. Except the eyes – they were the wrong color. Wouldn't they be brown?

But Khal wasn't smiling. It had vanished. He pushed me off him, looking tense, even annoyed, and left the bed.

"I'll go and put the coffee on." Khal slipped his jeans on and went downstairs, leaving me stranded, wondering what had just happened.

Confused and hurt, I slipped my robe on, went for a pee, and joined him downstairs.

Khal had already collected the paper from the floor and I could hear him clattering around in the kitchen. I hesitated before entering. He promised he wasn't going to push me away again. And yet, here he was, shutting me out. What was so wrong with what I'd said. Was he Egyptian? Being Egyptian wasn't that bad was it?

192

I didn't join Khal in the kitchen. Instead, I curled myself up on the sofa, thinking. He gave the impression that he was from England, round here somewhere. As if he'd never lived anywhere else. Maybe he hadn't and it was just his family heritage. But why react so strangely to it? Wouldn't he just say?

Khal came through with a coffee mug, handed it to me and sat on the sofa too.

"Thanks."

Khal's tension was still visible, distant, remote.

What did I need to say? What did I need to do? I didn't like this tension between us, especially after experiencing the most salacious night of my life. The pain was subsiding, and Khal loved me, didn't he?

"So what's the big deal then? Why are you pushing me away again? You said you wouldn't. You said you loved me."

"Abby, why can't you just leave it be? Don't spoil things now. Not now."

"Spoil what? Apart from the fact that you awoke a deep lust in me, I gave you my heart; something I'd never dreamed of doing."

I thought long and hard, tried to turn the tables; would *I* ever hold anything back? And I couldn't imagine one instant where I couldn't, wouldn't tell him if he asked. His aloofness had to stop. To share the most intimate of moments with this man, I couldn't have secrets. Not anymore. I'd made allowances before. We were just friends, not lovers. I needed answers.

"I know you think you do. But you don't really want to hear it." He watched the expression on my face, searching.

193

"God, I wish you wouldn't do that!" My anger was clearly visible.

"I'm sorry." His distraught expression revealed it all – he'd hurt me...again.

"Yes, I know. I know I've hurt you, pushing you away again. But I told you last night on the beach I would hurt you. I warned you. Told you that you shouldn't love me. But you were so insistent, so sure. I can't always give you the answers you're wanting. To give you what you're asking would mean lying to you, and I can't do that with you. And I also can't tell you the truth. You don't understand what it would mean, what would happen if I did. And I'm sorry for listening into your thoughts. But it helps me understand you, helps me know what you want from me."

Khal stopped talking, and I drank my coffee.

"I've never restrained myself like I have with you...and I've never given myself so completely like I have with you. That's why when you begin your questions I struggle. I can't fob you off. I want you to know, want you to see who I really am, what I am. I want you part of...of my life. Why do you think I allowed you to see my eyes, my friends, my tattoo. But you weren't supposed to know what it is. No one ever does." Khal hesitated for a moment. "Well, before we go any further, maybe you do need to figure this out. Tell me what it is you want from me. Decide now before it's too late. Because once you know, I can't stop your pain, I can't stop your anguish. And I certainly can't stop the inevitable result." Khal looked at me and waited.

"Before we go any further? Before it's too late? How can you say that? After everything I went through last night. After opening myself up to you. You seem to think you're

194

the only one who's exposed themselves in this. Well, maybe you're right. Maybe this should just remain casual, nothing more." Yes, I was angry. How could he say that? I would never willingly put myself through that much pain and agony for anyone else. I was a scaredy-cat when it came to self-infliction. But I'd also never experienced such ardent love-making which surprised me considering the number of men I'd slept with.

"Oh sweetheart. Please don't." Khal reached out to hold me in his arms.

I hesitated. Is this what I wanted? Him, unable to trust me, yet I had to put all my trust in him?

I reached out to meet him and he embraced me close, with a fervor like no other.

"I do trust you, love. I trust you more than you know…but this doesn't just affect me."

We sat quietly for a while, and I felt safe, secure in Khal's arms. But I didn't understand, except there was nowhere else on earth I would rather be at that moment in time.

I wasn't thinking straight. I knew that. I needed my breakfast, something to eat. I also needed a break, needed to take control of my fluctuating emotions as they pivoted on the edge of a precipice.

I went to the kitchen, got a bowl of cereal, and brought it back to the sofa.

I thought while I ate, wondering why I was here, like this. I wondered why I allowed Khal into my life so willingly, readily. Many of my questions for myself, I still couldn't answer. Jen had been right. I'd kept such a façade up regarding serious relationships that when it happened I didn't know what to do, or how to act. I tried to be myself but then I ended up in this mess with someone I loved unconditionally but knew so little about.

I enjoyed sitting on the sofa with him, having him so close and half naked, his chest bare, muscular and hairy. And when I looked at him the surrounding world didn't exist. The strange behavior, the unusual physical conditions, the secrets, all vanished into obscurity, and I just saw him.

My robe fell open as I leaned down to the coffee table placing my bowl down after I'd finished. I reached for my coffee, sipped my warm drink quietly, and watched him watching me.

We didn't need to talk. Words were unnecessary.

I imagined him naked again, and smiled. And I knew by the expression on his face that he was doing the same with me.

Khal took my coffee mug from me and leaned in to kiss me, ever so tenderly, and moved my robe away from my breasts. And I couldn't help but enjoy every minute of his touch, and enjoyed touching him too.

He lifted me up into his arms and carried me back upstairs. Not back to the bedroom, but into the bathroom.

"But you don't like water." I wasn't sure why that really mattered right now.

"I know," he turned to face me, peering down at me, and removed my robe, letting it fall off my shoulders to a heap on the ground.

"Why?" I stepped into the shower and Khal took his jeans off and followed.

"The cold."

"But the water's warm, and we can turn the temperature up more."

"No, not the water temperature, although that does help a little. No, it's the air temperature when I'm wet. England's too cold for me, even in the summer."

I watched the water run down Khal's hair and face and he looked miserable, quite pathetic, like a drowned cat.

I couldn't help but smile at the image, kissed him tenderly, and looked at his catlike eyes…

I turned around so my back was to him, thinking, jumbled thoughts running through my head. Khal had the soap and washed my back. I leaned into him. The hair on his chest was soft, his large hands wrapped round my waist. His eyes, his soft hair, his dislike of water. Was there a connection to the large cat sightings? Is that why Khal wouldn't talk about it? No, don't be stupid. That would be impossible. And anyway, he did talk about it. He was very knowledgeable…

I tried to snap out of my ludicrous thoughts, telling myself that such hocus pocus was for fictional writers, not for the real world. And anyway, half cat, half human – that was an Egyptian myth…

I spun around to face Khal staring wildly and looked at his amulet. Picked it up, turned it over. "Wedjat. A symbol of protection, of power." It was coming back to me.

"A protection for the afterlife, to ward off evil." I wasn't sure what I was saying. My head was spinning as I tried to find those little pockets in my brain that stored the information related to this.

I looked up at Khal. That pathetic look on his face was still there. Yet, there was also a pleading as if he was urging me on, telling me to keep going. I looked at his tattoo, the scarab – a dung beetle and the sun. "Resurrection."

Khal didn't move.

197

"Egyptian mythology. Half cat, half human. Your name. Immortal. Oh God." I swallowed hard, trying to dispel the panic surging inside.

I switched the shower off and got out quickly. "No, I'm not going there. This has to stop. Now." I was shaking, trembling.

But Khal followed me out of the shower and grabbed my arm. "You just won't face it, will you? Just won't take that final leap? And you wonder why I stopped earlier? You ask the questions, insist on answers, but when I give them to you, you won't face it."

"Won't face what? There's nothing to face. Leave me alone." I yanked my arm out of his grip but he pulled me into him, holding tight and forcefully kissed me. As he pressed his lips hard against mine, I started to forget what we were arguing about. Just being in his arms felt so incredible.

He quickly let go and with a determination I hadn't witnessed before, got a towel and proceeded to leave the bathroom.

"We need to get dressed."

I noticed Khal was struggling to shiver, his olive skin was ashen. He looked so deathly ill that I was shocked.

"I'm okay. Just give me a couple of minutes before you come through. Please." He gave an attempt at a smile but he didn't look fine. He disappeared quickly.

I picked up my robe and put it on. Then followed Khal into the bedroom as he was finishing getting dressed. He was nearly dressed already, and was about to slip his hoodie on. But there, on his unclothed, uncovered arms were thick blankets of black fur. I just stared, couldn't register what I was seeing.

Khal spun round quickly as if annoyed I had interrupted him, and finished pulling on his hoodie.

"Come on. You need to get dressed," and he hurried downstairs without saying another word.

I didn't argue. I didn't know how to at that point.

Chapter Twenty-Nine

I didn't have a clue where we were going, but I knew Khal had an agenda, one I was not happy about. Khal drove to one of the stately homes in Lincolnshire. As we approached I knew where we were. Alice had pictures on her wall of the house and gardens. And John had a book in his store about the stately homes in the area. I remember looking at this one thinking I'd like to go and visit it. Just not today...not like this.

The land that surrounded the home was sectioned off into different areas, like many historic places were. The layout of the gardens were from around the time when the house was originally built and apparently *Jane Eyre* was filmed here; which one, I had no clue.

Khal pulled into the gravel driveway and came round to my side of the car. He held my hand and started walking towards the house.

"Can't we look at the gardens first?" I knew I was stalling for time. So did Khal. But he agreed.

The gardens were beautiful and I enjoyed the stunning beds, the variety of topiary. Our last moment, in the shower, still preyed on my mind as we walked. Khal's inability to control himself last night, wanting to make love to me, and now his determination to get me to understand today. What had changed so much for him to give himself like that, to then want to drag me out here? And why wasn't

I happy about it? I was the one who kept pushing, kept asking the questions. Wasn't this what I wanted?

What was I so afraid of? And he knew I was afraid. Was that why he'd suddenly walked away from me when I did question him intensely? It was like a game of cat and mouse. If I figured out something, or asked personal questions, he shut himself off. And I gave him a hard time over how he should share things with me if he wanted us to be together. He then wanted me to know and I didn't want to anymore. If this didn't feel so serious, it would actually be funny.

He started to tell me a little about the history of the gardens. Talking about topics he was comfortable with seemed to help. He was doing it to help me...or maybe not. Maybe he needed this too.

He gradually stopped talking and slowly led us both back towards the house. At first I hadn't noticed, just enjoyed this time with him, pretending what happened earlier hadn't happened, forgetting about Khal's agenda. But as soon as I noticed that we were approaching the house I became all tense again, nervous, and tried to pull away.

My emotions were all over the place, completely irrational. But Khal was tense and nervous too – I could feel it as he held on to me. I couldn't cope with Khal's mood swings, when he shut me out, and I couldn't cope with this – whatever *this* was. I just didn't want to know.

"Khal. No. I don't want to go in there."

"Why not?" His pensive look of determination was something I'd never witnessed with Khal before.

"You're scaring me. I promise, I won't ask any more questions. I'll let you have your secrets. I don't mind." I struggled to hold back my tears.

"Abby, why don't you want to go in? You have a choice: tell me, tell me what you know, or we go in and I show you. You've been pushing and pushing, and now it's here you back off. No, you're going to know the truth, one way or another because I can't play these games anymore."

"But what if I don't want to know? It doesn't really matter. Honest. I don't mind not knowing. We can just carry on as we have been."

"It matters to me. You have all the pieces, you just won't put them together, will you? You think I want this? You think I want my life exposed, open for you to know everything? I'm scared, frightened that after I show you, you'll run away, never want to see me again. And then it'll be too late because this doesn't just affect me, it affects everyone else that I live with. And more. I asked you last night if you were sure. And I also told you that you didn't know me. Well, now you will know who, what I am."

"Okay, so you're Egyptian. So what?"

"No, Abby, that's not enough, and you know it isn't. Please, I need you to know who I am. I love you with all my heart and the idea of you not knowing is just too much to bear. If you love me you'll do this, for me. Please."

"And if I don't? Love you?"

"Oooh, don't you dare go there now. You can't decide last night that you love me to suddenly take it back because you don't want to face up to this, won't admit what's in front of you. You can't get angry over my saying that we have to do this before we go any further, to then throw it back in my face. You can't decide to ask questions about my name, my amulet, my tattoo, my cat features, to then back off when you don't like what you're seeing, don't want to admit what you're seeing. You're the one who believes that secrets shouldn't be kept if we give ourselves over to each other. Now, give me your hand." When he was like this there was no arguing with him. And I didn't know what else to do.

Khal paid for two tickets; he opted for the self-tour rather than the organized one.

Holding my hand, he guided me through the rooms, one by one. He chatted nonchalantly about each room, giving me an amazing account of the history behind the house, the rooms, and the pieces placed in each room, including the artwork. The knowledge he regurgitated blew my mind. I should be fascinated, enthralled with all he said, but all it did was confuse me. Was he trying to give me time to calm down? If he was it wasn't working. It just created more and more anxiety to the point that I was convinced I was going to have a panic attack.

Then he stopped outside one of the larger rooms, a room we hadn't been in yet. He paused, took in a deep breath then marched in. There was determination in his walk, and I couldn't pull him back. I didn't want to go into that room. A feeling washed over me, telling me I needed to be afraid. More afraid than I'd been so far. Something was telling me not to go into that room. But Khal kept pulling. He knew what my problem was so he hung on to my hand tighter and put his other arm around my waist to try and stop my physical protests.

"Khal, please. No. Don't make me do this. I'm begging you." But there were no reassurances coming from him. Nothing but determination.

Yet when we entered it was just another room, a dining hall this time, very long and covered with wood paneling. There was a large table down the center, surrounded by tall chairs.

A huge sideboard fitted along the far wall, and all around the room were full-sized paintings of past ancestors. They were all men, some old, some young, many in uniform, on horseback, or standing.

And then it happened. Khal stopped in front of one, grabbed my shoulders and turned me to face the painting.

I couldn't register what I was seeing. It was too surreal. I glanced round at Khal, hoping for him to just move on. But he wouldn't. I could see it in his face, his stature.

The painting was of a young man, elegantly dressed in a formal military uniform; the distinct red coat with gold buttons; the matching pants and hat; the rifle with what looked like a bayonet. The most gorgeous man I knew. Beautiful, perfect in every way. The small gold plaque nailed to the frame bellow the painting gave the details of the portrait. A relative, a distant relative whom he was named after.

And the resemblance, the resemblance to Khal was uncanny. Even the color of his eyes. A little younger, maybe, not really. But so real…

I whipped round to have Khal help me but he just looked at me, pleading for me to understand. But I just couldn't. I didn't want to.

"Khal, please…" and I couldn't finish. My knees went weak, my legs buckled underneath me as my head floated away. My body fell like a toppling tower of children's bricks.

Chapter Thirty

When I came to I was in Khal's arms on a bench just outside the room, and a young guide was asking Khal if I was okay, and if he needed any help.

"What happened," I whispered to Khal.

"You fainted, love." He stroked my forehead, held me tight.

"Are you sure she's okay?" the lady asked.

"Yes, I'm sure. She just overheated," he reassured her.

The employee left and we stayed on the bench for what left like an eternity.

And then it all came flooding back. The painting: the portrait. I snapped alert, pushed myself off Khal and looked at him, searching for answers. My whole body shook with fear. I moved forward so my feet could touch the floor and then wondered if I was stable enough to stand.

It took a couple of seconds to get my head to stop spinning. Then I ran to the room again, to the painting.

There, in uniform, holding a helmet in one hand, the reigns of a horse in another, standing tall, erect, was an image of Khal. I read the plaque: "Khaldun James Wynford 4th Baron of Willoughby de Eresby. 1782 – 1812."

Okay, so it was an old painting of someone with Khal's name. A historical twin. They happened; I was sure they happened. Famous people had them all the time, didn't they? It must be freaky staring at such a likeness of yourself.

Or meeting your doppleganger. It couldn't actually be him…Khal. That would mean Khal was…was…no. Just no. NO!

Khal stood beside me. I turned to look at him, tears streaming down my face. I couldn't help the sob escaping, sounding like a child's whimper. My stomach ached. No, I couldn't go there. I just couldn't.

"Yes, you can, Abby. Please."

"No…this must just be an ancestor. It can't be…you." I whispered the last word.

I was gasping for air.

"Abigail." Gravely, he didn't say anything else.

I turned to look closely at the portrait again. The eye color was the same: more green than gold but still the same.

"The eyes. They're different. This proves it isn't you." Now I sounded desperate.

Khal came closer, placed his arm round my waist, held me tightly. After all his determination to get me here, he was now his gentle self again and whispered, "It is me, Abby. You know it is, don't you?"

I wanted to touch it, to stay there forever. I wanted to check every detail of this painting, to find every fault in it so I could prove it wasn't him.

But there was no air. I needed air. My legs were failing below me again. I couldn't keep my balance.

"Come on. Let's go outside. You can come back again. I promise. I'll bring you here as many times as you need to come." His tranquil, placid voice had me agreeing with him. The man I loved. The man I couldn't imagine life without. And he was trying to tell me about his life, a life I couldn't comprehend, didn't want to know about.

We walked out of the rose garden, across the meadow and headed for the line of trees denoting the small forest. I just kept walking, and Khal followed along beside me.

This wasn't happening. I'd set out my whole life, mapped it out step by step. Get into NYU, be a doctor, then consider some kind of personal life. But that had all fallen apart. And I was supposed to come here to figure out what I was doing with my life. What direction I was going to take. And Khal came along.

Holiday romances: they were just stupid castles in the air for silly dimwits. They didn't really happen, and certainly weren't long lasting. That last bit was impossible.

But I met Khal and my whole world turned upside down, and I couldn't imagine him not being with me.

He came into my life; he pursued me. He made me fall in love with him. And last night...how could he allow me to go that far, go through all that pain? How could he let me fall in love with him? This was why I kept away from men – all they did was break your life apart, break your heart.

"This is crazy!" I shouted spinning around to face Khal. We'd reached the tree-line. "Impossible!"

I was angry. Angry at life; angry at him.

And I hit him – I got my fist and thumped it against his chest. "No! You're just trying to scare me. That, in there, cannot be of you. Reality doesn't work that way." I searched his face for answers.

But he didn't budge, didn't move. I did it again, and again, and again. Thumped him and screamed, "No! Myths aren't real. There is no reality with them. Never. You're just doing this because you knew I was right and you were wrong."

Pound, pound, pound: I never let up with my fists on his chest. "You can't do this to me. Not now. No! No! Why couldn't you just have left it? You didn't have to force it. You could've just left it alone. No. Oh, Khal. Please. You have to stop this. Take it back. It just hurts too much. Oh please, Khal. No."

And I just cried, completely and utterly broke my heart, beating his chest with my fists, wanting him to feel the same pain I was experiencing.

But he already was. I only had to look up at his face to see he was in complete and total agony. From me, from himself – I wasn't sure there was even a difference anymore. We'd become one, hadn't we?

He spread his arms out and carefully, slowly, brought them round my body, enveloping me completely. He shrouded me in his safety net, cloaked me with his sturdy frame.

And I just collapsed, sobbing.

Chapter Thirty-One

I had no idea as to the time, no idea how long Khal had been holding me. I had quietened down, stopped being so hysterical, and settled for the occasional snuffle.

And I could hear him, quietly, ever so quietly, humming.

Khal loosened his grip on me and moved his hands to my face. He tilted my face up to look at him and kissed me, ever so gently. On my forehead, my cheek and finally my lips. He'd taken his glasses off, knowing how much it meant to me to see his eyes.

We were completely alone, sitting by some old trees.

"How are you?" His voice was virtually a whisper.

"I'm ok." I lied. He knew. I wiped my eyes and cheeks on his shirt – it was already wet from all my crying.

"Do you feel like talking?" He asked me and then bent down to kiss me, again, tenderly. The tingling ran through my body. Showed me I was alive. Told me he was too.

"I don't know. Why? Oh Khal, this can't be. How can this be happening? This is impossible." I was fumbling, trying to get some kind of order to my head.

Khal didn't disagree. He also didn't say anything to hint that he agreed either.

"I can't. I can't." I shook my head over and over. More tears fell and I let them tumble in rapid succession until streams merged and dropped off my chin.

"How about we head home, and we can talk about it then?"

I couldn't argue. I needed time to calm down, think logically. And let's face it, going home was about the only logical thing in this mess. I nodded in agreement.

I felt drained. Confused. Cheated. What was I going to do? How could I continue knowing...what? What did I know? Nothing. I knew nothing. Not really. My life was in ruins and I hadn't a clue how to fix it.

The sky had become overcast and a light drizzle had begun. It was uncanny how the weather could so quickly change and reflect the feelings in my heart. No, that wasn't totally correct. Yes, my heart was bleeding, but it wasn't a slow bleed like the drizzle. It was like a summer storm in New York City where the rain pounded and bounced off the sidewalk rising inches above the concrete: where gallons and gallons of water fell from the heavens saturating everything in its sight; where inches fell in a couple of hours causing streams and small rivers to form rapidly; where within seconds you were drowning and raincoats and umbrellas were mere fashion statements.

No, my heart wasn't drizzling, it had broken in two, split in half and everything that had been inside fell to the ground where it had been stomped on.

It took hours to drive home. The weather had slowed traffic and because it was the middle of the day there were the occasional tractors on the road, slowing everything down even more. There were always large trucks taking goods to the Lincolnshire villages and towns. And the cars, there were so many cars today. Had everyone decided to come out for the day, to witness my humiliation?

Khal didn't speak. And neither did I. During the drive my brain had not stopped going over everything. It was as if a playbook had opened in my head and had gone back to the beginning to when I landed at Heathrow. No, that wasn't true; it had begun at Victoria Station, my hand on the door knob of the ticket office.

I looked out the window and watched the hedgerows fly past. Even at this slower speed everything around me moved too quickly to take in.

It may not have been the bus that came first but it – and the journey – was part of it. Had it all been a plan, something already laid out and I had no say in it? The first bus, the café, the second bus, the deli, the food. God, the food: he'd read my thoughts and done my shopping for me. How could I have been so naïve, so damn stupid. All the times we'd eaten together and I'd never registered that he didn't eat the same things I did so why would he be shopping...

I stopped there. No, I wasn't going to go there at all. No, stop it, I had to stop my brain from seeing the newspaper headlines. I had to stop seeing the slaughtered animals. No. Just...NO!

But it wouldn't stop. The images of our plates of food; his lack of interest in eating what I ate. And when I asked him if he was vegetarian he laughed and said 'no'. No, because he wasn't.

A cruel shiver ran down my spine. This kind, gentle man next to me was a monster. A monster: a serial killer of animals; a Hannibal Lecter of sorts. Only, wasn't Lecter more meticulous? Less brutal? Who was I kidding? Serial killers came in all shapes and sizes and there was nothing worse than having one appear…normal. I scoffed to myself – there was nothing normal about Khal.

By the time we arrived back at the cottage I wa a basket case, a huge bag of fearful nerves because I'd come to the realization: I was sitting next to a murderer, a killer.

I wouldn't say I was scared per se – Khal had never intentionally hurt me. But I had no way of knowing if that would stay the case. I had no way of knowing that now he'd gotten me in his trap that things wouldn't change.

It suddenly dawned on me that Khal would have heard everything I'd been thinking. God, I'd never get used to that, knowing he could hear everything going on in my head. If I'd angered him I would be in danger. I glanced across at Khal for the first time since leaving the stately home but he showed no acknowledgement, no recognition and no awareness that he'd been listening in. If anything, the way he gripped the steering wheel, he was trying his damnedest to *not* listen in.

I was relieved…but it didn't stop my anger…or change a thing.

We pulled up in front of the cottage and Khal turned off the engine.

"You set this all up, didn't you? You trapped me from the beginning. Pursued me and cornered me. This was your plan all along wasn't it? Well, I've got news for you, buster, I'm not a pushover. I'm not some simpering woman who'll bend and be placated into fitting in with what you want. I never wanted this. You knew that."

I took a deep breath and glanced Khal's way again – he hadn't moved. He showed no emotion. There was no pleading for me to stop. There was nothing. I didn't exist to him. I didn't matter. This really was a game to him. He'd lied to me; if he really did love me he'd show me…right now. But he didn't move.

He didn't love me.

"I'm not doing this Khal. I'm not going to continue with this fallacy. I don't want to be a part of it. I'm *not* going to be a part of it."

I opened the car door and stepped out onto the sidewalk. But before closing the door I leaned in once more to say one more thing before running to my front door.

"And if I ever – ever – see another headline of animals being slaughtered, I will point the finger in your direction."

"That wasn't me, Abigail and you know it. Do you really think I could do something like that? Do you really believe I would harm you? After all this time? Don't you think if that had been my intention I would have done it by now? Huh?" Khal raised his eyebrows at me.

"Right now, Khal, I don't know what to believe…except I don't believe you. I don't believe you about…anything."

"Stop being so dramatic, Abigail. You've had your say – yes, I was listening to everything going on in your head – but now it's my turn."

Khal opened his car door and slammed it shut. Then he marched to the cottage and opened the front door…with a key.

"Where did you get that, Khal? I never gave you a key." I followed him in.

"I took it. Just in case."

"You took it? Just in case of what? Khal, you don't just take things like keys. What gives you the right? And when? When did you take it?" I slammed my bag and keys

213

on the small hall table and followed Khal into the living room.

"Abby. Your anger has nothing to do with the keys. Come on. Sit down. I'll get you a coffee then we can talk." Khal led me to the sofa like a child and then went into the kitchen.

He was right. I wasn't interested in talking about the keys right now; that could wait for another time. I took a deep breath but it did nothing to calm me down. I got up from the sofa and went over to the fireplace. Then paced back to the sofa. Then to the window. I felt restless, nervous. I didn't want Khal here. I didn't want to talk about this. I didn't want to hear what he had to say.

"Abby. You have let your mind imagine the worst possible scenarios. You obviously need answers. You may not want to hear them but you are going to listen." Khal had come back into the living room with two coffees and placed them on the coffee table in front of the sofa.

"I can't promise you'll like what you hear. But I can promise you that nothing is as bad as you imagine it to be. Now please, come and sit down."

I hesitated. How could I sit next to him now? How could I let him touch me?

Khal stood up and came to me. He reached out and pulled me into his arms. I didn't resist. I couldn't resist. He walked me over to the sofa and as he sat down he pulled me into his lap and held me again as my tears tumbled over the edge of my eyelids in rapid succession.

"Why Khal? Why did you take me there? Why did you show me?" I pulled away from him and looked at him, pleading for him to make it all go away.

214

"I desperately wanted you to know. But I couldn't just tell you. Apart from the fact that we don't tell or show anyone, you'd never have believed me. But when you told me you loved me, I just wanted to take you, make love to you. And I realized I couldn't hide from you anymore. I wanted you to know what I am, share my life with you."

"All I know is that you are telling me you are over two hundred years old. That's it. I don't know anything else."

He caressed my hands, turned them round and round in his, played with my fingers.

"You know, Abby. You know."

I looked into his eyes. "But you said you hadn't killed those animals? You said you weren't a monster."

I could feel myself hyperventilating as I tried to see into Khal's eyes, read his expression.

"No, I didn't kill those animals. But Abby, I never said I wasn't a monster."

Chapter Thirty-Two

Khal watched the shock on my face. A hysterical laugh escaped as my mind conjured up images of vampires and werewolves, ogres and demons, ghouls and zombies.

Khal burst out laughing. "Okay, not that monstrous but I do need to drink blood. Fresh blood."

I pushed myself off Khal's lap so quickly I fell on my ass. But none of that stopped me from placing my hands over my throat so he couldn't latch on with his fangs. Then I remembered I'd never seen any fangs. And then I remembered that vampires' fangs only came out...or down when they wanted to puncture a person's throat. And that made me squeeze my neck until I almost couldn't breathe.

And then I remembered I didn't believe in such stupid stories. So I gave another hysterical laugh, picked myself up off the floor but moved over to the fireplace out of Khal's reach.

"Abby, I'm not a vampire. But yes, they do exist. And yes, they are...okay, let's change the subject. I do not drink human blood. Never have and never will. No, only animal blood. But it has to be fresh. I can't get my energy unless it's fresh. And it physically hurts not to have it."

"Not a vampire? So...what then?" I swallowed the lump that had formed in my throat.

"Sarjikris."

"Sar...what?"

"Sar-jik-ris. And I can only hunt in my cat form."

216

Khal stopped talking and went to put a log on the fire. I quickly scrambled out of the way, went over to the chair and perched on the arm. I wasn't trembling as much as I was before but I didn't want to be near Khal...not yet anyway.

"The large cat sightings? They were you?" I knew. Deep down inside, I'd realized this morning.

"Not just me...but yes."

I thought for a while. "A Shape shifter? Is that what you're trying to tell me? You're a shape shifter?"

"Yes, Abby. I am. Would you like a repeat of this morning just to prove it?"

"God no! No, it's okay. Let's just say that for now I believe you. How does this tie in with everything else?" I stopped for a moment. Slowly but surely the pieces were falling into place.

"Your eyes."

"Yes."

"Your Egyptian tattoo and amulet...the eye of Horus? Egyptians loved...worshipped cats."

"Yes."

"But that portrait." I wiggled my fingers in front of me as if I could magically make that painting appear. "What does that have to do with Egypt and their love of cats? I mean, are we talking the whole pharaohs and the afterlife and gods and goddesses and Sekhmet?"

"No, it's Bastet."

"Bastet? Half woman half lion. Wasn't she a defender of the pharaoh?"

"Yes."

"So what's the connection between you and Bastet? And what does this all have to do with the portrait?"

217

"That was the portrait my family had completed before I left to work abroad. A few years later I went to Egypt. I was twenty-nine when I left for Egypt; I had already been to India. I was due to marry when I got back. My family had arranged a wife for me. This was to be my last assignment and I was ready to continue the family requirements of eventually becoming an Earl. It was my duty. I already held the title of Baron, as you saw." Khal sighed.

I'd always wondered about his life before now, where his family was. He'd never talked about them, always veered away from answering any questions I had.

"But it wasn't meant to be. Our regiment was sent to Rašīd...Rosetta. It's a city a little east of Alexandria. We were sent there to help defeat the French but when we arrived, the place was quiet. We were sure we had the place covered, weren't going to have any trouble. But we were ambushed. Many died. I was injured. A woman took me to her home and bathed my wounds. I've little memory of this time. Apparently I ran a high fever and the woman was sure I was dying. That was when she called on Bastet.

"I remember seeing Bastet. She initially came as a cat. Do you know much about what the Egyptians believed in regarding the afterlife?"

"Only a very tiny bit. There were certain important steps that had to be followed."

"Do you remember the steps regarding which organ was considered the most important?"

I thought for a moment, trying to remember the process, remembering how I nearly threw up in class when the professor went through it all. I could feel my stomach going queasy now, just thinking about it. "Wasn't it the brain...no, the heart. Something to do with the soul."

"Yes, the heart. The idea being that the heart is considered the lifeforce of the human body. Egyptians believed the heart to be part of the human soul where all emotion and reasoning originates. How much your heart weighs determines your purity. The heavier your heart, the less pure you are, the less likely you are to pass on to the afterlife."

"Yeah, something like that. Something to do with a feather and being heavy of heart."

"Well, you know the scar you noticed on my chest? Bastet did that. She cut me with her claw and drained my lifeforce, my blood, from my heart. Then replaced my lifeforce with some of hers so that my heart would continue to work as long as I fed on blood. The heart is the one organ that makes that movement through to the afterlife possible because as long as it is given the potential of eternity, which is what Bastet gave me, it's then easier for the rest of the body to pass over."

Khal's face changed. I wasn't quite sure if he was looking sad or if it was just his way of remembering. I felt this sudden urge to go to him, to be near him while he talked. I acted on that urge and slipped across to the sofa and propped my leg up so I could tuck my foot under my knee.

"Bastet. She looked like a vision, almost an illusion, in the shape of a panther. Black. Once finished, she changed into a woman, placed the amulet round my neck and embedded the scarab onto my chest as a form of protection. I wasn't frightened, although the whole process was excruciatingly painful...and lasted many days...Are you okay? I can't hear your thoughts anymore."

219

"No, I'm fine. Just listening."

"Do you want me to keep going? Do you want to hear this?"

"Yes…yes."

"I don't know the exact time frame, how many days I was unconscious or how many it took to go through the process Bastet initiated. All I remember is waking up with no fever, and no longer dying. I thought I was better; I felt so alive, until I tried to eat normal food. My stomach rejected everything. As the days passed I had no energy, and quickly became weak. And the weaker I became, some terrible cravings took over. They were almost as painful as what I'd just been through. And that was also when the strange static began to happen. It was like my nerve endings were alive, a mind of their own. The woman who'd looked after me, explained how Bastet gave me life so that I could continue to experience human emotion and reason, and how now some of my senses would be exaggerated. And the first time I noticed it was whenever this woman came near me I couldn't hide the pain from the static that bolted through my body's nervous system. My whole body burned, felt on fire. It excruciatingly ripped through me and I would tremble uncontrollably. I hated myself for reacting so severely because she'd been so kind. But she seemed to understand, realize."

"Did she feel it too?"

"No. Not like you do. The strange cravings continued where I needed to find something to eat immediately but I wasn't sure what. The woman didn't tell me what I needed even when I asked her. So I left to find food.

220

"I ran through the streets, looking for something that would satisfy me, that I could actually keep down. And soon found that my nerve sensitivity amplified my ability to sense my surroundings, so I could feel things before I could actually see them. So when an animal came into my periphery I became uncontrollable; I gravitated towards that animal because I was hungry. They were so appealing and I didn't seem to care what it was: rat, dog, camel."

I shuddered at just the thought of what Khal must have gone through. And the idea of eating a rat or a dog. It just didn't bare thinking about.

Khal smiled at me then began to lean in towards me. He hesitated, looked at my face, honed in on my lips, then leaned in more and gently pressed his lips to mine. As usual the sparks flew and my heart raced. But I didn't encourage him.

I didn't stop him either.

Khal moved back and took my hand in his, entwining our fingers. "When I got close to something that I craved to eat, I felt my body change and I couldn't stop it. The more I craved the taste of that animal, the more my body wanted to alter, shift into something else. That first change took a very long time too. Hours.

"I changed into a cat and fed, satisfying everything within me. And after, as I felt fulfilled, I also became aware, shocked, repulsed at what I'd done. I'd killed the dog. Sorry, Abby, but yes it was a dog. I slowly changed back into a man and wondered the streets, not wanting to go back and do that again, sickened by what I'd become. I'd heard of scary monsters that fed on the blood of humans and initially I thought I'd become one even though I'd not tried to drink a human's blood, or even wanted to. Whenever I encountered

221

a human – male or female – I never felt the same urge as I did when it was an animal.

"I think deep down I knew I wasn't one of those creatures. However, I did need the blood of an animal and I was horrified at the thought of having to kill one just so I could survive like this. It felt different to killing an animal for a whole family to feed off. I never really touched the flesh, just the blood.

"I staggered around aimlessly, for days, losing energy quickly but not wanting to satisfy my cravings again. I couldn't. And the worst thing was, I wanted to die, leave this world. But I couldn't do that either. No matter how much I deprived myself, I just continued to exist. That's when Chaf found me, languid emaciated. He brought me back to health, showed me that I didn't need to be a gruesome predator. I could satisfy my bloody-thirsty nature another more respectable way.

"Chaf showed me an ancient tribal custom of 'bleeding' an animal. I didn't need to kill anymore. I didn't need to sacrifice another animal for my cravings. He also showed me how once I got used to drinking the blood I could actually eat normal food too, in small portions. Then he explained how the shape shifting worked and how to control it." Khal stopped and smiled for a minute.

"What are you remembering?"

"Well, as I said, when I first shifted it took a very long time. Hours. After that initial one, each time it got faster and faster as my body became used to the ability to change from one form to another. But I couldn't control it in the beginning. I had absolutely no control over what happened. So when I was able to change in seconds it became a problem because of my inability to control what I was doing. We need to shift to eat so whenever I had a craving to eat I shifted. That was not good...because sex made me hungry." He laughed and just looked at me, waiting.

"Oh!"

Chapter Thirty-Three

Yeah. The first time I wanted to…you know…satisfy my sexual urges – which at the time were quite prolific – the poor woman almost had a heart attack. Probably wasn't a bad thing because it was with her and another woman not long after her that I came to realize how much it hurts me to touch and be intimate with a woman. Sex with regular humans was out of the question for a long time. Anyway, Chaf taught me how to master my transformations and appease my appetite without losing energy. How to balance regular human food with my other needs so that I got the best of both worlds, and was able to blend in. That's why when I'm with you and that first time I saw your body, upstairs, when you were hurt, I could control my reactions. I'm able to switch my yearnings on and off. However, it was the hardest thing I've ever had to do in my entire life, walk away, from you that day, and why I kept forgetting when you were persistent. That's the effect you have on me, when I'm near you. And why when you said you loved me, I knew I'd have a problem." Khal stopped from a moment, thinking.

"Chaf's help went beyond just the initial mentoring. We were virtually inseparable for my first few years. But I was lonely. Even though Chaf showed me the communities of others like us, I missed home. And started wandering on my own, not knowing what the problem was, believing this life should be perfect and yet, it didn't feel it."

"Why you? Why were you chosen?"

"I just was." Khal shrugged his shoulders and looked away. I knew by his reaction that there was more to it than he was willing to say.

"Where does the meaning of your name come into this?"

"Coincidence. I don't know if my father knew or not. I was named after my father and I never asked him before he died."

"Is that why you came back to England, because you were lonely?"

"Yes. I needed to come back but as Chaf warned me, it would all be different and I would need to accept that and move on. I came home, but I couldn't go home. My family thought I was dead. They'd buried me. My betrothed had married someone else. My brother took over the family name and title, and life continued for them. I couldn't then show up as if nothing had happened, only for them to see that I wouldn't age."

"I'd forgotten about that bit. According to the plaque on that painting you are thirty but that was over two hundred years ago."

"Yes, I'm thirty. I was twenty-six when that painting was commissioned. I...changed a few years after. And no, I'll never age."

"Why do you look so unhappy about that?"

"It's a long time to stay at one age. If you meet someone who isn't immortal, they grow old and you stay where you are. It's tough, hard to live with." The way Khal put it, it sounded so sad. I just couldn't imagine what that would be like.

"Is that how you came to live on the farm? Because you couldn't go back to your family?" Khal nodded.

"I built the farm. Chaf joined me. By now we were like brothers. We had no one else. We're similar in many ways, enjoy the same things. And we wanted somewhere away from Egypt. My need to return to England had us both realizing we wanted to belong to a community here – we have a communal instinct, wanting to be near…others of our own kind. Back then the majority of the communities we knew were in Egypt. It was rare anyone left. I wanted somewhere near home where we could be isolated yet accepted. And it was important to us to be able to help others like us. We needed our place to be big enough that allowed communal living, and allowed others to come and go as they pleased. I was sure there would be those who struggled like me and wanted to live somewhere more isolated away from Egypt. Don't get me wrong, I love Egypt. I actually consider it home too. I go back regularly: every couple of months at least. I enjoy going back. But this was always home."

"So is Chaf's name like yours, shortened for something? And is it Egyptian too?"

"Yeah. Chafulumisa."

"And does everyone else have Egyptian names too?"

"Yes. Everyone except me is Egyptian by birth. Lisa is Lisimba, Rose is Omorose, Wali is Walidah, Zeb is Zuberi, Sim is Asim, Tali is Talimah, Dru is Badru." Khal looked at the shock on my face and sniggered.

"You aren't expected to remember them all you know."

"Thank God for that. So how did you meet the others?"

"Different ways. Some were newly changed some were around long before I was. Some wanted to leave Egypt

226

but had nowhere else to go. Now, there are other communities all around the world, but the biggest ones are still in Egypt, especially Zagazig, a town in Lower Egypt. There have been others, beyond who is there now, who have come and gone over the years."

Khal stopped talking. It felt like we'd been sitting there for hours. The light was fading outside, and the fire was almost dead.

I'd always enjoyed listening to him talk, loved the sound of his voice. This was the first time he'd been so open about his personal life. Every long conversation we'd ever had before was either about me or kept completely general. I wanted to keep him talking. I wanted to hear more.

"You said that you needed to have blood as food. But you've been living with me, staying with me."

"When you're asleep, I leave. That's why I took the key, so I could let myself back in without disturbing you. It doesn't take me long. And I run a lot faster when I shift. And I don't need to feed very often. Every week or so, sometimes longer depending on what's happening at the time." He did one of his thoughtful smiles again.

"What?"

"Well, as I said before having sex makes me hungry. I'm going to have to make sure I eat more often."

I couldn't help but smile. For some strange reason I couldn't imagine not making love to this man. I felt my brain shift to compartmentalize and separate the Khal in front of me with the one he was talking about. That way they wouldn't interfere with each other and I could continue with the belief that Khal was just a man, a normal thirty year old with nothing different about him.

"How do you cope with other women then? You've said before that you've had others."

"Yes, I did. But I generally keep it just friends. You do get used to the pain it causes and don't think about it if you find someone attractive. But I just can't...I feel as though I'm using women if I go with them for sex. It's something I haven't done since I changed. Let me put it this way – you're the first for a very long time."

"Oh. God, you must have been shocked when you saw in my head then, with how I do have men just for sex."

"No. Some of them on the farm are like that too. It's just not something I can do. That's all."

"So tell me about the Sar...Sarjik – whatever."

Khal laughed. "Sarjikris. There's very little written about us because we don't talk about our lives. We don't normally let people know, and we don't feed off humans so unless we tell them, humans rarely get to know about us and therefore little mythology exists. Many generic names are bandied about – were-cat, witch, shape shifter, undead, and yes, vampire – for those people who think they know something. Immortals know about other immortals. Some immortals talk openly with each other so that's pretty much how humans get to hear *stories*. We do have some tendencies that are the same as other immortals, some that are very different or complete opposites, especially with a vampire. Unlike many immortals, we can eat small amounts of some human food successfully. Although we do have to make sure we feed on blood first. It's more difficult these days because of all the processed foods out there; we have to stick with whole, organic foods. We can also drink a variety of things like wine and coffee. Like vampires we have increased senses just different ones: touch and feelings. We can *see* what you're

228

thinking at the time you're thinking it if we're close by. We have a strong emotional connection to people and cats. We can naturally experience love and human emotion, albeit with the volume turned up to an almost unbearable level. And we're strong, powerful – but we only use it to defend ourselves. We abhor violence. We much prefer to live in groups, communities than on our own. However, we will live away from our community for periods of time if we have a mortal partner. We just don't like being on our own permanently. And we don't normally...never tell our partners who we are. Or show them."

"Never? But you've told me?"

"I know." Khal whispered.

"Oh." I really didn't know what else to say to this.

"We can't control your mind to make you believe or feel certain ways like vampires can."

"Wait. You keep talking about vampires as if they're real."

"That's because they are. Well, what literature and other texts refer to as vampires or blood-suckers. Yes, they are very real."

He actually looked serious as if I should believe every word he just said. There was no way we were ever going to agree on this whole myth issue.

"We don't use our power to attack or hurt others just because we feel like it. We can control our cravings extraordinarily well, unless something is wrong with us. We don't have to kill to appease our hunger. We're not restricted by the rise and fall of the sun, and can move around freely no matter what time of day it is. We can sleep, albeit for only short periods of time. Our eyes are those of a cat. We cannot change into vapor, a bat or any other creature, only into a panther. We don't age. We have a more natural relationship with humans. Humans don't have to fear us and so therefore we don't have to shy away from them in that sense. I think that's all of them. I don't actually know a whole lot about vampires." Khal stopped for a moment.

I shook my head, sniggering. "Khal, Dracula was not real. I promise you. Bram Stoker made it up."

Khal gave a contemplative sigh and smiled a little.

"What about the slaughtered animals? The papers said how a wild animal had mauled them. If you didn't do that, then what did?"

"That's something else. That's not us. We abhor violence and will do anything to avoid killing another...animal. We are also no danger to humans. Our senses don't allow us to hurt our own species. We can't kill cats and we can't kill humans. They are also the two species that cause the incredible electric shocks whenever they're nearby, and we feel their own personal pain. Their pain can take over our bodies if we're not careful. So we learn to shut a lot of that out by switching off, blocking our brains from receiving any messages. It's like a safety mechanism I guess."

"So, go on then, tell me about these other immortals out there."

"There's an unwritten rule where we don't reveal them and they don't reveal us. As long as there isn't any conflict, we leave them alone and they leave us alone. We know about them. We can feel them. But we don't let the mortal world know."

"Oh. So you can't tell me?"

"Not unless circumstances permitted me to."

I should have known. This buttoning up and not telling just added to my belief that they didn't exist.

I couldn't think of anything else to ask so just sat quietly, not really thinking of anything.

"You seem more settled. Are you okay?"

"I think so." I was. I'd surprised myself. I thought I'd be forever scared of Khal, frightened of him.

But, surprisingly, I wasn't.

And even more surprising was that I could still admit to myself that I loved him. I loved him more than I ever dreamed possible to love another human being.

Chapter Thirty-Four

I thought you were going to tell me to go, leave you. Or you'd run back to New York and tell me you never wanted to see me again." Khal genuinely looked relieved.

"I...I was going to. I was petrified when you dragged me into the dining hall to look at that painting. And then when you followed me...everywhere." I still felt the adrenaline, deep in the pit of my stomach, telling me to flee for my life. But I was also experiencing an uncontrollable urge to cling tightly to him, to not let him out of my sight. There was also this irrational thought that I needed to please him, to do anything I could to keep him happy so he wouldn't leave me.

"I'd wondered a few times why you hadn't just come out and asked me. Why you never questioned more. And when I didn't answer your queries, why you didn't just call it quits and tell me to not come back. But then I saw your reaction with David and John, and it explained everything. It wasn't just me you didn't question; you're like that with everyone. You don't like snooping into other people's business. You see it as a private thing. But you also don't want to face what's in front of you. You would rather bury your head in the sand and pretend it doesn't exist." Wow, he really hit home with that remark. I couldn't comment, couldn't dismiss his description of me. Because it was true.

"Why did you need me to know? You said you'd never told anyone else before. Why me?"

"I don't know. You make me feel so complete. And yet, I didn't feel whole without you knowing. And even though you'd expressed your love for me, you decided that you would just take me as I am, not wanting to know anymore, until you noticed my scarab and registered what it was."

"Does everyone have the scarab tattoo?"

"Yes they do. But listen, Abby. You can't ask me about everyone else. We're all private people and no one is going to be...happy that you know so much. Even those of us that have had human...life partners before don't tell. No one ever knows. I don't mind you knowing about me; I want you to know about me. But I can't include them."

"I understand. Sorry. Have you had a life partner before?"

"No."

"But you've had partners?"

"Yes."

"How many?"

Khal smiled with an air of resignation. "Since my change just three until you. You make four. And I've only ever lived with one woman."

"Oh." I thought for a moment. "Does that include the two women you told me about...you know...immediately after you..."

"Yes."

"Do me a favor, don't ask me that question, will you?" All I could think of was the number of one night stands I'd had, completely outnumbering Khal's four, and I was only 21.

"I won't." He smirked as if there was more to this story than met the eye.

"Khal, you're thirty? And you said you've only had three after you changed? What about before?"

"Ah, you picked up on that...I was hoping you wouldn't notice that bit."

"Why? What's the problem. A bit of a philanderer? You're aware of my sex life – I could hardly be judgmental of yours."

"Well, I think you'll find mine a little more debauched than yours somehow. Back then, men were expected to know how to perform in the bedroom ready for marriage. A wife would be a naïve virgin, so it was up to the man to know what happens and how to behave. My father was a passionate, devoted lover to my mother, and believed that his sons should be the same with their wives. He detested how men treated women in our society, only seeing them as breeding machines or sex objects, that a woman couldn't be a wife and a lover. And so at seventeen my father chose an experienced *lady of the night* for me to learn from. I was to go to her once a week for a year where she would teach me all there was to know. Then she chose inexperienced *professionals* for me to go with to see how I faired. So before I was due to marry I would know how to please and respect my wife, and I would be able to gain my pleasure from her without needing anyone else."

"But you come across as so reserved, shy almost."

Khal shrugged with an air of resignation. "I wasn't one of her better pupils. I exasperated her female ego on more than one occasion. I never seemed to be quite up to par."

"Well, you could have fooled me. Your prowess in our bed was definitely the art of an experience lover." Khal grinned at the obvious compliment.

234

"Why, thank-you. Some good did come of all that training then…Hey, come here." Khal held his arms open, inviting me in. I didn't hesitate. I was a strong, independent woman, but there was something about Khal that I couldn't resist.

Chapter Thirty-Five

It was late when we went to bed. I hadn't let Khal go. I awoke in the morning and he was there, peering down at me, smiling.

"Did you sleep well?" I struggled to wake up, exhausted from the day before.

"You look tired. It's seven and I know you have to go to the store today. Are you up to it?" Khal stroked my hair away from my face and kissed my forehead.

"What day is it?"

Khal gave a smiling chuckle. He looked so happy, content. "It's Tuesday."

My brain tried to remember everything that happened yesterday, last night. I had wanted Khal to make love to me again but he wouldn't. And I'd been desperately disappointed. But he'd explained how he wanted to give me time to come to terms with him, with what he'd told me, so that I was sure I still wanted to be with him. I reluctantly agreed but knew there was no way I was ever going to think about what he'd told me...shown me.

"Did you go out last night?" I really didn't know why I asked because I knew I didn't want to know.

"No, not last night. I wanted to stay with you to make sure you were okay. I wanted to be here in case you needed me...in case you had a nightmare." He was no longer smiling and moved another stray hair from my face.

"Come on. You get ready for work and I'll put the coffee on." Khal left the bedroom wearing only his jeans. A habit I hoped he'd continue because there was no doubt he was certainly a fine specimen that deserved ogling.

The coffee was ready and there were a couple of slices of toast on a plate, buttered. The local paper was lying on the kitchen table, next to my coffee and toast. The headlines were glaring:

CARNAGE ACROSS LINCOLNSHIRE
LEADS TO NEW EVIDENCE

Khal didn't comment until he heard my anxious thoughts.

"I'm fine. You know it isn't me...any of us so there's nothing to worry about."

"But what about the posses? The farmers are gathering even bigger bands of locals to help them hunt the culprit. Look, here it says they are now hunting 'more than one large cat' so they aren't even considering it could be anything else that is doing this. They'll be all over the countryside."

"People are scared. But we know this place, know Lincolnshire's hiding places. We'll keep out of the way. And we don't go near other farms or farm animals. We have our own. There really isn't any need to worry." Khal was definite in his voice. It was obvious he knew what he was talking about. But I felt uneasy. No, scared.

Khal came over, kissed me and smiled.

I was never going to be able to resist that smile, ever.

Our day was quiet. I had little to do in the store. John came over for coffee but I wasn't in the mood for chatting.

"Everything okay?" He looked concerned.

"Oh, I'm fine. Just really distracted today. A lot on my mind. I'm sorry I'm not much company." I didn't like to disappoint John.

"Hey, I understand. Just let me know if I can be of any help."

John kept trying to talk about today's headlines but I just couldn't go there so every time he started a discussion on it, I changed the subject or found something that needed my attention.

He eventually got the hint.

"How about I take the banking around lunchtime today so that you can finish early?" John was a star and I thanked him profusely. It was just the type of help I did need.

He took the banking at two and I finished half an hour later. Khal waited for me outside. He'd been shopping.

We took the shopping home and went for a walk along the beach. There'd been rain, mainly drizzle, on and off all day but by the time we took our walk the sun shone.

We must've been walking for hours because by the time we arrived back at the cottage I was ravenous.

We walked into an inviting smell. Khal had been busy cooking and cleaning. I couldn't help but smile at his domesticity. He was comfortable in the kitchen, in a home. He knew his way around with ease.

"You enjoy housework and cooking, don't you?" Just the idea of either had me shuddering.

"Yes, I do. I've had my own place for a long time, and there's only me there. If I didn't clean, it would never get done."

"I thought you all lived together?"

"No, we all have our own separate homes. Well, Zeb, Tali, Sim and Wali share the communal house, and right now Rose and Dru are together, but the rest of us have our own places."

"That doesn't explain the cooking, though. You don't eat enough to warrant it."

"I know, but I love food. I love the aroma, the textures. If I cook I get all the pleasure and I find cooking actually stops me craving the food. So I cook for the homeless, poor, children's homes. I even worked in a prison as a cook once." That last revelation had Khal smiling, and me astounded.

"Now, your dinner's ready. Are you?"

"I'll change into my sweats first if that's okay?" It was still relatively early in the evening but I had no intention of going out anywhere.

"Of course," Khal answered and disappeared into the kitchen.

I came back down after having showered and changed, and curled up on the sofa. Khal had the fire roaring and the flame captured my attention that I didn't hear him until he sat on the sofa next to me. It wasn't a cold evening, but there was something hypnotic about a fire.

He handed me a bowl of soup and a bread roll on a plate, He'd already opened a bottle of wine and placed a full glass on the coffee table in front of me; he held his own and occasionally took a sip.

Our evening was quiet, calming; a very different day to yesterday. Yesterday felt like another lifetime, another life. Surreal, a bizarre dream.

I hadn't stopped thinking about everything Khal had told me even though I refused to acknowledge any of it. As far as I was concerned mythical creatures didn't exist. Period. And yet, here I was, virtually living with someone who told me he was a mythical creature. He even explained all the issues as if he was someone with an overactive imagination. I couldn't – wouldn't – get past my skepticism. But I also couldn't stop thinking about it.

Khal hardly spoke. I wasn't sure if he was listening to my thoughts or not – whether he'd been listening to them all day – but he never commented, never interrupted. He sat quietly, reading a book. I watched him while sipping on my wine, enjoying the flickering flame dance across his silhouette.

He read quickly, turning the pages swiftly, one, then another. I crossed my legs on the sofa, facing him, enjoying the view. His hair fell round his face, just the way I liked it, his parting invisible because his hands were constantly pulling his hair back. His eyes were virtually black in this light, the green hidden behind the huge pupil. I loved the green, found it sexy. But when his eyes became huge onyxes, my sexual desire for him ripped through every pore in my body.

He smiled. He was listening.

Khal closed his book carefully, and rested it on the coffee table. He crossed his legs on the sofa too and faced me. I giggled as he squeezed his long legs onto the width of the sofa.

"Give me your hands." He held his own hands out for me to place mine in his. I put my wine glass down and I gave him my hands.

Chapter Thirty-Six

"Close your eyes." I couldn't help but smile as I did as I was told.

"Now really concentrate. Empty your mind of everything. Every thought, every image. And keep it blank."

I tried. I really did. But every time I got to that blank space, something popped into my head: Mom, Jason, Dad, Alice, waves, sand. And I burst out laughing.

"No. Stop. Take that sand and close the door on it as if you're putting everything away in closets. Now your mum, and close the door. And stop giggling." He shook my hands, still holding on, and waited.

I gave it another go. Composed myself. Shut doors when something tried to come in. I got to that empty spot but struggled to keep it.

"Hang on to that. Don't let anything intrude your mind except my voice." I occasionally lost control, gave out a little giggle and tried again. Khal kept quiet until it went blank and then he talked again so all I could 'see' was his voice.

It was strange. When he talked, just talked, images fluttered into my mind. Then when he stopped, the images disappeared. He talked again, and different images came back. Sometimes they related to what he was saying, a word relationship, sometimes they were too abstract: love, friendship. Sometimes they were specific: cats, horses, cars, streams.

241

"Now, keep your mind blank when I stop talking, and listen really carefully to what I'm thinking." I peeked out one of my eyes to look at him wondering if he was really serious.

"Yes, I'm serious. Now come on. Concentrate. Close your eyes and get that mind blank again."

It took forever, keeping that emptiness in place without his voice filling the void. Then all of a sudden an image flashed across my thoughts. I couldn't fathom it; it was fuzzy, greys, blacks and whites. I tried to get my mind blank again, thinking it was me who put that image there, not concentrating enough. But it happened again, and again. It was incredibly fuzzy, a large space with someone in the middle that moved around. I couldn't figure out what it was, but it was definitely there and I found it impossible to stop it.

"Wait." I pulled my hands back off Khal and opened my eyes. He looked at me with a smirk on his face.

"That was you?" I was horrified. No. That couldn't be. "How?"

"Anyone can do it if they try. It just takes practice, patience – and someone who knows what they're doing. Also, people are too busy with their own little worlds, so caught up in the bustle of life, that they don't pay attention to what's around them anymore. If you learn to shut out the world, slow your life down and blank your mind to all images, you can feel the person next to you. Once you learn to feel them, and I mean really feel them, their force field will send you messages. I pushed that one forward so you knew what I meant. Normally you'd have to work a lot harder at it."

"Force field? You've been watching too much sci-fi."

"Yes. Everyone gives off energy. Have you ever sat in a room, alone, reading a book or something else that distracts you just a little, and notice a change in the atmosphere when someone else walks in? Why do you think that is? Everyone gives off energy. You, me, everyone. When a person or animal walks in with their own energy field and disturbs yours, you notice."

"Okay, I'll give you that logic. But that doesn't explain the other, the mind, the image transfer." I was not going to believe this in a month of Sundays.

"You really are so disbelieving, aren't you? Think about the logic of it. You've studied the body, how the nervous system is all connected. When you feel that shift in a room, what is it that senses the change? Your nerves, your aura. All you do is learn to focus that change and channel it to always reach your mind to create images." He made it sound so easy as if anyone could do it.

"Everyone could if they knew how, and were patient enough to learn." Well, I wasn't convinced. It was impossible. If all people were able to read other people's minds, then scientists would have discovered the concept by now.

"You really don't like things to not fit if society says it is impossible, do you?"

"No. That's not true. I see that everyone can be what they want to be. I don't like society dictating what it considers to be normal. But mind-reading isn't possible for everyone. I know there are people out there with special abilities and I see you as one of them. That's it."

"It's not possible because science says it isn't possible?" I thought about his question for a moment.

"I suppose. Yes."

"But science doesn't know everything, you know that. There's so much science doesn't know about the human brain. Haven't you ever had a thought about someone and then they call you. Or get a feeling that something is wrong and then you discover someone you knew died. Science can't answer these phenomena. Isn't that why we have God, religion?"

"Oh, don't go there. That's just as unbelievable. The majority of religions were only invented for crowd control, or to keep certain groups of people in their place. Look at how women have suffered over the centuries because of religious oppression, all in the name of God."

"That wasn't God; that was human cruelty. There's a difference. I take it you don't believe in God then? Atheist?"

"I don't know if I'd go as far as saying Atheist. More agnostic. Why?"

"No reason. Here, hold my hands again." He held out his hands for me to take. He dropped one of his legs down off the couch.

I gave him my hands and closed my eyes to concentrate, blanking my mind. It was easier than thinking about religion.

"Now, tell me what I'm thinking." I smirked again; something I struggled to stop doing, and tried to concentrate.

His hands twitched under mine, heated up until they felt like they were on fire. I felt the hair on the back of his hands stand up, felt the static build between us instead of diminish as it normally did.

Then an image popped into my head. Me.

My heart jumped wildly and I flung my eyes open. I knew exactly what he was thinking because I suddenly wanted it, wanted him too.

Chapter Thirty-Seven

His hands were clammy, his heat surged even more. Khal came in close and placed his forehead on mine.

"I love you. I'm sorry you find all this so unbelievably hard. And I know there's little I can do to help you. But I'll try and help if you'll let me." He turned his head to kiss my lips, moving his mouth to force my head upwards.

God, I loved him so much that I couldn't resist anything he said, anything he did. Tears fell from my eyes and ran down to meet Khal's lips.

"What's wrong?" He asked.

"I don't know. I couldn't help it. Sorry." I didn't know what was happening to me. I quickly wiped away the tears.

"Hey, you don't ever have to say sorry." Khal helped wipe my tears and kissed each of my eyes. It was so incredibly sensual that I could do nothing else but respond with my whole body.

I moved my hands to his t-shirt and lifted it up. I loved feeling his skin, touching his chest. Khal allowed me to lift his t-shirt off and I removed my shirt. My breasts were instantly exposed. I pushed Khal back gently so he could lie back, and I followed. It felt incredibly pleasurable being on top.

My smooth skin brushed against his slightly rough skin, and he wrapped his arms round my back bringing me down on him, closer. Our mouths stroked, fondled. He kissed my neck, my shoulder while his hands stroked my back, up and down, squeezing impulsively as the blood moved round my body, round his body, inflating his jeans below me.

My hands played with his hair, felt his two-day-old stubble. He regularly didn't shave and it suited him.

Khal suddenly lifted me up off him as if I weighed nothing more than a bag of flour.

"Sorry. Just hang on." He moved himself away and got off the sofa.

"What's wrong?" My mind was doing overtime – what had I done. Was he upset, had I thought something I shouldn't have done?

"Don't be daft. It's just uncomfortable. My jeans are too tight."

And I suddenly noticed what he was doing. A relief flushed over me and I smiled.

"Oh. Are you ok?" It was an amazing, sexy feeling knowing how quickly I aroused him.

He slipped his jeans off and came back. "Yes you do. You always have. I can't control it anymore. It has a mind of its own." He looked resigned to the inevitability of his body's faults, and we both laughed.

"Now, where were we?" Khal lay back down and lifted me back onto him. I grinned so hard I thought I would burst, and just laid there with my head on his chest.

He stroked my hair, moved it away from my face. I rested my chin on my crossed arms that lay on his chest and looked up.

"Why do you like my hair so much?"

"I don't know. It's soft, comforting. The color changes depending on the light – it captures my imagination. I see you in the meadow, or in the firelight, and your hair is flowing, shimmering. As you would say, it's sexy." He laughed and grabbed my ribcage and pulled me up to his mouth.

His hands began to stroke my back again and I felt the heat rise beneath me. His chest became hot, clammy, his boxers twitched and grew rapidly. And I responded in the only way I knew how – I gave myself to him completely.

The electrical current was a little stronger than I remembered, a little more intense than our last time together. But I wasn't quite sure if that was the actual heightened senses, or my sexual desire going into overdrive.

All I knew was I needed him to make love to me, to express his love fully and completely again. And I needed to combine our bodies into one again. I needed our first night back. I needed it to be real.

And Khal obliged with everything. He loved me, made love to me. Again and again. In front of the fire and then after he carried me upstairs. Our naked bodies moving together.

And I slept soundly, better than I had the night before.

Chapter Thirty-Eight

Khal and I were still spooning when I woke. I felt his breath on the back of my neck, slow and even. He was still asleep.

It was late. The sun's rays came through the drapes at a different angle to how they normally felt when I first awoke. I had always loved this room, how sunny it felt even on the dreariest of days. I turned round to face Khal. This was a first; I'd never seen him sleep. Actually, I'd never watched anyone sleep before.

I had my head on the pillow, my hand resting underneath. We were both still naked from the night before, still a vivid memory in my head.

And he didn't move, not a muscle. I could barely make out his breathing as I watched his amulet resting on his chest. He looked so peaceful.

I took his hand and held it in mine. Then decided to try the experiment that Khal had taught me last night. I closed my eyes and just waited until my mind was clear before I focused on him.

I kept my head on the pillow and just laid there, waiting to see what happened. And in my head an image popped: me.

I must've done something wrong. I tried again, emptied my mind and concentrated: me again.

"Of course it's you. What else did you expect." Khal stirred next to me and rolled onto his back, stretching his arm out to put it round my shoulder. I moved in to him.

"I don't know. Do you think of me a lot?" I didn't know why I wanted to know. It wasn't an ego trip or anything. I didn't know what it was.

"Always. You're always there, in my head. If I don't have an image of you, I have your images, the ones you're thinking." He squeezed me slightly, slowly opening his eyes.

I thought I was the only one. I'd been unable to get Khal out of my head for such a long time it was as if he'd always been there.

"Did I wake you?"

"No, not really. I was only napping. You know, catnap." He turned round to smile and kissed me.

"Just hang on. Morning breath. I need to go and clean my teeth." I moved to get out of bed.

"Want a shower? With me?" I was surprised by Khal's suggestion but loved the idea.

"Won't you get cold again?" I didn't want him to go through what he did last time.

"As long as I don't take too long, and warm up quickly afterwards, I'll be fine." He walked through to the bathroom and turned the shower on. This time, I made sure I gave him enough time in the bedroom after he left the shower to 'prepare' himself so I didn't see anything I didn't want to see…if you get my meaning.

Our morning vanished into nothingness. We didn't venture downstairs until lunchtime. I had missed a call from Jason so returned it after I'd had some coffee. Then I chatted for an hour with both him and Jen; yes, I told them Khal was a fixture in my life but didn't expand on that simple fact. I

249

couldn't; I didn't know what to say on the matter. I called mom and Ben afterward; I didn't mention Khal to either of them even though I knew Ben would be excited to hear about him. Khal was in earshot the whole time but I had nothing to hide so didn't even try to conceal what I said – then I remembered it wouldn't have mattered if I had because he'd still 'hear' me.

Then we chilled in the living room, reading the paper.

The newspaper wasn't really reporting much today. After the dramatic headlines of the latest killings, the reporters had backed off today and weren't going on about it like they did last time when a large wild cat was sighted. I was pleased because I didn't want to read about any of it.

Thankfully there were a few other articles of interest: summer information, sports. There were also a couple of local deaths that were unexpected due to the ages of the women but the reporter stated 'the authorities were not looking for anyone in connection with the deaths' although a coroner's inquest would be required. The description of the women gave the impression that they were prostitutes. And that was it. It was as if the reporter was dismissing this piece of news because the women were prostitutes and I didn't like that. Surely they deserved more than a page five brief article?

I discarded the paper and Khal didn't pick it up. He seemed to prefer reading books.

We played cards and even had a game of chess. Then eventually got dressed and went for a walk on the beach. We didn't stay out for too long. I liked hibernating indoors with Khal, letting the world carry on without us joining in. It was comforting to know that just for a day or two I didn't have to belong to the big wide world out there.

"I'm going to have to go out for a short while." We had been back inside for an hour or so, and were reading our books curled up on the sofa, my feet resting on Khal's knee. Khal went to move to leave.

"Oh. Can I come? No...wait...forget I asked that." Maybe it was better if I didn't join him, especially if he was...hungry.

He laughed. "No, I'm not hungry. Well, not *that* kind of hunger anyway. We don't have any more condoms left."

"All of them? Gone?" I was shocked. We'd been very good using protection. But I couldn't believe we'd gotten through all that we had.

Khal nodded and smiled.

We both walked down to the stores. The town was alive now the summer break was nearly here. The sun had almost set and there were some teenagers laughing and gallivanting around on the opposite sidewalk, enjoying the last of the sun's heat. There was still a little warmth to the evening but I'd put a cardigan on, just to stop the cool breeze making me feel chilly. I regularly felt a little cool after the sun went down – I put it down to having lived in New York for so long where the summers were definitely a lot warmer than they were here.

We entered the drugstore and found what we wanted. Khal was hilarious, collecting a variety of packets, different sensualities, flavors. "Do you think we really need all those?" I tried to sound serious, but it was difficult.

"Yes." Khal looked satisfied, determined, and I just laughed and shook my head.

He headed to the counter and I wandered around the store to see if there was anything else we needed while I was here.

"If you're going to be awhile I'll go to the bookstore; there's a book I've been wanting to read that I'd asked John to order for me. He probably has it in by now."

"Okay. I wanted to look at the makeup. Will you meet me back here?"

"Yes." Khal quickly kissed me then left.

I found the makeup wall and grazed over the large variety. I played with the foundations and lipsticks trying different combinations to see which ones I liked. Then looked at the nail polish to find matching colors.

"Hello stranger." Greg appeared at my side, attracting my attention by putting his face up close to mine and wrapping his arms around my waist. I jumped in shock at the sudden intimacy but Greg held firm and squeezed me into his body.

"Hello." I smiled a little but felt extremely awkward. I really didn't want Khal to see me in this predicament; the last thing I needed was two males strutting their stuff and staking their ground.

But I hadn't seen Greg for what felt like ages so I was actually pleased to see him...just not like this.

I maneuvered out of his embrace and turned around. "I've missed you, Abby. Where have you been?"

"I'm sorry. I've been really busy with work and...stuff."

"You're not busy now." Greg inched forward again and leaned in to kiss me.

I turned my head and his lips hit my cheek.

"What's wrong?" He stood up straight, his face serious.

"Look, Greg, I'm seeing someone right now. And...well...I've enjoyed your company. You've become a good friend. I can't...you know...make it more. It wouldn't be right." As I spoke I saw Greg's eyes physically darken, his face change to an almost frightening expression that, if I didn't know Greg, I would actually fear for my life.

"Then get rid of him Abby. Get rid of him now." His voice was deep and low, his eyes became wider and he moved his face closer towards me and looked directly into my eyes, trying to hold my stare.

I moved away. My heart was pounding and I felt trickles of sweat running down my spine yet I was cold and shivery. I pulled on my cardigan to fight off the sudden chill.

"Greg. I can't do that. No, that's wrong. I won't do that. Greg, I'm sorry. But...I love him." I tried to plead with Greg, to make him understand.

I heard a deep menacing groan come from the depths of Greg's chest; his breath came in short sharp puffs. I wanted to laugh because I swore I was about to see smoke come out of his ears.

"Abby. Get. Rid. Of. Him." Greg came in close again and repeated his stare-down.

"Will you stop doing that to me. I don't like it. And if you're trying to scare me it's not working." It was actually but I wasn't about to tell Greg that. Instead, I stood tall and pulled my shoulders back and never flinched when I looked directly at Greg.

A loud crash at the front of the store had me turning around quickly to see what the commotion was. Damn, it was Khal rushing towards me.

I looked around to tell Greg he needed to go and leave me alone but when I turned back Greg was gone. Completely vanished.

I looked around, wondering where he'd disappeared to...and why. Did he know Khal?

Khal came up behind me and roughly turned me around and squashed my whole body into his until I couldn't breathe.

"Khal. Let go. Khal." I mumbled into his shirt. "Khal. You're hurting me."

That seemed to do the trick and he loosened his hold...a tiny little bit...before stroking my hair and kissing my head.

"Okay, that was a little dramatic, you know. What possessed you to come crashing in here like this?" I tried to look around him to see if we were being stared at but I could hardly move.

"Nothing. I just...nothing." His breathing was eratic; his heart pounded under my ear. "I thought you were in danger. I thought you needed me."

"No. I'm fine. You can let go now." Khal hesitated then slowly released me.

"What do you think of this color?" It took a moment for Khal to come back to me.

"Mmm? Oh, I like it." He was still edgy and kept looking around and then towards the door.

By the time we were heading back to the cottage, Khal had calmed down and began swinging his bag, whistling.

Khal unlocked the front door and without hesitation, we ran upstairs to the bedroom, racing to see who could get there first, laughing as we went.

Greg had become a distant memory, a blip on the horizon, and our evening and night disappeared into oblivion.

Chapter Thirty-Nine

I woke up late again and this time something felt very wrong. I turned quickly in the bed only to discover Khal wasn't there. Okay, there was no need to panic; he was probably downstairs making the coffee. I bolted upright and tried to listen to see if I could hear him.

I quickly picked up my robe off the floor where he'd dropped it the night before, scrambled to put it on and quickly tied it as I went to join him.

But there was no sign of him. His sneakers were gone from the shoe rack by the front door, and his t-shirt that I'd flung over the back of the sofa was missing.

However, there was nothing in the kitchen to say he had started making the coffee, and the fire wasn't cleaned ready for tonight – he always cleaned the fireplace every morning.

And the dishes from last night were still in the living room; again, something he did every morning was clean up the dishes and wash them.

"Okay. Don't panic. There will be a reasonable explanation." But I was panicking.

I wandered from living room to kitchen and back again trying to think where he could be. "Milk. He's probably gone for milk."

I ran to the fridge and opened the door. I picked up the milk that was there, took the lid off and sniffed the contents. Fresh.

I then went to the bread bin and opened the sliding door to check the bread for mold. Fresh.

So he hadn't gone for milk or bread.

I ran back upstairs to check my phone to see if he'd left any messages or tried to call. He'd call if he was going to be late. Maybe he was caught up at the farm, a problem with one of the animals.

My phone was on Khal's side of the bed, plugged in. I switched it on but there were no messages or missed calls. I sent a text in case he was out of hearing range.

Then I quickly got dressed, forgoing the shower. I brushed my teeth and hair and pulled my hair back into a quick braid.

I needed to calm my nerves, to stop panicking. There was a logical explanation for why he wasn't here. There had to be. I went downstairs to make the coffee and while I waited for it to brew I remembered the newspaper by the door.

Quickly fetching it, I opened it up to the front page as I walked back to the kitchen, hoping…praying there wasn't anything in the headlines that would send me spiraling into an uncontrollable panic

Thankfully, there was nothing that could in any way relate to Khal. I put the paper down on the kitchen table and poured myself a coffee. I considered making myself some toast but realized I really couldn't stomach anything at that moment.

I scanned the paper, not really paying much attention to anything, then went into the living room and put a movie on while surfing the web and reading the comments on *Facebook*. Some of my 'friends' posted silly memes which always made me giggle; today, they didn't work.

I tried writing a few e-mails but it was a pointless exercise because no matter how hard I tried I couldn't stop the panic from rising inside of me to the point where every few minutes a tear would escape.

If only he'd answer his phone. If only he could hear me. If only I knew where his home was so I could go to him…somehow. I'd even get my bicycle out and cycle all the way if I knew which direction to go.

The doorbell rang and an instant feeling of relief ran over my body. He'd forgotten to take the key.

I raced to the door, and breathed a sigh of relieve as I flipped the latch. But my relief was short-lived as I saw who was at the door. It was Chaf.

An overwhelming sense of disappointment came over me and the tears I'd been fighting came tumbling down my cheeks.

"Hey. Chaf. I'm sorry but Khal's not here."

"I haven't come for Khal." Chaf stood rooted to the spot, not moving.

"Oh. Okay. Please, come in." I moved over to let Chaf enter. Chaf looked extremely hesitant, nervous.

I wiped at my face with the sleeve of my sweatshirt and closed the front door.

"Is everything okay? I'm afraid I don't know where Khal is. He went out early but…he's probably caught up at the homeless shelter…or with the farm. Oh, you'd know if he was there, wouldn't you? Well, maybe it's work related. Or something…" I stopped talking and wiped my moist face again.

I felt my breaths becoming shorter and shorter as Chaf stood in front of me not staying a word.

258

I knew something was wrong – why else would Chaf be here. None of them had ever come to the cottage before. Except Khal. But Khal wasn't here.

"Can I get you a coffee? Sorry, tea? Yes, let me put the tea-kettle on and make you a cup of tea."

I turned to go to the kitchen. "Abby. He's okay. But he's asking for you."

"No. No, he'll be back any minute. I'm sure. If you have some tea, you'll see." I didn't want this, not now. I shook my head as the tears cascaded of the edge of my face and down my sweatshirt. I knew. But I didn't want to know. Yet I couldn't think of anything else to stop Chaf from saying what he had come to say.

"He was shot…early this morning."

"No, Chaf. No. You're wrong. He's fine. Look, he'll be back soon. I promise. No." I shook my head even more, my tears spilling faster. And I felt my legs give way underneath me.

Chaf caught my fall and held me to him. I heard him grimace and it took me a moment or two to realize why – I was hurting him. I reached behind me for the stairs and sat on one of the steps so Chaf could let go. I hadn't felt a thing but as I looked up at Chaf it was obvious he had, even though he was covered with a sweater and jeans.

My body trembled uncontrollably and I gasped for air.

"He's okay, Abby. Honestly. But he's asking for you and I said I'd bring you to him." Chaf had stood back, away from me. He waited there, until I was comprehending what he was telling me.

"Where is he?"

"He's at home, at the farm."

"Okay. I'll just grab my things." I fumbled my words, my brain racing in my head, and I ran upstairs. I grabbed my bag and stuffed my phone and keys inside. Then I went to the bathroom and washed my face hoping it would make me a little more presentable. When I looked in the mirror I saw it had been a waste of time. I wasn't normally such an emotional wreck. Maybe I was entitled to be this time.

I shoved my feet into a pair of flip flops and went with Chaf out to his car.

Chaf drove quickly, zipping through the country roads. I had no idea where we were heading, my mind was full of Khal and the thought of him being shot. Chaf said he was fine, but fine could mean anything.

Eventually Chaf turned onto a dirt road. It appeared to go to nowhere. The land for miles was virtually flat and there was nothing I could see in front of us or to the sides that would indicate a dwelling of any kind.

I lay back, resting my head, closing my eyes to try and calm myself. Chaf said he was fine, so I had to believe he was. The last thing Khal needed was to see a blubbering idiot appear when he was the one suffering. And Khal told me he'd been hurt before and survived. He was strong, healthy. There was no reason to think he wouldn't be fine.

I wasn't normally one for praying to God, but I couldn't help it. I said every prayer I could think of…could remember hoping that at least one would reach the Almighty and hear my plea.

I had no idea how long we'd been travelling down the dirt road before Chaf slowed down. I sat up to take a look. Ahead was a tall hedgerow hidden amongst a small gathering of trees. I wouldn't call it a wood or forest; they gave a feeling of being thick brush and vegetation rather than something more. In a gap among the trees and the two sides of the hedgerows was a pair of enormous wooden gates bridging the road; it was only visible once we were so close we were almost on top of it. As Chaf approached, the gates opened and Chaf slowed even more as he came through the gates. They closed behind us.

There was a large square gravel courtyard surrounded on each side by what appeared to be living quarters. The homes were three sides of the square, stone, with thatched roofing: two stories and very long. A large oak door was opposite us as we came through the gates and an archway split the right building in half. Through the other side more buildings could be seen, and another courtyard, this time laid with brick.

Wali, Tali and Rose were outside in the gravel courtyard, heading our way.

Chaf parked the car and we both got out.

"Hi Abby. He's fine. He's waiting for you." Wali spoke as they approached. Seeing all their faces helped calm my nerves but until I saw Khal I couldn't stop shaking.

"This way." Chaf had come round to make sure I was okay. Everyone, Chaf, Tali, Rose and Wali led the way to the longest building on the left.

Another large dark oak doorway was approximately half way along the stone wall. It swung open and out came Khal. He stood in the doorway wearing jogging bottoms and a t-shirt, and holding his stomach and ribs.

I went to run over to him but as he moved away from the door someone else came out of the shadows with a smug look on her face and her arm around Khal.

Lisa.

261

Chapter Forty

Khal leaned down to say something to Lisa then moved away from her. I was dying to know what he'd said, and what her response had been. But I was also determined not to give Lisa the satisfaction of knowing I was jealous. Then I remembered – she could read my mind. Shit.

Khal shifted his body and jerked his head to indicate he wanted me to come over to him so I did. This was neither the time nor place to act churlish over something that could have been innocent. I looked behind me at everyone else. All their faces were blank...except Wali's. Wali looked angry and when I turned to see who he was aiming that anger at I smiled. Lisa. At least I had someone on my side.

Once I reached Khal, he led me into what I assumed was his home.

It was dark inside and it took me a little time to adjust to the lack of light. There was a large stone fireplace with a gigantic oak mantelpiece to the left of the room. Above it hung two large swords, crossed. A sweeping oak staircase to my right led to an enormous balcony looking directly down onto the sofa, two chairs, large coffee table and fireplace. There was dark oak everywhere, much of it carved. It was incredible. And so old. Well, old compared to what I was used to back in The States. And it also reassured me that this was Khal's place – no woman would live here.

I walked with Khal over to the huge leather sofa that sprawled in front of the fireplace. I thought that America was the place for everything enormous but I'd never seen anything like this before. And when I sat on the sofa, it sunk: soft, luxurious, conformed to every curve of my body.

"Yes, it's comfortable isn't it." Khal eased himself down.

"Do you need anything?" I understood why Chaf said Khal was okay. He looked well, exceptionally well, apart from obviously being in a lot of pain.

"No. I'm fine. Just having you here is good. So what do you think to my home?" Khal grinned, and looked excited when he mentioned his home.

"It's amazing. Very masculine. Suits you." I got up to look at some of the artwork hanging round the room. They were mainly paintings of people, young and old. I didn't recognize anyone, but a couple of times I stopped to take a closer look, as if I'd seen a face or two before but couldn't place where.

On the left side of the fireplace, there was a painting of a sweet young girl, dainty, graceful, walking through a meadow on a spring day. I guessed her age to be around fifteen, sixteen.

On the other side was a painting from a similar era of an older woman, in her early to mid twenties, holding a baby in a christening gown. A young boy stood next to her, and a handsome man stood erect behind them all. She wore a pretty smile, kind.

"These are the same person, aren't they?" I turned to look at Khal.

"Yes. Elizabeth. She was going to be my wife. That was her family. I bought the paintings when her family sold them after her death. I should really take them down."

"Why would you want to?" I came back to the sofa and sat with Khal.

"Because of you. I don't want you to have to look at my past, see it every day."

"It doesn't matter what I think. This is your home." Every day? Was he expecting me to move in with him? That was definitely not a good idea. Everyone here may be used to my being around, but they had all made it very clear I was only accepted because of Khal. To live near them all would create too much animosity.

"I've never shared it with anyone before. Ever. You're the first person I've ever had here that isn't Sarjikris. It's strange because I'd planned on bringing you up here after you finished working at the shop, hoping you would like to have a few days away from the cottage. I wanted to be the one who drove you here, to show you around. I wanted your first time here to be special." He actually looked disappointed that his plan hadn't worked out. This place meant a lot to him.

"Well, you can still show me around, when you feel better. I'd love to see it. So, are you going to tell me what happened or am I going to be left guessing."

"Oh, it was stupid. After I talked to you yesterday about being aware of your surroundings, and I didn't pay attention to mine. The farmers got me, early this morning. Dru and Rose thought they saw something last night, so early this morning I went out to take a look. And, I needed to come home to change my clothes and see the animals so it just seemed like a good idea that I be the one to look and see if I could find anything." Khal took a break for a moment, wincing, holding his side.

"Find what?"

264

"Oh, nothing for you to worry about. Maybe a wild dog that was hungry. But it did mean I didn't pay attention as I should have done. I didn't notice the group of farmers and locals. They were out and spotted me. I was stalking in some tall grasses on the edge of a thicket, paying attention to what I could hear in the brush, and not to what was happening in the far field. They got me with a rifle. It went in and out of my side." Khal stopped talking again, shifting himself to get comfortable. He wasn't looking too hot; his appearance had quickly changed and he appeared pale, almost gaunt.

"I'm sorry I worried you. You must've been petrified this morning when you woke and I wasn't there. I've become quite used to the way you think, the way you see things."

"That's okay. Chaf did his best to reassure me. How does it feel now?" I reached for Khal's hand to play with. Intertwined his fingers with mine.

"I heal quickly. In a day or two I should be completely better. We don't have a problem getting better. There isn't a lot that can destroy us. I just had to come home so Chaf could help me." It was strange to hear Khal talk about home and needing Chaf. He rarely talked about his home, and he'd always seemed so independent.

"Would you like me to show you round?" Khal was keen, excited. I couldn't resist.

I held my hand out for him to take as he heaved himself off the sofa. He walked slowly towards a door along the back wall. It was a large heavy oak door that led to a huge fully equipped kitchen and dining room. The dining table had fourteen large oak chairs surrounding it and an enormous empty fruit bowl. The size of the fruit bowl suited the size of the table.

The kitchen was open plan with pans hanging from a cast iron rack above the cooktop. The floor was stone across the whole expanse.

The back wall was a blanket of windows, ceiling to floor, and in the middle were a set of French doors that opened to a formal garden where a large ornate rose bowl fountain trickled quietly in the center.

"Khal, this is wonderful. It's like your own little oasis." I stood at the back door looking out at the garden.

"It's open. You can go out if you'd like." Khal was leaning heavily on one of the large chairs, his hand gripping the top rung. He needed a walking stick.

I gave him a smile and reached for the door. The house felt cool compared to the air outside. There was hardly a breeze; the garden was completely enclosed by high hedges and large trees, mainly deciduous. The air was warm, sweet-smelling; a variety of birds gathered round a bird feeder and some bathed in the fountain. Squirrels played games, running up and down the large trees at the back of the garden, and there was a pair of rabbits chewing on the juicy clover on the lawn. They looked up at me but soon carried on with their dinner.

Khal hadn't come with me so I didn't stay. I came back quickly and closed the French door behind me.

Khal looked a heck of a lot worse than when I left him. He looked deathly pale. His eyes glowed and had a wild look to them. And he was shaking uncontrollably.

"Khal? What's wrong?" I rested my hand on his arm but he jumped a little as if it hurt him, something that he'd never been so obvious about before. He looked my way but I wasn't sure he was actually seeing me. And I suddenly became irrationally petrified that he was dying.

266

"Khal? Do you want me to get you back to the sofa?"
He was scaring me. I could move him with his help, but right
now he was stood rooted to the spot, not willingly moving at
all.

I needed to get him help…fast.

Chapter Forty-One

I started shouting and ran towards the kitchen door to make my way into the living room. But before I got to the door, Chaf flung it open with Wali and Lisa at his side.

"What's wrong with him?" I asked. I didn't care who answered.

They obviously knew immediately what the problem was but no one talked. I shook, worried as my mind worked overtime with what could possibly be wrong. He'd been shot, infections could set in. Maybe he needed to get to a hospital. Who was I kidding? He *did* need to be in a hospital; he shouldn't have come home.

Chaf and Wali helped Khal through to the living room and Lisa held me back.

"No. Stay here."

"But, Khal. I…"

"No, Abby. You need to leave him to Chaf and Wali." I didn't understand. One minute he was fine, the next he looked like he was about to die.

Lisa didn't give me a choice and pushed me to the garden to a little bench where she forced me to sit down. I wasn't protesting very much. I didn't know what to do.

My trembling got worse. I took in some deep breaths hoping to calm myself down. I tried to stop my tears but they wouldn't obey. I leaned forward putting my head down a bit. This emotional rollercoaster ride that I'd been on for the last few days – the elation then shock, then a sexual high then insurmountable worry – was getting out of hand, and now this was making my irrationality go even more haywire than it normally did.

"He's going to be fine. Chaf told you that earlier. Nothing's changed." Lisa spoke with a firm, impatient voice.

"I don't understand. What happened? Everyone else seems to know but I don't." I swallowed hard, choking on a lump in my throat.

"I'm scared. I'm petrified that now I've opened myself up to him, allowed him into my life, I'm going to lose him. And I don't think I could cope if something happened to him." I looked at Lisa, pleading with her to at least try and explain to me what was going on.

Lisa looked at me as if she realized just how much Khal meant to me. "The bullet, it hit Khal's spleen. It isn't as serious as it sounds. He won't...die. But he needs to keep his energy up so that he heals quickly. If he doesn't then...well, he just needs to. You being here, he forgot he needed to...eat something. And that's the result. So Chaf and Wali are giving him something to help."

"So why didn't he say anything. I would've understood." I wanted to go to him, tell him it was okay. But Lisa grabbed my arm, quickly let go of it once I was sitting back on the bench.

"No Abby. You have to leave him. He needs to do this on his own, without you. He's with the men and they're helping him.

"But you don't understand..."

"Yes, I do. You think that because you love him it's okay, you can now share everything."

"But Lisa, I already know about Khal. I know that he needs..." I took a deep breath and told Lisa. "I know he

269

needs blood, fresh blood, and he needs to...change in order to do that. So, it's you who doesn't understand. And I need to go to him."

I felt stronger now and stood up to my full height, towering over Lisa's small frame.

Lisa looked shocked. It took her a second or two to come round to what I was saying so I took advantage and headed towards the French doors.

As I opened the door, Lisa flew in front of me and blocked my way, pushing me back. She was strong, a lot stronger than I was.

"So, he told you. Well, that doesn't change a thing. Just because you think you know, doesn't mean you understand. Otherwise you'd realize what danger you are in if you go to him now. He's injured, an injured animal. And an injured animal is dangerous. He knows that. And you know it too if you think logically for a moment. Why do you think he couldn't talk to you before? It took all his power to stop himself from changing there right in front of you. If he'd wanted you to see, don't you think he would've just gone ahead and changed? Now, I can either take you home now, or you can wait for Khal to...finish. He won't be long." Lisa stood firm by the door, her legs in a wide stance, her arms crossed at her chest.

And she didn't say another word.

I sat quietly for a while, thinking about what Lisa said.

"Khal told me how Bastet changed his...lifeforce. Is that what happened to all of you?"

I waited patiently. I wasn't going to let Lisa win. I was part of Khal's life now and she needed to get used to that fact. I wasn't sure whether she was listening into my thoughts or not but I saw her persona change before she answered me.

"Khal's unique."

"What do you mean?"

"He was part of the enemy's regiment in Egypt. He was considered British even though his father was Egyptian."

"So because he was hurt and in Egypt at the time that meant he was...changed?"

"No. Khal was wounded trying to save an Egyptian woman and her child. His men, the British Army, were ready to fight and she got in the way. Khal tried to stop the advancement but it didn't work, so he ran to save her. But one of his own men shot him. He kept going, not letting the soldiers get to this woman and her baby. But once he got her to safety, he was dying. She called Bastet to come and save him."

"He never said that's why he was chosen."

"No, he wouldn't. He doesn't talk about what he did, what happened. He doesn't talk about his life to anyone." Lisa abruptly stopped. She must have realized what she'd just said because Khal had talked to me about some of his life.

"Are you Egyptian?"

Lisa didn't answer me.

"I know...you all have this connection and I'm an outsider. I've always got the impression from you that you don't like my being part of Khal's life."

Still, no answer.

"Why don't you like me, Lisa?"

"Not everything is about you, Abby."

"What do you mean?"

271

"When Khal first met you, showed an interest in you, none of us understood just how much you'd affected him. We just thought it was another woman. Someone he'd hook up with for a while and drop when he'd had enough." Lisa stopped for a moment and gave me a smug grin as if she knew something I didn't.

"Don't worry, Lisa. I don't have a problem with his past relationships. He's talked about them." And I smiled back at her, a sickly sweet smile.

"Well, he's had a few, not as many as the other men but quite a few. We get used to it so we didn't take any notice of you to begin with. But Khal changed. Something happened and it was like he'd become possessed. The majority of us didn't understand but Chaf did when he saw you with him at the beach. He knew straight away what you meant to Khal even though Khal wouldn't admit it. And when Chaf said you might come out with us, we didn't like it at first. But then we met you and we realized what Chaf was saying. We don't mix with the partners unless they're one of us, so you're very different from that point of view. You are the first outsider to come here."

Some of what Lisa was saying contradicted what Khal had told me and there was something about her body language that screamed at me she was lying. But I knew she wasn't lying about everything – I just wasn't sure which bits.

"What about you. Don't you want a life away from here?"

"I haven't been back long. Me, Tali and Rose, well, we prefer to be here and don't like to mix with outsiders. It's not the same for us."

"Oh yes, Khal mentioned it hurts you more than it does the men."

Lisa looked annoyed...no, angry again and didn't respond immediately.

"Only if we go with human men. And they all know that so if we want some...fun the men are happy to oblige." She shrugged but there was an undertone in her words that I couldn't put my finger on.

"Over the years, we've partnered up with each and every one of them. But Khal's only ever been with me." Oh my God, was Lisa Khal's lover? Was this an ongoing thing? Is that why Khal wouldn't sleep with me for so long?

"Oh, dear. I thought you said you knew. When you said you'd talked with Khal. Damn. I'm so sorry."

Chapter Forty~Two

It's okay. I was just shocked. It never occurred to me. That's all." What Lisa was saying didn't gel with what I knew about Khal. It wasn't just what Khal had told me but also how reserved he was around women. No, Lisa was lying again, I was sure of it.

And then I remembered Khal saying he'd lived with someone. Was that Lisa?

Lisa looked at me with a strange expression that I couldn't decipher then turned to walk back into the kitchen. I waited before following her. As I came inside and closed the door I heard shouting in the other room and quickly went to see what was going on.

"Get out of my house. You had no right, Lisa. Fuck what she needed to know. That was not your place to say anything...to tell her."

Khal turned to me. Out of the corner of my eye I saw the front door open then close; I presumed everyone else left, including Lisa.

"You're feeling better now?"

"Yes. I'm sorry you had to see that."

"Seeing you? That wasn't a problem at all. I wanted to help. But obviously my help isn't good enough." I knew I was being bitchy but after what Lisa had just said and then my overhearing Khal, I was in a bitchy mood. I'd obviously got it wrong, Lisa wasn't lying.

274

"Abby, don't start. You know you need time to get used to all this. And both you and I know you don't want to face any of this. And I'm certainly not going to push anything on you."

I took a deep breath and let it out slowly. He was right. I knew he was right. But I was hurting. And I'd been frightened, not knowing whether he'd live or die. And now with all Lisa had said, my insides were churning to the point where I felt sick.

"I frightened you, unnecessarily, and I'm sorry. If I'd just been a little more careful, it wouldn't have happened." Khal held out his hand for me to take. The color was returning to his skin, his eyes no longer looked wild and…frightening. I came closer and sat next to him on the sofa, taking his hand in mine.

"Lisa wouldn't let me back in."

"Mmm, I know." He looked annoyed.

"Don't be angry with her. She did what she thought was the right thing."

"I'm not cross with her about holding on to you. I asked her to. You needed to stay out of the way. No, she shouldn't have told you about me, and her. That was not her place."

"So it was true? She's the woman you lived with?"

Khal really did seem perturbed by Lisa's comments.

"What's the big deal?"

"Nothing. It's nothing." Khal flinched when he moved off the sofa and walked, limping, to the fireplace.

"Are you both still…intimate with each other?"

He moved around quickly and held his side in obvious pain. "No. No, of course not."

"Well, something's wrong. You do this when you don't want to talk to me. Walk off and blank me out. You build a wall between us. How can I be here if you won't talk to me? I thought we'd come a long way with being more open with each other. What changed?"

I wasn't feeling angry or hurt or even confused anymore. But he'd promised that he'd be open and honest with me from now on, that he wouldn't shut me out. "We aren't just friends anymore, we're lovers, partners, playmates, call it what you will. But how can our relationship continue if you don't trust me enough to tell me what the issue is when I ask?"

"You never used to want to know. You didn't want to know about me. You weren't prepared to face it, so please, don't give me the lecture on being open." Khal actually seemed bothered by my presence. He pressed his fingers to his forehead and dropped his chin to his chest.

"Look if you don't want me here just say and I'll go. I'm not hanging around just so you can get upset because I ask you a question you don't want to answer. I'm trying my best here to understand."

"She was pregnant." Khal turned round and looked at me. "With my baby."

Okay. I hadn't expect that. Lisa only said that her and Khal had been together. She'd made it sound like a hook-up, a way to scratch an itch. I never expected their relationship to have been that intimate. A family together?

Did they still live in the same house then? I was shocked, and I certainly never expected him to just blurt something like that out.

"We don't live in the same house."

"Lisa was here when I arrived. She was with you." I tried to remember all the times I'd seen the two of them together, wondering if there was something that I'd missed.

And Lisa's anger at me when I first met her. She hated me.

"No, Abigail. She doesn't live here, with me. I've already told you I live on my own. She was just here because I needed some help, and she wanted to talk about her new book. She has her own place. And she doesn't hate you." He walked over to the sofa and sat next to me, carefully.

If he really thought Lisa didn't hate me, he had a screw loose. And he didn't know women very well.

"But yes, Lisa is the one I lived with. We were together for many years. We lived as man and wife in a little North Yorkshire town. We were happy, just the two of us. We were always led to believe that Sarjikris couldn't have children and because we don't feel the same static pulses that we feel with humans there was no need to take any precautions. We'd been together for fifteen years and just enjoyed life. We were happy. Lisa taught little children in the local school; I worked at the university in the nearby city. It filled our lives and we loved being part of the local community, feeling...normal." Khal hesitated for a moment and began rubbing his head again. He closed his eyes and frowned.

Then he turned to me with a solemn expression. "She's upset right now. She doesn't want me to tell you. She's sorry she even mentioned our being together to you." Khal held my hand and looked resigned to the fact that he needed to continue. A part of me was about to tell him to stop, that it didn't matter, but another, smaller part of me couldn't speak.

"Lisa was sick. All the time. We couldn't understand why. She kept vomiting, retching like crazy and no matter what we tried she couldn't control it. I brought her back to the farm, weak and delirious, to see Chaf and Rose. And that's when we discovered she was pregnant.

"God, we couldn't believe it. We were ecstatic. Lisa had always wanted her own children. She loved...loves children. But she couldn't keep anything down which had everyone – but especially Lisa – worried about the baby. When I think back now, it was frightening. There we were about to be parents, something we never thought would ever happen, and she was, well...we didn't know what would happen, to Lisa or the baby." Khal fidgeted again, turning himself so he could lie back. He waited a couple of minutes before talking again, looking tired, worn out.

"This was when Chaf discovered a herbal remedy that we could take to help improve our digestion of regular food. Up until this point we could eat small amounts of human food but only if we fed off blood first. We tried it for Lisa to see if she would keep something down. It worked. She was able to switch to mainly regular food until she was half way through her pregnancy, and then she was able to go back to feeding on the animals. She just had to keep each meal small so she could keep it down.

"She looked incredible, and loved being pregnant, feeling our little boy moving inside her."

"You had a boy?" I looked around the room to see if I could see a painting of a little boy that looked like Khal.

"No, you won't find one."

"But why, Khal. He's your own flesh and blood." I stopped when I saw his face, a face full of grief and anguish.

"Khal, what happened?"

"Lisa...she went into labor too soon and it was too long. She lost a lot of blood. She'd never completely gained all her strength back from those first few months. And he was too weak. He just couldn't survive the trauma of the birth. Charles, after Lisa's father." Khal got up, and looked in complete and total agony. He rubbed his head over and over, squeezed his fingers into his temples, jerked his head as if saying 'no' to someone. I guessed it was Lisa.

Didn't she realize that he had a right to talk about this if he wanted to? Surely she could not listen in if she couldn't face hearing any of it.

"Did you consider trying again? If it happened once, surely there was a chance Lisa could fall pregnant again?"

Khal shook his head and started to look sick again. His face was pale and drawn. "There was too much damage during the birth. And there have been no other recorded pregnancies among Sarjikris – a Sarjikris male impregnating a human or female Sarjikris, or a human male with a female Sarjikris. Therefore no children. It just doesn't happen."

"Poor Lisa."

Khal stopped moving around and clung to the fireplace for a moment. Then lifted his chin to look at me and shook his head.

"I can't do this anymore. I have to go to her. It's killing Lisa." Then he left.

Chapter Forty-Three

I couldn't believe he meant that his talking to me about his son was really physically killing Lisa. However, I also didn't want to dismiss her distress regarding this matter. I couldn't imagine what she must be going through, after hearing what happened. It was obviously still very fresh for them both. It then had me questioning just how long ago the two decided to go their separate ways. Was I a rebound for Khal?

No, I couldn't see that. He seemed too well grounded...until now.

One thing was very clear to me – Lisa still loved Khal.

I went back to the paintings hanging on the walls around the living room. I began to wonder who all the other people were. I had no plans to ask Khal about them. He'd been through enough. My curiosity could wait.

As I approached the last one I realized I was cold and hungry. I had a protein bar in my bag that I found to eat, but I hadn't brought a jacket with me. I looked in both the kitchen and living room to see if Khal had anything for me to throw over my shoulders. There was nothing. So I went upstairs to see if I could find a sweater.

The stairs creaked as I climbed them, the old joints rubbing against each other. They were solid, dark, with an ornately patterned burgundy runner up the center. The carpet followed along the top hallway to what was obviously the master bedroom.

A set of double doors faced the balcony: again, dark oak with ornate carvings. I opened one side and walked into an incredible master bedroom. A four-poster bed proudly took center stage, and large armoires and dressers covered two walls. The bed was turned down and on the bedspread was one of Khal's jackets. I picked it up and put it on.

I turned to leave the room, not wanting to pry into anything personal. But as I turned towards the door, a painting captured my attention. Hanging on the wall, over a dresser opposite the bed, was an incredible life-sized painting of me.

I was wearing my white Capri pants, blue t-shirt and my pink bra. I was laughing, kicking my leg as if trying to splash someone, and holding my flip flops in my extended hand. But there was no one else in the painting, just me.

"Still cold?" Khal was so quiet when he walked in that I never heard him enter and almost jumped out of my skin when I heard his voice.

"Sorry. I didn't think you'd mind." I went to leave.

"You aren't going to ask me about it?" Khal nodded towards the painting.

"I thought I had put you through enough today. I've already been too nosey. How's Lisa?" I needed to know she was okay.

"She'll be fine. It'll just take her a little time. She just couldn't handle hearing it. But the painting; you like it?" Khal came up and put his arms around my waist. But there was something that was different. He seemed...remote. Resigned. And sad.

"I love it. Did you paint it?" Khal nodded.

"I did it as soon as I came home that night. I wanted to capture your laughter, your energy. I think I did."

"I didn't know you painted. It's incredible. I could never have dreamed I looked like that." I loved art, loved how it expressed a person's feelings.

Khal turned me around in his arms and brought his lips to mine. They always felt so soft and warm. I loved the feel of them, the taste of them. I deepened the kiss, my tongue playing with his.

Then as quickly as our kiss began, it stopped. Khal moved away abruptly, his face a mixture of anguish and...anger.

"Khal?" I wondered what I'd done, wondered what had happened? Had I caught his wound? Should I not have kissed him back?

Khal turned away from me and really seemed to be battling about something as if...oh my God, he was arguing with one of them. And I could guess who again.

I couldn't believe it. Was she really going to do this now? Hadn't he been through enough today?

Khal suddenly ran downstairs. I followed. But as I reached the bottom step it was obvious something was very wrong with him again. He was doubled over and groaning. His skin was ashen, his eyes glazed, almost haunting and he was trembling.

I went to reach out and touch him, but remembered what happened last time, how he flinched.

"Oh Khal. Okay. So don't panic. He's okay." I quickly ran for the front door and began shouting. "Chaf! Wali!"

Over and over I shouted until the two men walked towards me. "Please. He needs help."

Neither said a word. And neither smiled or registered I was even there. They walked into the house, picked Khal up between them by the arms and practically dragged him out the door.

"No. You'll hurt him." I ran after the two of them.

"Stay back, Abby." Chaf said.

"But you're going to hurt him." I began to cry, sobbing Khal's name. I swore this time he really did look dead.

Oh God. A cry of anguish left my body and I tried to reach for Khal again.

Out of nowhere Lisa came and stood in my way. "Why? I don't understand. I asked for help and they're treating him so cruelly. He doesn't deserve that."

I looked at Lisa. "What were you saying to him? Why were you arguing with him? He had a right to tell me, you know. Charles was his son too. I'm sorry for your loss but don't punish Khal for something that wasn't his fault. He didn't know. How could he?"

"Leave it Abby. You haven't a clue what you're saying. Now go inside and shut the door and wait." Lisa was treating me like a child again but I had little choice. I backed up, wiped my face and went inside. I went to the kitchen to get a drink of water. And just cried.

These last few days had been unbelievable. I was on an emotional rollercoaster and I needed a break. This wasn't supposed to happen. I came here to help Alice out and take some time to think about my future, decide what I wanted. And I'm more confused now than ever.

I wasn't sure how long I'd cried for. It felt ages. I knew it was at least a couple of hours, probably longer. I finally slowed the sobbing down. Crying helped me realize this was all going too fast, and I'd lost control of my life.

Khal was ill and I was just a hindrance, getting in the way. Chaf, Wali and Lisa had made that very clear.

Lisa had also made it clear where I stood with Khal. And the more I thought about it, so had Khal. Lisa still mattered a great deal to him. I wasn't convinced he still loved her but Lisa definitely loved him. And if I wasn't in the way she could try and get him back. Didn't she deserve that chance?

Even if it didn't work out for the two of them, I needed this time to fix my own life. I needed to go home, back to the cottage. He needed to be with his family so they could look after him and so he could be with Lisa. They were all able to give him something I couldn't and I needed to accept that fact.

I had also reminded myself that he couldn't be everything for me. No one could. I had to stand on my own two feet; leaning on Khal wasn't an option. I also wasn't keen on a long-distance relationship. I wasn't good at relationships to begin with; having the extra strain of three thousand miles made the ending inevitable. No, I needed to put my future first. I couldn't have anything...or anyone standing in my way. I needed to get back on track.

I turned to go through to the living room. I needed to find Khal to let him know I needed to go home.

"Chaf's waiting outside for you." Khal was at the door. He knew.

He looked a lot better in his color. I was grateful.

He was also no longer angry, or in pain. I was grateful for that too.

But there was a look of knowing. He knew what I'd been thinking. He knew that I'd put two and two together about him and Lisa. It was written all over his face.

"Khal. It's for the best. We both know this now." I was resigned to this fact and decided I wasn't going to be resentful towards Lisa. She'd been through enough and she obviously needed him more than I did.

"Look, if you want to go, go. I'd never hold you here against your will. But don't you ever tell me I don't understand how important your future is to you. Or that I agree with your decision to leave me. When you love someone, you give everything to them unconditionally. I'm prepared to do that for you, but you seem unwilling to grant me the same respect."

"That's unfair. You've held yourself at bay from me for weeks. And now that you've thrown everything at me you expect me to just accept it. You're the one with the weird life, not me. I just have a normal life that I have to live to the best of my ability. And right now, I'm drowning and I can't get my head above water. My emotions are all over the place and I don't belong here."

I couldn't believe we were arguing about this. The tears welled up again. "Oh, and by the way, I wasn't telling you anything. You were listening in, again."

I went out to the living room, picked up my bag and stormed out to the car where Chaf waited for me. He drove me home…in silence.

As Chaf pulled up to the front of the cottage I told him 'thank-you', but got no response in return. I didn't have a clue what I'd done to him or Wali or Lisa for them to shun me in this way. Were they all siding with Khal? Probably with Lisa. I could understand that; I'd probably do the same if this was Jen or Jason.

I climbed out of the car and walked to the cottage. I took my key and unlocked the door. Then walked inside and closed the door behind me. And never once looked back.

Epilogue

I was in trouble. Serious trouble. I loved her. She had quickly become my life like no other. And now she was gone.

I was in trouble. But not because I loved her. Or even because of all she'd felt and said. No, I was in trouble because I'd told her – and shown her – who I was. And now they all knew what I'd done. I'd risked everything and I couldn't take it back. Not that I wanted to. I couldn't have lived with myself – and her – and not told her. She needed to know the truth.

After being dragged away, I was given the opportunity to get some nourishment. Not that I wanted any. Now, I didn't want anything. If I couldn't have Abby I'd rather die.

Huh, if only life – or death – were that simple.

Lisa. She didn't let up once, making it very clear she hated Abby, hated my relationship with Abby. I hadn't been surprised really; I'd expected it. I'd just hoped, given time, she'd come round, come to see how much Abby meant to me. I'd obviously been expecting too much from her.

It wasn't even because I'd told Abby about me...my life. Oh no, as soon as Lisa discovered that Abby knew about the Sarjikris, she went crazy. So my telling Abby about Charles was the icing on the cake.

As I emerged from the barn into the sunshine, Chaf was pulling up into the driveway. I wanted to ask him if

Abby was okay, if she said anything on the way home. By the look on his face, I'd say the answer to both of those was 'no'.

They were all outside. Chaf joined the others as I closed the barn door and approached them

Lisa was at the head of the group and I waited in front of her. I decided then and there that I had nothing to be ashamed of. Nothing. Head held high, shoulders back and straight, I waited for her to begin her tirade.

"Yes, you should be. You should be ashamed, Khaldun. You've put all our lives in danger because of your ego." Lisa shouted in my head just as she'd been doing while I was talking to Abby. Under normal circumstances it was easy to block each other out of our heads, but with my injury and Lisa being older than me and her pushing her thoughts at me with everything she had, I'd been unable to stop the bombardment.

"Lisa, I know what I did goes against everything you believe. You've made your feelings abundantly clear — including your jealousy. But I disagree. I always have. I've kept our secret, our lives private from the outside world all this time. But no more. I cannot live like that. Not with Abby. She's my life. She's all I want. All I need. And she had a right to know who I am."

"No. She. Didn't. You think you're the only one who's ever been in this situation. Look around you. Yet not one of us has ever revealed the truth to a human partner. Not once. Those are the rules. That is the law. And you broke it. You deserve to be reported to Bastet. And you deserve to be punished for what you've done."

"Lisa." Chaf breathed out on a sigh of frustration. Everyone knew what that meant.

288

"No, Chaf. You encouraged him. You brought her into our group. If you hadn't −"

"What, Lisa? If I hadn't accepted that Abby means the world to Khal? If I hadn't encouraged him to bring her to us he would have left. Don't you get it? He would have left us to be with her. Then who would deal with the Watcher, with Grigori? He's here somewhere. We've felt him, seen the destruction he's caused. The only one who can stop him is Khal. Are you really prepared to explain that fact to Bastet? That your ego got the better of you and he left?" Chaf's frustration got the better of him and he walked away, turning his back from the group.

"Khal wouldn't have left us. He wouldn't." Wali added. I wasn't sure if he truly believed his words or not. "But he also wouldn't have risked our safety if he didn't believe Abby could be trusted. I trust her."

"Aargh. Why can't you all see it? Why do you keep defending him. Her. You heard her: she doesn't want to believe it, she fights her feelings for Khal and she can't cope with it all. Now, she's left him and there is a good chance she won't be back. You all felt her, you all heard her thoughts. She wants nothing to do with him. And what does that tell you? How can you be so naïve to think she'll keep mum?"

"I didn't listen to her Lisa. Abby was right that day in the pub; her thoughts are none of our business. And are you forgetting how kind she is? How accepting she is of others? She's more like us than you want to see. I'm beginning to agree with Khal; it's your jealousy that's driving you to this extreme. We are a family and yet you're willing to betray one of us." Wali said.

"I'm betraying us? Khal's the one who broke the law and exposed us all by telling that…that Yank."

I was angry now. It was one thing for Lisa to go at me, to speak of me and to me in this way. But I would not listen to her bad-mouthing Abby. *"Lisa, no matter what you think of Abby – and I'm very aware of your thoughts on her, believe me – she will not say a word to anyone. And she hasn't left me. It was just too much of a shock for her and too much for her to cope with all at once. She just needs time."*

"Khal." Lisa was no longer shouting in my head but her stance was firm. *"You're a bigger fool than I took you for if you believe that. But you know, whatever you choose to believe is moot. It doesn't change the fact that you broke the rules. You broke one of our most coveted laws for your own gain. There was no other reason for you to let our secret be known to Abby except to benefit you. And that is inexcusable. Inexcusable. Bastet may say she needs you to complete this mission, but there are plenty others who could take your place."*

No one else said a word. Not even me. I knew Lisa was right. Everything she said was true.

But I wouldn't have changed a thing. Except Abby's reaction. Given time, I knew she'd come around. She had to.

I knew Abby. I knew how her brain worked, how she had to think things through, work through everything in her head first. And I knew, beyond a shadow of a doubt she would come around.

I gave Lisa – and everyone else – a nod in recognition of what Lisa had said. Then walked to my home. I opened the door. Then closed it behind me...quietly.

Time. She just needed time. But I didn't know if I now had the time to wait for her.

Because I knew what Lisa intended to do.

Glossary

Bastet: a goddess in ancient Egypt – over a long period of time (starting in 2890 BC) she was known as the goddess of cats, protection and love.

Grigori: a name given to Watchers.

Khaldun: a panther shapeshifter and Bastet's chosen

Mount Hermon: a cluster of mountains where the summit borders Syria and Lebanon.

Nephilim: a hybrid – the offspring from a union between a 'son-of-god and a female human.

Sarjikris: shapeshifters made by Bastet

Watcher: angels sent down from heaven to watch over humans. They are sometimes referred to as fallen Angels.

Zagazig: a city in Egypt

Acknowledgements

I send out huge thanks to Ria Jessop and Phil Pearse. Without you both taking the time out of your busy schedules to read my drafts, I would be lost. Also, thanks go to Katy Pearse and Erin Carroll for reading my very early drafts – you were both very brave!

To my Family: thank-you for putting up with my frustration while writing, and my grouchiness when it doesn't go well. And an extra thanks to Phil – not only did you read and reread, you helped edit and proofread too. You are a very brave man. I love you with all my heart and couldn't have done this without you.

Excerpt from: *Paradox*

By the time I arrived outside, it was dark. I didn't mind. New York was the city that never slept. It seemed like there was always something going on.

Heading down 3rd Street, I was thinking about Bastet and Khal, and wondered what Khal was up to. I realized the time difference meant it was after midnight for him, but that made no difference. Knowing him he would be keeping himself occupied with some kind of project.

It was still stifling in NYC, the heat of the day trapped by the brick buildings and vast expanses of concrete. It was almost oppressive, and very different to the weather in England. I wondered what Khal would have made me for dinner tonight: probably a salad. He would be annoyed with me for my poor eating habits recently. But I couldn't help it. I just wasn't hungry.

As I walked through the city – a city I'd called home for eighteen years – it suddenly came to me that it wasn't England I missed anymore. Going back had fixed that. But since arriving back in New York, I desperately missed Khal. I missed him every second of every day and not a moment went by without his image attaching itself to a memory. I'd be in the shower and I'd think of Khal, eat breakfast or lunch and think of Khal, listen to a lecture and think of Khal. I hadn't quite figured out why he appeared in that last one, but he did…every time.

I crossed the road, trying to avoid the black garbage bags awaiting pick-up. These side streets became clogged with garbage before collection day. I needed to get the image of that night out of my head, blank my mind like Khal showed me so I didn't have the nightmares return. I really couldn't cope with anymore sleepless nights or something that stopped me from eating. I was never one to worry about my weight or anything, but right now, I looked terrible.

"Mmmmph...mmmmrgh." I screamed but my screams were stifled by a rag squashed on my face by a bulky hand. It smelled of oil, tasted gritty. A colossal arm grabbed my waist and lifted my feet off the ground. Large, towering above me, he dragged me rapidly into the alley. He must have been waiting there, camouflaged by the dark.

Kicking frantically with my sneakers and gnawing on the filthy rag, I fought back, with everything I had. I tried to get my brain to remember all the rules – don't fight it, run into it so your attacker loses balance, don't scream, shout fire or police or help. But he was too strong and I'd been too preoccupied to notice him. I tried to find his weak points: I scratched for his eyes and tried to bring my legs up to kick him in his knees and groin.

His hand loosened on my mouth. I took the opportunity to spit the rag out as quickly as possible so my voice could be heard. As I went to shout, the monster let go of me for a split second. My chance to run. I bolted, not thinking or looking in his direction. But something hit me across my stomach. I doubled over in agony; it stopped me from moving, stopped me from screaming, but I didn't fall down. I looked up with my eyes and saw a plank of wood, hard, rigid. I groaned, but couldn't catch my breath, gripping my abdomen, hoping in some way to stop the excruciation that had me rooted to the spot. I tried to scream again, cry for help. I took in a deep breath so I could let it out, loud and clear. He did it again, swung the plank of wood. He hit me across my face. The pain seared through my jaw. I fell. My head smashed on the concrete ground, and bounced to hit the ground again.

I tried to groan but the pain through my face and jaw was too much to bear.

Khal, Khal, where are you? Help Khal. I shouted silently, begged him to come and help me, prayed to God to give Khal the chance to hear my plea. But that would be impossible. Khal was too far away. He said he needed to be close to hear me. And even if he could hear that far away he couldn't possibly run across the vast ocean. *Khal. I'm sorry.*

The monster yanked me over onto my back. My pain took second place to the realization of what his intent was – rape. I kicked my legs up, scratched in front of me with my poised talons. A knee came down hard on my right hand, a vice squeezed my ribs. The man was on top of me, ripping my shirt, breathing his foul breath all over my face. I couldn't breathe. My left hand was free grabbing whatever it could get hold of: stones, screws, anything lying on the ground. I tried to loosen his grip so I could at least catch a bit of air, pulling at his clothing to get him off me.

I felt him move pulling at my jeans. *No! NO!* I screamed inside, mumbled whatever noise I could make.

And then nothing. Instant relief. I gasped for air rapidly, taking in large gulps. But the pain was agonizing torture as my body reeled from what had just happened.

His heavy weight on top of me was gone but I struggled to move.

I didn't want him to come back, get a second chance. *Move!* I told myself. I knew I had to at least try to escape. I turned over onto my hands and knees, my right hand now unable to take any weight. Like a limping dog, I scrambled along, pulling myself away from the alley, searching to see if I could see him anywhere.

I froze. Up ahead a deep and menacing roar echoed against the tall buildings.